◦◦ THE WILD HUNT SERIES ◦◦

Shadows

of

Solace

H J REESE

SHADOWS OF SOLACE

THE WILD HUNT
BOOK TWO

H J REESE

Cover designed by MiblArt

ISBN: 978-1-7389528-5-4

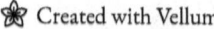 Created with Vellum

DEDICATION

To the friends and family that have taken me in along the way.

To Erin.

CONTENT WARNING

Shadows of Solace is book two in the Wild Hunt books. Though these novels are *not* dark romance their content warnings include: swearing, hunting/animal related triggers, violence, death, and sexual material not intended for readers under 18.

SUMMER COURT

Angus, God of Love
Gift: His Daggers

I am the water
The river runs through me

AUTUMN COURT

Gael, God of Forging
Gift: His Hammer

Hope lights the fire
Fury fans the flames
Courage carries me through

SPRING COURT

Daina, Goddess of Fertility and Air
Gift: The Berserker

With a song on its wings
And life at its feet
Wind guides us all

WINTER COURT

Bruma, Goddess of Ice
Gift: Frost Witch

Frost quiets my mind
Ice hardens my soul
I will persevere

EADHA ISLAND

BY MAP
MAKER TEAL

WINTER COURT

SPRING COURT

SUMMER COURT

AUTUMN
COURT

THE COURT OF
SHADOWS

GALEAIRY STRAIT

THE COURTLESS

THE MAINLAND

MAP TO THE
SCALE OF A
MERMAID'S TAIL

1

KADERYN

Once upon a time there was a virgin on a cliffside
Who had large breasts and an even bigger backside
She held their gaze, and the fire blazed
With a heat the males mistook
And when they tried to have their way
They met her strong right hook

I THREW MY HEAD BACK AND LAUGHED. "That's not how it goes. I distinctly remember it being far viler than that," I said into Valentina's hair from where she sat before me on Malvasia, my horse.

She had modified Jairek's song and had just used our mind-speak, our newfound ability to communicate mind to mind, to share her version.

"I guess you haven't figured out how to close your mind to me yet," she said, turning to look at me as a delectable smirk crossed her face.

"Maybe it's impossible to keep you from my thoughts."

The sun was low in the sky by the time Valentina, Jair, Teal, and I reached the road to Blackwater Junction. The soft pattering of rain on birch leaves rang out before the sky opened up and unleashed herself fully. Then every step forward was like walking through a wall of water.

So much for drying our clothes back at the waterfall.

But I had finally done it. I'd regained a part of my shadows that had been locked for centuries in an iron chest hidden in a nuckelavee cave in Spring Court's Yegevani Mountains. I splayed my hand on Valentina's belly and pulled her closer to my chest, tugging her further under the cloak I had fished out of one of the bags at my thigh.

General Mohr from Autumn Court was chasing her down across Eadha Island. But unfortunately for him, she had tied herself to me with a Caterina del Aamod scarf in Autumn's Fortress. The Caterina del Aamod ties were relics from the gods, sexual ties meant for lovers and only found in Summer Court.

Valentina and I had gone back and forth trying many different ways to close the mindspeak that my magic in the nuckelavee cave must have opened. I wondered if it had to do with the ties around our wrists, like some magic of the gods, or if it was just terrible fucking luck blasting a hole in a nuckelavee —a sea beast that found its way into Spring Court—to save her. And when Valentina would answer my mindspoken questions out loud, I knew I hadn't figured out how to close the door between our minds yet. So, we kept trying.

But the rain smelled funny, and it had me tensing up—in a familiar sort of way, in a way that I didn't want her in my head for. So, I hastily pictured shadows clouding the connection of the mindspeak we shared.

And the rain continued to tumble down.

"Hey," she shouted over the downpour. "You did it. I can't hear your thoughts anymore."

Relief tried to settle in, but there was something in the air. "I blocked it with shadows. Jair!" I called up ahead.

Jair turned around; his golden hair was matted to his head. He looked as miserable as a wet cat. "I smell it. Let's keep moving."

Teal, the one-foot-tall, blue-skinned pixie, was tucked, grumbling, inside his hood. Her little pointed hat drooped low over her large eyes.

"Where's your balance, Teal?" I shouted up to her.

"It's unnatural
This rain that we're in.
Cities are not supposed to swim.
I'd be less concerned
But it smells like . . . him," Teal growled.

Blackwater Junction was a sleepy faeless town at the apex of the three northern courts. I'd come this way long ago, the first time I tried to get to the chest. After learning Kyrrahalyn was still standing after coercion from Winter, I wondered what Blackwater had given up for its sovereignty.

Lord Aborys was trying to wipe out the faeless, a magicless group of fae on Eadha. To what end? I did not know. I'd never considered the faeless a threat, but from what Oir Winnetiren, my advisor back in Shadow Court said, faeless could reproduce quicker than the fae and live just as long. Oir did not know what sparked a faeling—a term for all fae younger than eighteen —to be born without magic; just that it did not discriminate. Two full fae parents could birth a faeless and two faeless parents could birth a fae; along with any combination between. Magic skipped generations, and I never cared enough to ask why. I would have said luck was involved, but I knew better; I knew how the gods worked.

The road led us to a courtyard shrouded in fog, and in the middle sat a large fountain, moss covered after years of unuse. Murky water poured over its basin sides as I watched the rainfall pool into soft streams along some worn, eroded cobblestone. It washed downhill until it flowed into a river that I didn't remember being there before.

Bags of grains were stacked against the rushing river, acting as a makeshift wall, holding it back from taking over the town. The smell of mold rose over the smell of the sea and that damn demigod. I groaned. I couldn't think of what value it was to Adrian, the son of a sea god, to be involved with the faeless town of Blackwater Junction. What could he possibly want with such a town?

Jair guided us on, following the fuzzy lights of the shops along the road to the tavern and adjacent inn where we were hoping to stay.

And still, it rained, soft but steady like an afterthought to a thunderstorm.

We tied the horses to a swollen rail under a covered awning and made our way through the drizzle to the door.

"Think she'll welcome us?" I asked Jair, shoving the Caterina del Aamod ties under my shirt sleeve.

He heaved the door open an inch, needing a little more arm strength to pull it past the waterlogged door jambs. "With a drink and a song, Kade. We'll stop here for a day. Two at most, resupply, and head north. All will be fine." Jair gave a lopsided smile and threw the door open to a noisy tavern smelling of warm food and damp corners.

"Avika!" he called, launching his arms wide in a greeting to the faeless behind the bar.

Frown lines marked her deep brown skin, the color like red oakwood, and fury lit her light gray eyes. "Get out, all of you."

Avika slapped a damp rag onto the bar top. It landed with a squelch.

The rest of Blackwater Tavern's patrons grew quiet and stilled as they shifted in their seats. Valentina tucked closer to my arm and instinct had me stepping sideways to shelter her from view. I didn't think firefae would come to this town, but Mohr was bullheaded, and anything was possible.

"We were hoping for warm food and a place to get dry. But I fear we were drier in the river," I said, pushing off my hood as Avika came to the doorway.

She was small-boned, almost hungry looking, though her baggy clothes suited her well. Damn, I'd forgotten how much she looked like her sister. But she carried an air about her, one of confidence and control even if she didn't have a single magic bone in her body. The faeless before us dropped her hands onto her hips. If anyone knew why this town reeked of a demigod, it was going to be Avika.

"One meal, one night, and one drink," she said, holding up a finger like we were too stupid to know how to count, *really* driving home how happy she was to see us.

"I'll concede on the first two, but we've had a nightmare of a trip and could use more than one drink," I said.

"Well, come on, close the door. You're letting the river in." She led us to a booth. "I don't carry that vile Solanci Ipsum you make in the Shadows, Kaderyn."

I pulled the bottle out from under my cloak. The obsidian liquid sloshed inside. "Quite fine, I've brought my own."

I guided Valentina to sit down first, and I slid in beside her.

"I'll send Sloane over. Let her know what you'd like," Avika said, leaning her calloused hands on the table, glaring with a ferocity to compete with Autumn Court's tempers. "Keep your heads down and don't cause any trouble."

"You won't even know we're here," I answered, trying to

give an innocent smile, but her glare continued. I was going to have to work on it.

Teal took it upon herself to tell everyone what to order. My roasted lamb came with a side of cooked cinnamon apples, which I unthinkingly passed to Valentina's plate even as she pushed half of her meat and steamed beets onto mine.

Valentina went to take a sip of her mug, filled with whatever they'd brought over, but I set my hand flat overtop. I pulled both her hands and the mug over and smelled it as she raised an eyebrow at me. Water.

"Drink nothing in this court without Jair or I checking first," I said, setting down the mug before looking up into her wide eyes. "Please."

Sloane was a friendly little light-haired faeless with skin as fair as the silver birches we'd passed coming through. She beamed at us with almost sleepy, hooded eyes. Val gave her a warm smile once we had finished scarfing down our food and she returned to grab the last of the dishes.

I would need more information before I could ever close my eyes in a town that smelled so strongly of a trickster god. But I was fae—at least some form of it—and like it or not, I couldn't lie. And I couldn't think of a single fucking way to bring up Adrian without calling him the prick he was.

"Avika tells me you'll be staying the night. I'll clear this and go make up your rooms shortly," Sloane said with a sweet smile as I drummed my fingers on the table and swished my drink between my cheeks.

And thank my hounds that Jair had more control over the situation. "You're not afraid to have the Shadows and the Courtless in your tavern?"

"Oh no, we are protected." She looked out adoringly at the rain. "The noble god, Adrian, has been shielding our town."

I choked on the Solanci I was guzzling as she continued, "I

know you mean us no ill will. The rain he gifts us with protects us from those who mean us harm."

"You mean Winter Court?" Valentina asked, leaning forward.

She nodded. "And the firefae to the east. They cannot step foot in the rain without shriveling up like vines of grapes left in the sun," she said with a vulnerability and an innocence that rivaled Valentina's.

And I wanted to warn her that Adrian was an absolute piece of shit, but Avika had a backbone stronger than most fae and she'd kick us out before I got the words out. I should have just risked the trip to Arnprior. If we'd done that, we'd have bypassed this fucking town entirely.

"Adrian just . . . protects you . . . out of the"—I leaned forward and cleared my throat, trying to get these words out—"goodness of his heart?"

She nodded, her hooded eyes dazed as she said, "He loves us."

I took another pull of the bottle because, *fuck's sake*, that couldn't be it. Adrian liked three things: his wine, his appearance, and causing others misery. I grumbled into my deep onyx drink; we were going to get nowhere with Sloane. Clearly delusional.

That's not nice, came Valentina through the mindspeak.

Neither is Adrian, I answered the same way.

Who is he? she asked.

A giant pain in my ass.

Sloane walked toward the kitchens with our empty plates. Teal followed close behind as the two chatted about everything Teal'd been missing in Spring. I knew she was eager to catch up with the stories of her home court before she'd found herself in an ogre's cage.

"Well, I see a pile of dimas with my name on it," Jair said as

7

he heaved himself up and sauntered toward a table of faeless males playing cards and a stack of dimas, Eadha's currency, in the middle.

They greeted him well enough, but I wondered how much of it was out of fear. Jair, as beings of Eadha go, was a calm creature. Unless he was mad. Then even I stayed out of the lion-shifter's way.

Valentina yawned into my arm as I took another drink of Solanci.

"What is that?" she asked. "It smells like oranges and vanilla, but it looks like the night's sky."

She was right, the drink was black with small white sparkles running through it.

"It's called Solanci Ipsum. You smell blood oranges grown under shadows and the ash of vanilla bark harvested in Gillies Forest. There may also be a touch or two of rice alcohol," I said. I halted the bottle halfway to my lips as the memories of my Hunters crashed into my thoughts. Quieter, I added, "It's the closest drink I could make like it is back home."

"In The Court of Shadows?"

I swallowed down the Solanci and the damn pain in my chest that sprang up whenever I spoke of this. "In the Underworld."

I looked down at her as her eyes closed against my shoulder. By my hounds, she was beautiful. In deflection to thinking about her or the Underworld, I cleared my throat. "Let's get you to bed."

"Mmhm."

Later that evening, Sloane led us to our room, and I steered far clear of any more conversations with her. I was bound to put my hand through the nearest wall if I heard any more of her delusional opinions about Adrian.

Avika would love that.

I shucked off my shirt and lay in the middle of the bed, giving Valentina plenty of arm's length to get herself ready on the other side. My mind was rattling as I watched her lay her red and yellow daggers on the side table. The gods' daggers that I damn well knew could cut the ties between us. But I feared she would leave, so instead of being an honest fae and telling her the truth, that with one swipe of those daggers she could be free of me for good, I watched her in silence.

Water from her damp hair dripped a path down her chest. It trailed past a crude watermark tattoo on her clavicle and soaked into my black Court of Shadows' shirt she wore that was three sizes too big. I looked farther down at the fox-fur Autumn . . . underthings—as far as I was concerned—she was wearing. She looked like an enigma, a mash-up of the courts, and I didn't have to wonder if she felt like she fit in on this island. I knew what it was like to be different. The difference was, I had a feeling she cared.

"We can go in the morning and get you some proper-fitting clothes," I said.

She looked down at herself with a startled expression. I tried to pry inside her mind to see what had her so preoccupied, but she'd learned—clever creature—to keep me out.

"Are there faeless in The Court of Shadows?" she asked, ignoring what I said, and I dragged a hand down my face. Where, pray tell, was she going with this?

"No."

She turned to me and rubbed her fingertips over her full lips, contemplating something. Her eyes were blue and wide as the sea, and they were doing funny things to my insides. "Do you think the faeless will survive Lord Aborys?"

I yawned, sprawling out further onto the bed, wondering how much truth I should tell her. I settled on honesty. "With the lords and ladies of the courts doing nothing about it? No."

"And yet, *this* town still stands," she argued.

I threw an extra pillow to her side and eyed her cautiously. "Please don't mistake whatever Adrian is doing as kindness."

She huffed and crossed her arms. No matter my actions, I couldn't coax her to the bed. "Do you think so highly of everyone?"

I stilled and looked up at her face—her absolutely pissed-off face. What the fuck was going on? I raised an eyebrow as I tried to open our mindspeak again, but she was closed off entirely. Fuck.

I swung my legs over the edge of her side of the bed and pulled her to me. I trapped her between my knees, holding her still, with no more intention than to drive home the understanding of what I was about to say.

"When my shadows exploded across the wastelands, turning those faeless who were roaming there—exiled by their own courts—into Shadowfae, we needed supplies. Food and shelter. And we were turned away. Every time, for far too long. It wasn't until our numbers grew and we began to make our own concoctions from Gillies Forest did they want anything to do with us. And it all stopped again when the fae went missing."

Her features softened. "Even the Courtless?"

"Their heir to the throne was missing. They kept to themselves until I returned him to them."

"Jair?"

I nodded.

She rubbed her bottom lip with her fingertips again, contemplating what I told her.

I traced the subtle movement with my eyes, like a pendulum, ever curious to know what those lips felt like. That impulsive brush of a kiss I gave her in the Fortress had only served to tease me. So I did what any noble fae would do; I tried a third time to forcibly pry inside her head to see where she was going with this. I was met with a thick black wall; she had barred me out completely and wasn't giving in. Which was probably a good thing, considering the direction of my thoughts.

And like a cold bath, those piercing eyes shot back to me as she said, "So you'll do nothing? About Lord Aborys's attacks against the faeless or if The War of Many finally comes crashing down?"

Ah. Here it is. My mouth twitched. "When I get my shadows back, and I will, I will protect my court and the Courtless as best I can. But the other courts? They can squabble and steal and rip themselves apart for all I care."

She looked down as if she wished to not see me, and my skin prickled at her reaction.

I was becoming increasingly aware that I cared what she thought of me. I was letting her down, and something inside me was *hurting* with this knowledge. "You don't like my answer?"

She pursed her lips. "When my water magic left me . . . I felt —I feel, helpless. And I hate it. But that's how these faeless in Kyrrahalyn and Blackwater and across the island feel every day. And you sit here with all this power. These shadows," she said, gesturing to them as they trailed up her legs, "are pulsing in waves I can feel through my entire being."

She was doing bad things to my ego.

Keep going, I urged through mindspeak.

Her eyes locked with mine again. "And yet, you do nothing."

Ouch.

I tugged her toward me, pulling her off her feet. I wanted to coax her out of her misery. She relented and landed on my chest with a huff. I tucked her into the curve of my body, spooning her. And I wanted to tell her to sleep and enjoy the soft bed we had for the night. To leave the problems of the island for the morning. But I knew her mind was whirling like spokes on a spinning wheel.

And the worst part? She had me thinking, too. Thinking about how she was infinitely better than anything else on this fucking island and how selfish I was to want her to stay with me while I trekked Winter, got my shadows back, and left, possibly forever.

I looked over at the traitorous gods' daggers on the bedside table. The ones that would cut this magical gold-and-silver tie that bound us to each other. She'd be free to go. And I feared it more than ever, that if she wasn't tied to me, she'd leave. Because what in me was there worth her staying for?

I sighed. "What is it you'd have me do? If I were to get involved?"

"Help, Kaderyn. I'd ask you to help them."

2

VALENTINA

I T TOOK ME FAR TOO LONG TO FALL ASLEEP. I
listened for Jair's light footsteps and Teal's drunk laughter
before I could close my eyes for good. Kaderyn was
comforting against my back and, though I barred him out of my
thoughts, I listened to his steady breathing.

I yearned for his power and was frustrated at his inability to
care about the island. But even that frustration was quenched
with the reminder that Kaderyn had been through things I
knew nothing about. He'd seen and done things I was inexperi-
enced to.

I traced his palm with the tip of my finger; the very spot he'd
shown me where an angry, red scar lay. Branded into his skin
was the shape of an iron key we were now using to get to his
chests. Now it was smoothed over, his fae glamor doing
wonders to hide his imperfect skin. But he'd shown me that
night in Kyrrahalyn, so I traced it all the same.

I traced it until sleep finally came.

I awoke sometime in the early morning to find my limbs tangled with Kade's, my head resting on his chest and my cheek pressed into his bare skin. His body was warm and hard under mine and there was a safety in being wrapped up in his arms. In my groggy state, I pressed my hips into his thigh as my thoughts waded back to memories of our naked bodies embracing in the pool outside the nuckelavee cave. I thought back to the way his fingers had curled through my hair, slightly tugging, entreating me to trust him.

And everything now smelled like him. The sheets, my shirt. Me.

I pressed again, but it just lit the desire I felt burning inside, this *need* for closeness with someone I could finally trust. Strong fingers pressed up under my chin, tilting my lazy head up to his face. His black eyes were desperate as he rubbed the pad of his thumb over my lips. First softly, then again hard before he dropped his face down to mine with a predatory gaze that froze me.

His breath tickled my lips as he leaned down and brushed our mouths against each other with delicate curiosity, promising satisfaction. Much like he had in the Fortress so long ago.

Though my body wanted to find out *exactly* how we could get these ties off the proper way, my mind flicked back to our conversation the night before. Because this was it, wasn't it? Even if I trusted him, he had a one-track mind for his shadows. And I didn't think I could ever ignore the problems of this island ever again.

His hand slid slow and sleep ridden against my waist, before it tightened and pulling me harder into his thigh. His mouth moved closer and—

"You're really to do nothing about the faeless, then?" I asked into his curved, warm lips.

He stilled, either wishing I had stayed silent or thinking of a way to salvage the moment. But I'd spent too much time last night thinking about Terna, the Autumnfae at the Fortress, and her faeless sister, Jassa, in Kyrrahalyn; about Teal and why she had a fear of caves; of Jair going missing for decades; of the fae stolen from their own courts, never to be heard from again, and the massacres committed by Lord Aborys.

The island was in a state of chaos. And those with power were doing nothing about it.

Kade didn't have time to answer before someone hammered at the door.

"Kaderyn, he's here," came Jairek's voice from the other side.

Kade's black, piercing eyes shot to mine before he brushed a strand of hair off my face. His voice was heavy and harsh from sleep. "Stay behind me. Please."

He pulled himself back on the bed, kneeling between my legs as he pulled on his shirt. His face had gone unreadable, and I worried I'd pushed him too far on the topic of the faeless.

A few minutes later, we descended the creaking stairs to a busy tavern full of excitement. In the middle of a buzzing crowd in the tavern's main room was a male clothed in a deep-indigo tunic edged with silver embroidery. The blue was the same color as the Faebric Kade kept in his pocket that housed the iron key. This male's smile was large, and his teeth were stark white against a rather small but gorgeous face. He stood with the arrogance of any fae male, an arrogance I could not ignore. I slinked back behind Kade's shoulder as I peeked at the dark-haired male before us.

Something was different about him. There was no urgency, no force in his posture that most of us—but especially those of Blackwater—carried. Something lay underneath that calm, something unpredictable, an unhurried sense of peace lined with anarchy. He was beautiful, but he carried that knowledge with him. Back at the theater in Elaria, Sisaria carried this air too, but she used it mostly for money or applause. I didn't know this fae's asking, and that made him dangerous. But most noticeable was the way this male carried himself, like he ruled the world. And maybe here, in this sleepy, backward town—he did. I had to guess this was Adrian.

The faeless kissed his fingers and bowed at his feet, and I wondered if I should do the same. What was the protocol here? I'd never met a god before—demi or whole. A sharp growl from Kaderyn warned me not to drop to my knees alongside them.

"Kaderyn!" Adrian, the demigod, shouted with his arms wide as if greeting an old friend. His voice was beautiful, in a singsong way. "What a surprise."

"They were just leaving, Adrian," Avika said as she straightened her posture and pulled back her shoulders.

"Oh, what a pity." His face crumpled into a pout. "I would have liked to show you around this town that I'm so *generously* saving."

"You mean drowning," Kaderyn growled, leaning against the worn railing of the stairs.

I turned to Teal, who sat seething on Jair's shoulder. Jair appeared relaxed, but I knew better by now than to think he was.

"The courts north and east of here cannot step under it. This town of beautiful faeless are protected." Adrian caressed the cheek of the server, Sloane, who knelt at his feet and looked up at him like she owed him the world. "Be pleased I completely forgot about either of your courts when I fortified this town, or your skin would have run from your bones three steps in." He tossed something in his mouth and chewed.

Kaderyn's shadows swirled around us slowly, menacingly, and I gripped his arm tightly as he moved to step forward.

"Another year and that river will engulf the town entirely," Jair said.

Adrian tossed something in his mouth again, and I realized they were nuts of some kind. I squinted. Hazelnuts maybe.

"And what are you two doing that's better, I wonder? Other than screaming across the island about your lost shadows. Ah, pixie! There you are! Last I saw you, you were one chomp away from being an ogre's toothpick."

"One chew
And I'd be gone
No thanks to you," Teal fumed.

I cleared my throat, suddenly uncomfortable. Had he heard our conversation upstairs?

"And what, pray tell, do you have attached to your wrist, Kaderyn?" he asked, stepping between some revelers, knocking them to the side. They affectionately brushed at their clothes where he touched them like trying to soak in his essence.

Kaderyn shifted himself to stand in front of me. "You're losing focus. You were going on about your magnanimity in saving the town."

Adrian let out a big belly laugh that bent his lithe body backward. "You can try to hide those ties all you want; I smelled a god's relic the minute I walked in. Though Angus's daggers on the hips of a—" Adrian stopped talking as he stared at me.

Kaderyn swirled his shadows more, covering me in darkness. "Leave it alone, Adrian," Kade said in a warning.

I braced for impact, and my heart slammed in my chest so fast I felt like I might have flown away.

"How did *you* manage to find the Siphon?" Adrian's voice was one of wonderment.

But I was sinking, swallowed whole, as a dizzying sensation enveloped me. What did he just call me?

Kaderyn looked down at me, and his furrowed brows brought up a guilt I carried for not elaborating about *why* Mohr chased me when Kade had told me so much about the shadows. I still hadn't told him I could take pain away.

He gritted out, "I know I'm going to regret asking this, but —*what*?"

"Everyone out," Adrian shouted, but his eyes, even through the darkness, did not leave mine.

My gaze darted around at how quickly the tavern emptied out of fear or awe of this demigod.

Adrian lifted his hand once the room had cleared and pointed to me. "The Siphon. Her. Leashed on your wrist with Angus's Caterina del Aamod tie, you *absolute* dunce," Adrian said as he sauntered, swayed really, straight up to Kaderyn's twirling shadows.

My lips parted in anticipation.

Adrian waved a hand through the air dramatically, trying to shoo away the shadows between us. "Do you mind?"

Did this demigod know what was happening to me? Did he know why I couldn't use my water magic? What else did he know? I squeezed Kaderyn's hand. "It's all right," I told him. But when he didn't move them, I stepped forward out of the darkness, and the golden ties between us dropped from Kaderyn's sleeve, clashing with the blackness of his shadows.

"Valentina," Kaderyn warned.

"What's happening to me?" I asked in a whisper, face to face with a demigod.

"*Valentina*," Adrian said my name, working it around his mouth like a fine wine. "Oh, what a beautiful rarity you are." He ran a thumb down my cheek before Kaderyn's chest bumped into his, shoving him out of the way.

"Hands to yourself unless you want to lose them," Kaderyn snapped.

"Oh, sit down, Kaderyn. You and I can go a hundred rounds and still make it to first call when Avika starts serving. Don't bore me with empty threats."

"I'm not the one wearing Angus's daggers," Kaderyn said, drawing attention to what I had holstered around my waist.

Adrian's nose twitched, but he proceeded to ignore Kaderyn and he turned back to me. "I bet you only feel the magic of those in your proximity. I bet here in a town full of faeless you feel nothing at all. As though you are no more fae than one of them. I suppose the exception would be the invasive Shadowfae tied to your wrist and the lionshifter holding up the wall over there. And of course, your ability to pull another's pain into yourself. You're a Siphon, Valentina, of magic and pain."

Tears overflowed across my cheeks. Adrian *knew*. But my blurry eyes sought out Jair, who leaned up from the post, watching intently. *Oh gods*, he was going to know what I did in the Narrows. He had been shot by one of Winter Court's hollowood arrows when he stepped between me and the small Winter's general, Helle. He was going to know I took his pain.

"You are one of a kind, beautiful Valentina, and it would be my honor to show you what you are capable of. You were very strategic in tying yourself to her, Kaderyn. Kudos to you for finally planning something for once," Adrian continued.

Tears were streaming down my face as my eyes flicked to Kade's. I could barely comprehend what he was saying.

"I want nothing from her. Don't twist this into something it's not," Kaderyn ground out.

But Adrian just smiled. "As she stands there in nothing but your shirt."

Did you know what I was? I asked Kaderyn in mindspeak because I was choking on tears, and I couldn't find my voice.

Don't listen to him, Kaderyn's desperate voice came through. *Please.*

"Where have you been hiding?" Adrian said in a singsong voice, eyes shining.

"Say nothing," Kaderyn growled, pulling me away.

"Summer Court," I found myself saying. Was this why I couldn't feel water magic anymore? Because I was too far from Summerfae? The strongest and eldest fae lived next door to Father and me when I was a faeling in Willowspeak. Before Winter came when I was six and changed my whole world. And then in Elaria, faeless never could afford our performances in Otti Theater anyway.

"That explains why Angus was so generous to grace you with his daggers. And I almost don't want to ask why you're tied together by a blessed scarf, but I do love a good romp story. I just heard the catchiest little tune of a virgin on a cliffside." He started humming the verse.

"I am not fae, then?" I asked, leaning in. Desperate.

"Oh, you're something else entirely. Afraid someone was mucking around the day you were placed on this earth." He went back to humming that vulgar song. "I heard the other gods babbling about a Siphon once when I returned to get . . . something for a friend."

"You have no friends," Kade said, but I ignored him.

"The gods? How do I call them? Can you bring them

down?" *What was I to do, throw rocks at the sun? Yell? Pray?* No doubt, I'd done that enough since I'd been taken.

Adrian burst out laughing. "Oh, they would not listen to me. Afraid I've done some mucking myself."

"What else?" I wiped at my tears with shaking hands. "What else do you know?"

Adrian stopped his humming and his eyes flashed, almost victorious. "Well, I also know those daggers at your waist will cut the ties on your wrist. And I have a feeling I'm not the only one in this room who knew that." His eyes danced to Kaderyn, who became so still beside me. "You could be free to go anywhere you choose. And into my company is always an option."

I recoiled like I'd been slapped. Kaderyn knew these ties could be cut by the daggers? Hadn't I asked him about this back in the cave? What did he say, again? My mind was reeling. Did he want to keep me tied to him for what I could do? If not for being this—this Siphon—but for being the keeper of the gods' daggers and being able to touch iron, which he very well couldn't.

"By the parents of the gods, Adrian. I swear I will find a way to kill you before I'm through with this island."

"Oh, there's a threat I hear twice weekly, Lord of Shadows. Yet here you are, still so far from your band of Hunters. Plus, you're swearing on my relatives, and I can promise you, they don't much care which way the fates of Eadha flow."

Kaderyn stepped forward, wrath and vehemence spinning wildly in his shadows. Adrian's resolve stuttered for barely a fraction of a second. But Kade kept walking, almost dragging me with him, before he shoved Adrian back. "Decades ago, you left us in Bran's lair," Kaderyn said as his shadowsword materialized in his hand.

"You made it out," Adrian snarled, but relented and backed up a step.

"Through no help of yours," Jair said, his arms flexing as he took Kaderyn's side.

But this seemed to crack something in Adrian that even Avika, who had stayed and witnessed this entire ordeal in silence, spoke up. "Adrian—" she warned, her normally powerful voice now shaky.

"Help?" Adrian snapped as static hit the air, magic so strong it was palpable.

Worry shot through to my toes. What good would angering a god do?

"Don't lecture me about helping. You spend your days crying about your shadows while I'm here, protecting this town from Winter's wrath and Autumn's cruelty. You think it's easy pulling rain clouds from nothing? You don't think I'd rather be having a strong drink in a tall tower with good company?" Adrian tugged at his tunic, straightening himself out.

But Kaderyn couldn't let it go. "Why do you protect this town, Adrian? What's in it for you?"

"Reasons far more important than sitting here arguing with you lot. You question my motives? Why don't you give it a try?"

"Adrian, don't do it, we need you—" Avika pushed between the warring demigod and the Lord of Shadows. If she was scared, she didn't show it.

But we all heard the sudden dissipation of rainfall on the tavern roof. The once steady pattering slowed, then ceased altogether. We all looked toward the windows and sure enough, sunlight streamed in, in a rainbow array of colors onto the tavern's moldy floor.

"This town's extermination will be on your hands,

Hunter," Adrian said. I turned my gaze from the windows to him to find his eyes staring at me. "I'll be seeing you again."

And with that, he disappeared in a cloud of brine-smelling mist. I blinked at the spot he'd disappeared from. I had heard that some of the gods could turn into nothing at will, but Adrian was the first god I'd met, and my mind failed to understand what my eyes were seeing—or not seeing. Luckily, Avika was there to pull me back to the room with her fury.

"You absolute oafish pile of black smog!" Avika hollered, facing off against us.

But a crowd of faeless faelings had congregated outside and their laughter filtered in through the cracks in the framework of the wooden tavern.

Sloane barged through the door, shoulder first, eyes searching for the god who had left. The one who had taken the rain with him. "Where is our savior? Where is God Adrian?" Her frantic, pale face was drawn into an expression of disbelief.

"He left you," Kaderyn grumbled, moving to go back upstairs.

In the open doorway behind her, I saw faelings tentatively splashing in puddles, squealing. They had no idea what the lack of rain meant. This town had nothing to bribe the fae with. They didn't mine metals or forge weapons. They had little to trade in food, as the rain had hampered what they were able to grow. And they were so far into Spring Court it would take days riding to get word to Scarlotta, the capital of Spring, to ask Lady Fede for soldiers to spare. If, that is, she cared about what happened to Blackwater Junction at all. And judging by what Adrian had just said, he had been providing—or drowning—them with rain for ages.

"We'll stay," I found myself saying to Sloane's desperate eyes and Avika's piercing stare. Ignoring the looks from Jairek and Kaderyn.

"Of course you are. You four are protecting my town until I get back," Avika said, crossing the room and leaning over the worn wooden bar to grab something below.

"And where are you going?" Kaderyn asked.

She pulled out a holster of daggers and snapped them around her muted orange pants. "To look for Adrian, a god who can mist at will across an island, who either cares little for my safety—Breena! Come downstairs!" she shouted, before continuing, "Or is bound on seeing me and my kind wiped from existence. And you," she said, as a little faeless faeling—*no, not faeless,* I thought, as power bounced off the little female trotting pensively down the stairs, "are going to make sure the town is still standing while I convince an immortal sea god to continue to drench our town with a protective rain at no perceivable benefit to himself."

"So you don't know either? Why he does it?" Kaderyn said before I whacked him across the arm.

"That's not the point, Kaderyn," I said, watching Avika interact with the small faeling. They were discussing food to gather and horses to ready. The little one was not much older than ten. "You're bringing a faeling with you? Will it not be too dangerous?"

Avika straightened from where she had stooped over, giving orders to the young fae, and squared her shoulders. The new sunlight glinted off the bronze metal daggers now secured at her waist. "I trust my daughter at my side more than in your care."

But I didn't fully hear what she said because the ends of those daggers had my blood pumping to my ears in recognition. There, on Avika's dagger handles, was Cillian's insignia—the wolf's face howling inside a beast's paw. I looked wildly between the Avika and her daughter. They both had deep brown skin and dark hair, not unlike Roshan, my best friend from Summer Court. But the female she called Breena looked up at me and I gasped. Did she just say daughter? There, staring up at me, were Cillian's telltale green eyes and his hard mouth.

Oh gods.

He had a faeling. And Avika . . .

I looked up at her as my brain stuttered against itself. One thought crashed into the next too quickly for me to come up with any idea other than she was somehow involved with Cillian.

And I realized why he was so agitated that Autumn was sending forces to Blackwater Junction. It had nothing to do with protecting his court. It had to do with protecting a family I didn't know he had.

Cillian had a family.

I repeated it on and on in my head like it was somehow going to allow me to come to terms with it.

Easy, Valentina. Deep breaths, came Kade's voice from our mindspeak.

But I needed details I couldn't find out. How? When? Why?

Why come see me in the theater? Why pry into Daria three years ago about what I was? Why lead me on if only to be his . . .

Oh gods, he knew of my ability to take pain and he used it quite extensively. Would Cillian do that? Use me for sex and what I could do? But why didn't he tell me I could siphon others' magic as well? Kept caged in Otti Theater, he always knew where I was. He always knew how to get what he wanted.

My mind was reeling, spinning out of control. All memories of Cillian altered; all of the touches he pulled back from, all the looks he turned away from. It was clear in the hard stare now meeting mine that his thoughts had been here with this deep-skinned, gray-eyed faeless.

Avika and Breena left out the back door of the tavern, back where we had kept Malvasia and the mare for the night.

And because my mind hated me, I started comparing myself to the strong, capable faeless, Avika. I thought back to my last night with Cillian, when he stormed out, leaving me in pain on the bed we'd just spent the night in. How weak I was to almost beg him to stay.

"By my hounds, Valentina. Have a drink. For both our sakes." Kaderyn was grimacing after hearing where my thoughts had gone. He held out his bottle of Solanci.

I snapped my attention to him as his pained face was staring at a moldy spot on the floorboards. I had some vague idea Jairek was talking down a nervous, hung-over Teal, but otherwise we were alone in the tavern.

I licked my lips before snatching the bottle from his hand.

A sea god just told me that I was something capable of taking others' magic. And I found out the male I cared for, the one I thought was across the island searching for me, had a family he'd never thought to mention.

I chugged the inky, citrusy liquid. "Oh gods, why does it burn?" I choked.

But before he could answer, I lifted it to my lips and chugged more.

The pain of the burn was taking my mind off my problems. Because what was hitting me too was that we were now responsible for a town we'd effectively stayed in for less than a day.

Teal and Jair stared at me. Jair's eyes were full of a compassion I wished I'd never seen because the pity was gut wrenching. I leaned a hand on the railing, not coming up for air from the bottle until I could properly drown my traitorous mind like the town we were now stuck protecting.

Teal broke the silence first.

"The gods can condemn

Now there's two of them," she whispered in awe—and not in a good way—presumably talking about Kade and his obsession with this stuff.

Kaderyn. Lord of Shadow Court. Leader of the Wild Hunt. Who didn't tell me what Angus's daggers could do. Did he know what I was and was he planning on using me the way Cillian had?

I pulled the bottle from my mouth. "And you!" I rounded on him, and he went as wide-eyed as the rest of them. "You knew these daggers would cut these stupid lovers-ties, and you said nothing. For days we've been traveling, stuck together with the daggers at hand."

"Come, Teal, let's keep a lookout," Jair said, nudging Teal.

I waited until the door shut, drowning the cheers of the faelings outside. "I trusted you," I whispered, tears running down my face.

"And you still should," he urged, but his words were terse as if he wanted to say more but wouldn't let himself.

I felt completely and utterly betrayed by everyone. But worse, I felt stupid. And I didn't have time to figure out if I was taking out all my despair on Kade, because last night's conversation reeled through my mind. And we'd just doomed this town of faeless to those who wish them harm. "If I cut these ties, you'll stay and protect Blackwater and not leave these faeless to their fate."

His mouth twitched. "Valentina—"

"No," I interrupted sharply, sucking in a deep, shaky breath. "This is what's going to happen. I'm not cutting these ties until Avika has found Adrian. Until Blackwater is safe." I shoved a finger at him. "You don't get to give up on the faeless."

"Valentina—" he tried again.

"I'm not finished. Until they get back, you're going to train me to use your shadows. They're constantly dancing across my body. I might as well use them."

"I won't leave you," he ground out. But his eyes drew down, intense and full of worry that I almost wished to cut the ties just to get away from the pity in his stare. "Valentina, do you want to talk about—"

Did I want to talk about Cillian? Or how I had no magic unto myself and had to rely on those I was around? Or that too many on Eadha Island now knew I could take others' pain? Or that Kaderyn kept from me the power of the daggers?

"Never," I answered.

3

KADERYN

WHAT WAS I DOING? What, in this giant mess of things, was I doing? I sent out shadows slick and neat, hugging dark corners and barren streets.

I'd visited Blackwater prior to this venture, back when the rain was just a mist and alleys hadn't turned into rivers. But there was no faeling of Cillian's here then.

I pushed the shadows out farther, over moss-covered ground, and through mouse-made tunnels, worming my way deeper into Spring Court.

Searching for the Berserker.

Searching for Cillian.

I was going to string him up from the tallest of trees or bind him to the base of one for the birch hounds to find.

Or better, give that dog a bath in the brine waters of a certain nuckelavee cave.

My shadows slowed, then halted altogether. I furrowed my brows, forcing the darkness on, but hesitation built in my gut. If I pushed more, I'd have to pull shadows from elsewhere.

Slowly I retreated them back through Blackwater's streets, past empty gutters that were overflowing a day prior. Past soft, fearful crying because the one protection this town had was gone.

I dropped my fucking fae glamor and rubbed a calloused hand over the parallel scars on my chest.

Adrian left because of me. Valentina's mind had gone somewhere dark, and I didn't know how to pull her out.

I was not meant for this island.

I was not meant for her . . .

4

VALENTINA

I 'M A SIPHON, I thought.

Siphon.

I moved the word around in my head like, if I did it long enough, clarity would hit me and I would be shown what I was. What my purpose was. Was it greater than spending my days in Otti Theater?

Si-ph-on.

"Honestly, Valentina, I'm all for brooding," Kade said as he sat wedged between a small bath and the wall in one of Blackwater Tavern's upstairs bathrooms. "My hounds know I've been exceptional at it for quite a few years—"

"Centuries," I mumbled, dipping my mouth back under the cold bath water. It was steaming hot when I got in over an hour ago.

"You can correct me all you want as long as it gets your mind off saying that damn word again."

If words were titles, then what was this? What did mine

mean? Kaderyn was a Harbinger, a leader. Cillian; the Berserker.

But I siphoned. I *took*.

"They call me 'soul stealer' don't forget," Kade said darkly.

"Get out of my head."

The golden Caterina del Aamod ties draped over the bath edge between us. They glinted in Blackwater's newfound sunlight as it streamed in through the small window.

And I'd taken away Kade's freedom.

He stilled beside me before growling, "Don't say that."

I rolled away from him, and the water sloshed against the stone tub walls in answer. "Have you heard of a Siphon?"

He cleared his throat. "Well . . . I didn't spend much time paying attention to the happenings of the island, Val."

"Gods, you've had such your head up your ass."

"Perhaps before," he said softly.

Siph—

"That's it. Come on," he said, hoisting me out of the water with tender care. "My legs are cramped and numb, and the water is freezing."

He placed me down on the small bathmat and wrapped me in a towel from chin to knees, snugger than necessary. If he saw me naked, I did not care.

"What I have learned from dark thoughts is that the more you focus on them, the louder they get. When you can't replace them with something else, distraction is the answer."

"I thought you were going to say drinking," I said, my teeth chattering.

"Well, one thing at a time. Let's find a place to train."

AND SO, WE TRAINED. HARD. FOR THREE SOLID DAYS.

Jairek patrolled the first night and day in lion form as Teal sat atop the steeple of their tallest building. In most towns we'd passed, the largest structure was a shrine, dedicated to the gods that looked over them. Summer had one for Angus. In this town, it was for Adrian. A place Kaderyn refused to step foot in.

The streets, though no longer flooded, revealed their distress in the newfound sunlight. Compacted clay lay bare where the cobblestone had washed away completely.

I grabbed a pair of bronze Autumn-forged daggers sitting idle in Blackwater's empty hall from a dusty table against the far wall. If they'd ever used this building for a gathering, it couldn't have been recent. The daggers were like the ones Cillian had given me, but without the heavy insignia on the hilts. This made them considerably lighter. I twisted them in my hands. Maybe a little too light.

I faced Kaderyn who, because of the ties, was forced to follow behind me into the old festival hall. He crossed his arms, looking positively bored as I held up the daggers in a ready stance.

"I don't think so," he said, reaching out and snapping the daggers from my hands by their dulled blades.

His black eyes locked on mine like intense and devouring black pits as he pulled the gold and yellow gods' daggers from my waist and placed them hilt first into my hands.

I pointed them down quickly. One cut and he could die.

And through my misery, this fact echoed painfully in my head —and my heart. "Did you leave your brain in the nuckelavee cave? We aren't practicing with these."

"I could tell by the way you grabbed those other ones that their weight is off. There're no wooden swords in battle, Valentina. When we return to the safety of my court, you can putter with them all you want. Let's go," Kade said, materializing his shadowsword. He backed up as far as the ties would allow.

I ignored his mention of us returning together to The Court of Shadows. I had someplace I needed to be. "And when I kill you, I'll just . . . what? *Drag* you to Elaria?"

"No, you'll cut the ties. Be free to go back to that sunshine you crave so badly."

I stared at him. Did I *want* to return to Elaria? I had pulled them into a battle with General Mohr from Autumn Court. He'd made it clear he'd hurt them if I didn't return to him. But returning to him was a death warrant. It was no longer about what I wanted. I *had* to return to Elaria. I was the help, after all. And was my worry about Kade leaving me here alone to defend Blackwater baseless? Was I just stalling, refusing to cut the ties?

I'd spent those weeks across Autumn and Spring coming to terms with being attached to Kade, so much so that the very idea I could cut us apart seemed to send me into a panic. He said he wouldn't leave me, but he had refused to tell me that the daggers could cut the ties to begin with and I was already spiraling under Cillian's secrets. I didn't know who to trust.

Breena looked well into her tenth year and Cillian and I had only met a few years ago. The fact that he never told me about his life, like I wasn't worth the effort, hurt my heart so much it felt like it wanted to leave my body.

"If we're going to go spiraling with these thoughts again,

little lion, I'll be needing more Solanci." But Kade dropped his sword a few inches and softly added, "I know you're hurt, and you feel betrayed. I am here to talk about it if you'd like. You can trust me, Valentina."

No. I didn't want to talk about it; I didn't want to open the floodgates to all the emotions I didn't want to deal with. I didn't want to break down while we were stuck here, protecting a town of faeless. So, "I hope you're quick," was all I said.

"And I'd be more than happy to help drown these Cillian thoughts with you when you so choose. Let's go."

I slashed my dagger out first—at the mention of *his* name—but carefully, as if I were sparring with a faeling. Kade knocked his sword down hard enough that the yellow dagger I had just thrust out was ripped from my grip and went clattering to the floor.

I frowned. "That's Angus's dagger."

"If he's displeased, he can come down and show me himself. But something tells me"—he shook his arm with the Caterina del Aamod ties—"that he's having a rather good laugh wherever he is. Again," he urged.

I grumbled but kept my eyes on him as I stooped to pick the dagger up. Then I attacked—harder.

After half an hour of him shouting at me to stop pulling back and thrust further, I found myself pressed up against the dusty wall, both of us breathing hard. His knee was between both of mine as he pinned me to it.

"If you cut the ties, we can spar a little farther away," he panted. His sweaty face looked down at mine, but his dark eyes were shining, full of humor.

I quirked up an eyebrow. "I was just getting comfortable being so close to you. Besides, I thought you wanted these ties off only one way . . ."

His black eyes flicked to my lips as his brows furrowed. He pressed his warm, hard body into mine and only pushed further when I laughed and tried to squirm free.

I licked my lips, remembering what he'd said in the rowan trees in the Narrows. "What was it? 'To fuck me so well that me and my naive soul are satisfied enough that the gods will release the scarf.'"

He froze inches from my face, and his shadows swirled slowly, suspending themselves in midair. Shock or anticipation ran across his face, I wasn't quite sure which. And I didn't dare breathe as I lifted my free wrist and held my yellow dagger to his temple—but a healthy distance away because, though I was entirely confused at what I wanted, where I was supposed to be, and who I was, one constant factor remained: I did not want Kaderyn to die.

His eyes flicked to the dagger, and he let out a low groan and backed away. "Come on, I need a bath."

THREE DAYS HAD PASSED SINCE ADRIAN HAD LIFTED the rain and Avika and her daughter had gone off searching for him, for the god who had slowly been washing away their town, in one constant never-ending downpour. I worried for Avika and her daughter's safety. Because no matter the truths that Cillian held from me, I couldn't put his blame on them. Though the comparisons to Avika did not relent.

Once the novelty of the rainless sky wore off, the faeless spent the first day cowering inside their homes, beckoning their faelings inside, as they realized what the rest of us feared. But by day two the grains were sprouting, shooting four feet tall, and we found them all out in their fields again.

The faeless didn't waste a minute planting and harvesting what they couldn't before. We were in Spring after all, a court for fertility and air, and the grounds took well to the shining sun. They were resilient, these faeless, I couldn't help noticing. Just like Terna in the Autumn Fortress.

With a song on its wings
And life at its feet
Wind guides us all

I recalled Spring Court's mantra that I learned from Cillian. Bleh, Cillian.

Not a day later, that same hall we sparred in was being used to host a celebration. Flower garlands were strung up around the roof; hawthorn sticks were weaved together to create baskets. Faelings ran around with them, collecting cocoa-covered sweets their parents—or guardians, as was the Eadha way—had been hiding around the courtyard. I learned there were faelings who had never seen the sun before, as most of the Blackwater faeless had been too frightened to ever leave Adrian's rain. But now they were thriving, and it was beautiful.

I sat, sipping a mugful of Nightale tea in a corner booth inside Blackwater Tavern. Teal brewed it strong. She said it was to give me reprieve from my aching muscles and tired mind.

Kaderyn, at first, tried to go easy on me with training, but we both found that the harder we practiced using shadows and trying to turn my old dance-fighting skills into actual attacks and defenses, the quieter my mind became. So he stopped holding back and my body was feeling it. I stretched my left shoulder, grumbling. It wasn't like I could take away my own pain.

I watched an elderly male faeless through the green, moldy window, working away at the once rain-flooded fountain, and it startled me when water started shooting out of its top. I pressed my nose closer, my heart leaping when a band of small faelings rejoiced around him. And I smiled for what felt like the first time in ages.

The heat of Kaderyn pulsed beside me as he dug into the leftovers of the turkey pot pie Sloane had made. She'd taken over running the tavern, which I'd soon realized was the town's local gathering spot.

I absently watched Kaderyn chew, watched the flex of his stubbled jaw. I'd not relented in our training enough to allow him to maintain a smooth face. And if he knew how to use glamor to do it for him, he didn't show it.

"Can you tell when I'm using your shadow magic?" I asked, pulling apart a baguette.

He swallowed before answering, "It was always curious they'd follow you around. But now that you're intentionally trying, I can tell. It feels like a . . . a pulling." He took a sip of water and glanced at me. "How do you feel using them?"

I looked to the swirling shadows that always encompassed us as I called them to me. "You know," I said, controlling their swirling, using them to push his water glass across the table, "when firefae were around, I thought I was being burned alive."

He stopped mid-bite and looked at me.

"The very heat of the swelling magic rolling through my veins scared me. And I'm terrified Mohr is going to find me again and—don't get me wrong—I despise the general, but I almost feel bad for Autumnfae. They have this boiling heat burning through their bodies *all* the time. It so easily wants to present itself as anger. Because with Summer"—I stopped, the memories choked me—"with Summer it was like floating through calm waters, a magic that clears the mind, like at the waterfall outside the cave," I clarified, but memory of the passion we'd shared in that moment had me looking away from his steady black eyes. "Water magic is soft, soothing but powerful like rapids down a river."

He pushed the rest of his food away and turned to face me. "And ice?"

I stilled; I didn't know Winter's mantra. Summer's had been engrained in me since I was born, and Autumn's I had seen etched outside the Fortress. What was it again?

Hope lights the fire
Fury fans the flames
Courage carries us through

But Winter's? I didn't know. I just knew how I felt near that small general they called Helle. So, I stilled the shadows before releasing them altogether, snapping them to Kade like a bent stalk of grass releasing the dew.

"Silent. Deadly," I settled on, as different memories flooded me.

I was pulled from my thoughts when a miniature band of horses with their Hunters materialized out of the shadows before me. Kade's hands twitched as he morphed the shadows to show six Hunters chasing something I couldn't see. Together they galloped, with swords or weapons high in the air, their other hand twisting in the reins of their horses, running like one moving unit. I laid my head on Kade's shoulder and watched.

"And shadows? How do they make you feel?" he asked, rubbing his cheek against my head.

I lifted my hand, twirling the shadows into the form of myself, a long-haired female with a self-made waterdrop tattoo, standing before the hunting party. Hair of inky swirling shadows whipped wildly by an unseen wind. It was a shaky projection and my feet kept disappearing as I was just learning to control the shadows.

"I feel like myself," I finally said, because it was true. There was no urgency as with fire, no unnatural calm like with water, no deadly promise of violence like ice, and no strong-hearted courage like when I was around Jair.

And we watched the Hunters still their galloping, moving their horses to a gentle walk as they approached the shadow-me. The leading Hunter at the front, the one I instinctively knew was Kaderyn, his own shoulder-length hair flapping in an unseen wind, reached down, grabbed ahold of my shadow-self and pulled her up onto the magnificent horse he rode, before they all returned to gallop on the spot again.

We watched their dancing hooves and my eye caught on another Hunter, two back from Kaderyn, with a steady dot around his feet, like the shadows were avoiding him. I'd seen this before when Kade had distracted me with his shadows back in Autumn's fields of heather.

"Who's that?" I asked, pointing to the projection.

"Zedekiel. He liked—" he stopped and cleared his throat. "*Likes* his boot buckles of polished gold. It feels wrong to crowd them in shadows." He was quiet as if stuck on a memory, gave a hearty laugh, then continued, "If you think I'm irritable, don't find yourself in his company."

I looked up at him, his black eyes swirling in memories he couldn't get away from. His desperation to return to these Hunters was no different than mine to return to Elaria. We both had a responsibility we were trying to get back to. I opened my mouth to say something gentle because here I was, holding him back in Blackwater Junction.

"Come on, let's go see about getting you some clothes," Kade said, first standing from the table then absently reaching out for my hand.

We had tried to get clothes as soon as Adrian left but the one shopkeeper had stayed closed. Sloane said its owner was an elderly faeless who needed more coaxing than others at Adrian's departure.

We strolled down the narrow walkway, half torn up and washed away as the sun beamed down and a forever-light breeze blew down from the north. Not long after, we found ourselves stepping through a stained-glass door of storefront named The Sunny Bramble. It had a sign above it engraved with a needle and thread, but the word 'Sunny' was seemingly crossed out as it had a four-finger-wide piece of wood nailed over top of it at an angle. It had not been sunny here in decades—if not more, and I supposed this was easier than renaming it.

A little golden bell rang out as Kade opened the door. It was a sound too light and cheery for two fae desperately deep in nostalgia.

"Be right there," came a voice from a room behind hanging strips of cloth.

The room was packed, absolutely jammed full of clothing and fabrics. I ran my hand against cool silks, probably from Hawrenthia and rougher cottons more native to this court, when my fingers brushed a small paper clipped to a particularly stunning pale auburn cotton shirt. The marking of dimas on it had my stomach in knots, along with a further acknowledgment that I would never be able to pay Kade back. Not even when I got back to Elaria and regained my position at the theater as in-house pain reliever and an occasional dishwasher. I was never given a wage. Daria and I had made a bargain when I was ten that traded services for room and food. She would never let a renegotiation happen.

"I can't pay you back for this, Kade."

His shadows swirled once, achingly slow, and I realized I'd forgotten to block my thoughts from him. But his stare grew dark, furious, and menacing.

Before he could answer, a little elderly female shuffled out from behind the strips of cloth dividing one room from another. She had thick glasses hanging off the tip of her nose and moved with a considerable hunch in her back; the posture of someone who worked bent over a table.

"Hello, dears. What are we after? Have you noticed the sun shining? I haven't seen sun coming through my windows since —well, it's been a while now. Oh, do control your shadows, Lord Kaderyn, my eyesight is poor enough already."

If she was afraid of him, she didn't show it. But he continued to stare at me, so I gently pulled at his shadows like he taught me, reeling them in from the small room we now shared with the shopkeeper, coaxing them to me.

"Whatever she needs, Glynnera," Kade answered, his voice deep and low.

"Pants?" I said to both of them; one, as an asking if she had any; two, as an asking if it was all right with Kaderyn. Pants seemed like a fantastic idea in a windy court. I noticed that most faeless here had ones that had large slits up the sides and tightened at the waist and ankle.

Not long later we were walking back to the tavern—in proper-fitting clothes—and something felt lighter inside. Glynnera had stitched laces in the sleeve of a top so I could get it on and off with the ties.

"You can finally have your shirt back," I said, watching the last of the faelings that were playing in the water fountain be ushered into a nearby house for lunch.

"Keep it," he grumbled, but he grabbed my hand, and it did wild things to my heartbeat. "Valentina, I'm sorry I didn't tell you the daggers could cut the ties."

The sun beat down on my neck as I shrugged. "I don't know why you didn't. You've been complaining the entire time we've been tied together."

"I didn't want—" he stopped, pulling me hard to a stand-still. "Valentina, your hands are ice cold."

I looked down at my hand in his, and sure enough saw mist

rising from my skin, like ice melting in a warm sun, half lost in his shadows.

"Get inside your homes!" came Jair's bellow from the north path into town. "Everyone, get inside and hide. Kaderyn! Winter is riding in."

5

VALENTINA

ADRENALINE AND FEAR had me racing beside Kaderyn to the tavern. The euphoria of getting my new clothes had been washed away because the worst possible outcome was happening. Winter somehow knew Adrian's rain had left.

Teal fluttered from the open door as we met Jair in the entrance, helping some faeless find shelter. I couldn't see or hear Winter, but I could feel it in my bones and on my fingertips.

"I've rounded up the faeless from the fields." Jair was out of breath, panting, as he ran his fingers through his jaw-length hair. He must have shifted somewhere on the path, as he was now shoeless.

I dropped the bags to the ground as Kade jammed the door closed.

The faeless were well practiced in shutting the town down quickly. Within minutes, the only sound from the courtyard was the bubbling of the newly fixed fountain. But cloud cover had rolled in and it scattered the sun.

We hustled the faeless who came here for safety into the corner of the tavern then took up posts near the door. Except for Jair, who stood directly in the center of the room, hands flexing. If I didn't know better, I would have said he was welcoming a fight.

The first arrow missed Kaderyn's head by a foot and lodged itself into the swollen wood above me to the right.

"That was a warning shot, Hunter," came a female's voice.

"Where was that grace in the Narrows when you shot my friend?" Kade huffed back.

"I see Autumn's furs on my lands and I shoot. I expect no less from them, as they would give me the same courtesy."

"What do you want here, Helle? It's a sleepy, soggy town. Hardly to be noticed by your soldiers."

"I'd ask you the same thing," came a strong male voice, piercing the air.

Kade froze at my side and, for a moment, the shadows stilled, but I couldn't read anything from his mind. He'd all but shut me out.

I placed my fingertips on the windowsill and turned to peek out of the glass, squinting through mildew and watermarks.

An old fae, with a white beard and magic pulsing off him in waves, dismounted his silver horse behind the small female I recognized from the Narrows as Helle. She had her bow up and was ready to fire one of those white-wooded arrows. She held her stance, bow ready to let loose. Her soldiers stood the same.

The male dismounted far more nimbly than I'd thought he would. He stood regal-like, clad in sky-gray cloth under bronze armor engraved in intricate designs inlaid with blue like the arms of a snowflake. Armor I'd seen when I was six. His attire was far more elegant than Helle clad in all matte-black scales beside him. But they had the same nose, and that terrified me.

"Kaderyn, Lord of The Court of Shadows," he said, his

voice carrying across the fog-covered courtyard, clashing with the soft sound of the bubbling fountain. "My daughter told me she'd seen shadows watching her soldiers train in the Narrows. What brings you on the path to Silvermere?"

"Sightseeing," Kaderyn yelled back though no humor marked his words. "You're not welcome here, Lord Aborys."

"And you're a long way from home, Hunter, and I don't mean The Court of Shadows, whose own sky threatens to buckle under the weight of your ungodliness."

"Is it a coincidence the last of my shadows are stuck in your court, then?"

"Your shadows are of no concern to me, nor do I ever fear your hounds. I know exactly what is waiting for me when I pass and I can promise you, I'm not leaving Eadha anytime soon."

"Bold words from the lord killing innocent fae."

Lord Aborys's voice grew severe, and the air chilled so quickly my breath left a fog on the glass. "There is nothing *fae* about them. The faeless are a blight against our bloodline. They become ill with ease, have no magic to protect what's dear to them, and breed like snow hares. Their constant interference with the true fae will bring Eadha to its knees. They need to be wiped away. The future of Eadha depends on it."

It was quiet a moment longer before I strained to hear his next words. "They failed me in my time of need, Kaderyn."

"And you're taking this upon yourself?" Kade shouted.

"These courts need to remember that it was my god who caused the glaciers covering this island to recede and allowed the fae to thrive. And their way to show their gratitude is to squabble with each other like faelings. No, first I clean the island of the faeless, then I return to my rightful place as ruler of Eadha and fix this mess between the courts.

"I'll allow trade between your kind, Kaderyn. We will all thrive with my ruling."

47

It became silent.

Where was the bubbling of the fountain? I slide my hands along the windowsill, and peered to the far right to see what was going on. The water that had once cascaded down its sides had turned to ice. Frozen solid.

But my heartbeat, though I was terrified, never picked up. The steady ice magic was calming, not like water, but in a readiness for the attack, in tune with a prickling in the air that told me we were not getting out of this without a fight. My senses sharpened, and I rose to the balls of my feet in anticipation. Ice magic was allowing me to sense every bit of movement, and I was using it for all it was worth.

I noticed Lord Aborys's mouth moving like he was speaking, but no sound came out. They were methodical movements; was he chanting? And as I focused on the ice magic coursing through my veins, frost ran up the windowpane from where my fingers touched the windowsill, branching out in little twigs across its surface. I followed the staggering lines of frost until I noticed sky-blue eyes on me through the dirty and frost-lined window, those of Lord Aborys. I whipped behind the wall out of view.

A chill swept through me and out of panic or something else, I found myself tucking into Kaderyn's side. All my faeling-fears of seeing Winter again were coming true. Because Winter, again, was seeing me.

"Tell me, Kaderyn. What do you seem to have hidden in there? What is pulling at my magic so seductively?"

Kaderyn stared down at me so intensely my knees wanted to shake as he said, "These shadows are only the beginning."

"I'm not talking about you or the Shifterfae."

"Regardless, they'll stand in your way."

Metal clanking rose, but I didn't dare peek out the window again as faeless whimpered from where they hid.

"Pity, I'd offer you safe passage across my lands. You'd be able to reach your shadows in two days' time if your horse is well suited. Be off this island for good. Isn't that what you want?" I stared into Kaderyn's black eyes as the lord continued, "Just send out what I can sense is in there."

Jair and Kade shared an intense look I couldn't decipher, and I was shaking now because frost had found me. It didn't burn like fire, but its slow, comforting caress of strength and totality had me in awe and horror. Kaderyn swirled shadow magic around us.

Stories filtered to Elaria that it took weeks to chip out my neighbor's bodies from the frozen blocks they'd become, and that was even under the blistering heat of the constant Summer sun. He'd just promised Kade everything he wanted in return for me. Could I outrun the lot of them? Cut the ties and take the road south? But I'd be leaving the faeless to their deaths. No different than floating to safety down the Robinswallow River when I was six.

Metal clanging on the soft wooden floors in front of me startled me from my dread. I turned to see Jair throw down his weapons at my feet. The amber-brown eyes of the Shifterfae met mine as he cracked his neck and fell forward, shifting into a massive golden lion in the moldy, small Blackwater Tavern. And in a very Jairek-like move, he let out a low growl that rumbled through the floor, clang dishes together, and further dissolved pieces of the cobblestone walkway outside.

"Hold!" I heard Helle yell to her soldiers.

"In case you missed that," Kaderyn shouted, tugging on the ties, pulling me closer to his side, "Jairek says to 'fuck off.'"

I shook out my fingers, willing shadows to take ice's place, to flow through me as I clung to Jairek's resolve, to the brave-hearted lionshifter now nosing the tavern door. His forelegs were fixed in a ready stance.

He'd apparently had enough talking.

"I have no qualms with Shadows or Shifterfae, Kaderyn. This is your last chance to leave the faeless to their fate and keep peace between our courts."

"Well then, it seems we're at an impasse."

"These beings are a blight on our land, magicless and ill equipped. And one must really ask oneself . . . What. Is. Their. Point."

A murmuring rose around us, a violent whisper like the trees in Autumn, coming from the faeless around us. Slowly they rose from their hiding places, slowly their fear turned to anger. Until a cry rang out from across the square that made me look back out the window. Lord Aborys be damned.

"C-come and t-try!" came a male's shout from a storefront along the side street. I could see his figure in the small crack of a window that was still uncovered.

Helle stood strong, not bothered by the boldness of the faeless to her right. Her eyes stayed fixed on the tavern door, the one whose wood Jairek was splintering as his claws tried to carve their way out.

"Can we wait this out?" squeaked Sloane's voice from behind me. I turned to see her clinging to a frying pan, her pale face white as ever.

"Wait out the attack of our impending assailant? I'm afraid lionshifters are not that patient," Teal said from Sloane's shoulder, and we all looked down at Jair's razor-sharp claws as he shredded the floor of the tavern.

The air was sparking with an unmet desire for battle. This was it.

"Stay behind me in the shade of the shadows. Hold tight to

your daggers," Kaderyn said to me. Then louder, addressing everyone else, he said, "If you want to brave Winter's wrath, choose to do so freely. They will not hesitate to kill you. Sloane, dear, go to the back kitchens."

Sloane's hand trembled as she held the frying pan. "But first, I'll umm . . . I'll get the door for you."

She slid past a snarling Jair to heave what was left of the door from its latches; its bottom half lay entirely in shambles.

Jair did not hesitate. With a leap, he cleared the courtyard and bore down on Helle.

Apparently, he had a bone to pick with her.

Kaderyn and I ran out the door after him, clouded in shadows, which seemed to signal to the faeless that this was their moment, their time to make a stand.

Fear for Jair drove my steps as he bounded toward Helle's notched arrow. But she did the most surprising thing. She dropped both bow and arrow to the frost-covered ground and, with a smirk, pulled two short swords from hidden scabbards, and leapt into the air to meet Jairek halfway in a crash of claws and bronze.

Kaderyn had shot up his shadows into a black wall of magic and Winter's soldiers were busy trying to hack through them. Behind me, I sensed the closeness of the few faeless who wanted to fight for their town. Kaderyn sent out his shadows, grabbing soldiers by their ankles and tossing them backward. Some fell into the rain-made river beside Blackwater, some flew back farther into the forest beyond. If any were able to breach the shadows, Kade took care of them with his shadowsword slicing through thick Winter fabrics and bending bronze swords against his.

Lord Aborys stood, ever the regal leader, watching the battle like it was a set of curious moves on a game board.

I looked down at my gods' daggers. One nick, Kade said, would kill. But I'd never killed before. Could I?

I wasn't given the choice when a soldier came up around us. The hair on the back of my neck stood up, letting me know I was in danger, and I turned to see the bronze sword of a Winter soldier ready to slice across my face. Before I had time to raise the daggers, a blue blast shot out into his back, and agony marked his face as he crashed to the ground at my feet. I stumbled back, bumping against a battling Kaderyn. Teal's arm was extended where she flew in front of a trembling Sloane, who still held the frying pan.

"Blackwater is closed to tourists!
Push them back through Kinswood Forest!" Teal
seethed, her little face full of fury and bravery I was
proud of and envied at the same time.

I bounced on the balls of my feet. Oh gods, I was going to have to fight; I was going to have to kill, or someone I cared for was going to get hurt. But I couldn't do it tangled up with Kaderyn. He fell back into me, and we broke lines with the faeless we fought beside. I dodged around him in time to lift a dagger to stop the thrust of an enemy's sword.

Kade's ability to fight was stunted being tied to me. He couldn't lunge far enough or spin or dodge quick enough without putting me in harm's way. And the thought of accidentally cutting Kaderyn made my heart stop. I couldn't reach Winter's soldiers when his sword kept them so far away until they were too close to do something about. I needed space to fight. More importantly, Kaderyn needed his sword hand back.

We jostled again as they rounded up to our other side. Bronze met shadows. The air sparked blue.

I looked over at Jair, desperate to see that he was alive. And there, the small Winterfae general dodged a swipe of Jair's long claws and let out a small, wicked laugh. *How was any of this funny?*

She was a hailstorm riding in on a behemoth. Five-foot-nothing of frigid fury.

Helle's hand shot out, coating the ground under Jair's feet in a thick sheen of ice. He stumbled, trying to get purchase, but lion's paws were not meant for Winter's blights. His feet wanted to go different ways, which Helle took advantage of. She leapt onto his back, wrapped her arms around his thick neck, and twisted him to the hard surface of the ice. She held a dagger at his throat and my heart stopped entirely. I screamed something incoherent that couldn't be heard over the battle as I tried to run to him but the ties pulled me back.

But instead of slashing through his neck, Helle, General of Winter Court, with that ever-present smirk, leaned down, pressed one hand into Jair's massive snarling face, and she . . . licked his snout.

Jair rumbled out a growl before connecting his back feet with her chest, kicking her to the ground. My breath came out in spurts as I watched him find his balance in the melting ice and stalk toward her.

Damn it, I couldn't help anyone if I was tied to Kade. I was going to have to hope he stayed and protected Blackwater of his own will.

My hands trembled, and I couldn't breathe. I sliced my dagger against the ties that bound us. It cut through them like air, but I had put too much force into the motion.

I fell back.

6

VALENTINA

B REAKING THE CATERINA DEL AAMOD ties
dropped me to my knees like the blunt end of a knife to
the back of my skull. My vision turned black and in
panic, I tried to scramble to my feet, searching through pain-
filled stars for Kaderyn. My plan was to run to an opening, to
get away from accidentally hurting him, but the minute the ties
broke, a shock ran through my body so hard I lurched to the
ground.

My insides were shattered and torn.

I searched for Kade, who had faltered backward of his own
accord and was spinning wildly around to see what had
happened. His wide, worried eyes met mine as shock and an
ache ran down my spine. The ties fluttered, soft and surreal, to
the ground in two pieces between us.

But we didn't have time to focus on what this meant as
more soldiers, all with white eyelashes and eyebrows, came
barreling toward us.

The glistening of bronze against the newly found sun

sparked in the corner of my eye. I gasped, falling backward more as the sword of a Winter soldier came down, having just enough sense to thrust my dagger up in self-preservation. All of a sudden, the heaviness of his blade was flying away in Kaderyn's shadows, and the soldier was dangling upside down by his feet. I looked over, but Kade was fighting three fae and one was desperately trying to use their ice magic on him. Kade stopped it short by cutting off the soldier's hand, and the resounding scream that came from the fae curdled in the air.

Ice was creeping across the ground, unnaturally made, slicking the courtyard in a frozen state. Making every step we took a challenge.

"Help!" came a shout.

I whipped my head around and my gut churned at what I saw. The frosted ice magic that was dampening my steps was slowly climbing up a faeless's legs. He had dropped his weapon in his panic and was now forced to dig with broken nails into the hardening ice crawling up his body.

I jumped to my feet and bolted for him. I'd seen this before in a town a court away and I would not sit by and do nothing. I quickened my pace, not allowing the ice at my feet to grab a solid hold.

"Stay off the ice!" I screamed to anyone who could hear me as the remaining faeless scrambled back into houses along the courtyard. "Get back inside!"

I slammed my body into the frozen faeless, where the ice now crept up his calves. His screams of agony sent sweat through my body. His thick hands pulled at my hair. He clung to my shoulders like he was drowning in a sea and it was only I that could keep his head above water. Jabbing my daggers down, I used them as axes, hacking at the frost spreading across his pale spring pants, praying I did not touch his skin.

Again and again, I smashed at the ice until a large piece

broke off big enough to get a leg out. It seemed to renew his bravery, and he began thrashing to free the other leg. Eventually, he broke free, and we fell to the ice-slick ground in a jumbled mess.

"Go! Get inside!" I yelled, pushing him to move as ice threatened to crawl up any part of him it touched. And I felt it coursing through me, steadying my heartbeat and sharpening my eyes. "Barricade the cracks in the doors!"

I pulled at Kaderyn's shadows enough to send thick black trails behind the faeless's feet. As they closed themselves inside their safe holds, I sent the shadows into the cracks around the door jambs.

We were outnumbered. There were far more of them than us, and the faeless who were brave enough to meet Winter head-on now fled for their lives back into their homes. This was a losing battle.

Across the courtyard, Kaderyn grimaced and slammed a large black boot into the hard ice, smashing both the ice crawling up his pant leg and the ice below it. It shattered into reflective rainbow shards.

Jair and Helle were still locked in a snarling, snarking mess. But there, on the other side of the fountain, frozen into a statue of solid ice, knelt a soft-mannered blonde faeless who'd greeted us in Blackwater Tavern just a few days ago. The ice coursing through me may have steadied my heartbeat, but I couldn't breathe as I stared at Sloane, frozen in prayer posture, eyes hooded, as she smiled up at the fountain under a thick layer of ice.

"Sloane! Get up! Get up!" A bubbling gasp escaped my lips, and I found my feet running before I knew what was happening.

Through the shimmering ice, I saw her hands pressed neatly together, and the blue of her eyes were still visible. I pressed my hand to the ice, desperate to take her pain. To rid her of this blight, this anguish she must have felt until I could get her out.

But nothing siphoned into me. Nothing happened. I couldn't penetrate the thick ice around her. I smashed the daggers into the ice, the same way I had just done with the other faeless. But I had caught him early enough; I had made it in time.

But with Sloane? Tears streamed down my face as I smashed my raw hands into the impenetrable ice. I willed the shadows to try, but they couldn't, or I, at least, didn't know how.

And ice . . . could I take it away? I didn't know how to try without making it worse. I had no experience with this. I couldn't save her.

My tears dropped to the frozen surface, leaving indents in the cool ground, and I sank to my knees. What was I thinking? I couldn't protect the faeless; I couldn't *help* them.

Not against fae like Lord Aborys.

What self-preservation I had left allowed me to sense something behind me and I tried to turn around. Snot bubbled out my nose as I reached for my fallen daggers just as Kaderyn shouted my name across the yard.

"Valentina!" his voice boomed, a roaring sound as dark as the shadows that exploded out from him, pitching us into inky blackness.

And that was when the real screaming started.

From directly behind me came a shrieking scream and a soft thud as whoever was trying to sneak up on me met their end. They dropped in a heap to the ice at my back.

Then from everywhere all at once, weapons fell, and the muffled sound of bodies falling to ice blocked out my sobbing. I clung to Sloane, frozen in Winter's wrath like I could save her, but really, we were in the middle of an island not meant for fae like us. No matter her soft and trusting demeanor, now frozen for all to see, encapsulated in Winter's fury.

When the screaming stopped, when the darkness receded to the Lord of Shadows, his piercing black eyes stayed on me. His face was full of twisted emotion I couldn't decipher, his breathing heavy. Teal's little blue face peeked out of his hair, and her eyes went wide when she saw what I was holding.

I searched the courtyard for the one responsible for this all, Lord Aborys. But where he once stood had become a cage of ice and inside, movement of colors, mottled bronze and blue.

Helle, her expression shocked and her white-blonde hair wild, looked around at her fallen soldiers before limping to her father's side where he stood encapsulated in ice.

Jairek stalked to my side with a low snarl as Kaderyn moved between us and the enemy.

In a swift move, one of strength and fluid motion, Lord Aborys's sword sliced through his icy cage—the one he'd crafted himself as protection against Kaderyn's shadows—smashing it to pieces in a deafening roar. Ice scattered in chunks across the wide cobblestone.

Helle picked up her discarded bow and arrows with one last look at the lionshifter by my side.

"Kaderyn, Kaderyn, Kaderyn . . ." Lord Aborys taunted, stepping out of the half-broken ice enclosure. His mouth moved again in flicking motions, but no sound came out before he continued, "What's your plan? When you've returned to the Wild Hunt in the Underworld? You think you can protect your court? Or the Siphon behind you?" His eyes fluttered to mine and my heart stilled.

I pushed shakily to my feet, pulling on Jairek's brave-hearted resolve, stilling the uneasiness in my voice.

"You're an absolute monster," I spat with as much venom as I could for everyone mixed up in the pain and suffering these lords were causing. For my father, for our village, and for Sloane, frozen at my feet.

He contemplated this for not even a second before saying, "You think so now, perhaps. But maybe not always. You'll see one day, what I'm doing and what its purpose is."

"You're done here," Kaderyn growled.

"You can't protect this town forever, Hunter. Nor her, nor your court."

A silver horse trotted up beside him and a white thick-coated mare beside Helle. They rode off back into Kinswood Forest, leaving their fallen scattered across the courtyard. Helle's piercing, wild blue eyes stayed on us as she looked over her shoulder until they'd reached the cover of the trees.

"Water," I choked. "I need water."

Which felt—for the seventh time this journey—like a slap in the face for being from Summer and not being able to use water magic. But I couldn't dwell too much on that now. Sloane was stuck.

I grabbed a stray feed bucket as faeless emerged from their stores and houses. Tired and crestfallen, I hobbled to the river's edge, dunked the bucket in, and dragged it back to Sloane. I ignored Kade's pitying stare as I poured the bucket, sloshed it even, onto her frozen statue. Blue sparks littered the air where Teal had her arm outstretched, desperately trying to blast her way through the ice.

Back I went, to the barricaded river's edge, climbed green-molded grain sacks and back again. By my third trip, I passed a resident of Blackwater carrying their own bucket. He followed suit and dumped it on poor Sloane.

But the ice was frozen unnaturally strong and this struggling back and forth on an icy courtyard was going to take ages. We were losing what edge the sun was giving us.

I looked to the rooftops where wooden gutters ran along

almost every edge, which were useful when a demigod had enacted an ever-flowing rain. I climbed atop a rain barrel along a shop wall and with careful prying, heaved off the gutter, pulling it free of its nails, and jumped to the ground with it on my shoulder. I grunted, landing hard under its weight and the unevenness my shoulder provided. But I had to get her out.

In a swift motion, the weight lifted from my shoulder, and I struggled to grasp its edges as it was taken away from me. I looked back wearily to see Kade heft it onto his shoulder and saunter back to the faeless and their sloshing buckets.

Jair, now in fae form, ripped—with one hand—the gutter off a neighboring house. Shouts rang out as the faeless figured out the new plan.

"Build a channel, funnel the water from the river to—" I said, choking on the words, "to Sloane."

I had built a picture frame in Summer to take away pain from a full theater all at once. I could do this, too. And everyone moved at once, finding the strength to grab tools, to create the channel, and we began pouring water down its crevice, coating Sloane in six bucketfuls a minute.

When a joining broke farther down the line, Kaderyn's shadows swirled out and held our channel together as Sloane's poor head slowly, achingly slow, was freed from the ice.

I held her lifeless head still, brushed the blonde tendrils of hair off her fair face and closed her eyes. Cursing the damn god who abandoned her. But regret and guilt settled themselves into a home in my chest. It was us that made him leave. We should never have come to this soggy town.

And eventually—almost an hour later—the rest of Sloane's limp body slumped into my arms. Finally free of its icy casket.

I passed her to her friends as she had no immediate family, which was almost laughable. So many fae and faeless had lost those they cared about due to feuds over court lines or blood ties that even the immortal couldn't survive.

My legs trembled as I staggered into the tavern, soaking wet and starving, aware of Kaderyn's presence at my side. He'd waited, leaned against a post as Teal and I mourned Sloane before the weight of our misery hit us hard enough we had to walk away. But now we fell together into a booth near the door, and he looked as exhausted as I felt.

"Are you all right?" I asked, regarding him through puffy eyes.

He looked at me, blinking once, then pulled me into his side. He hugged me tight, and I basked in the strength he carried.

Jair flopped down into the opposite bench seat with such force that the booth shook. He rubbed the heels of his hands into his eyes. Teal flew in before the tavern door had fully swung shut, dropping the broken Caterina del Aamod ties onto the table.

I stared at them. Now broken, the gold seemed ruddy and the silver was tarnished as if it lost its shine, looking no different than a dinner napkin.

But the feeling when I cut the ties, the heart-wrenching agony of separating myself from Kade, flashed to mind even though he sat beside me now. I wondered how he felt, and pieces came through our mindspeak—one I was surprised but thankful we still had.

It was excruciating, he grumbled.

But before I could apologize, for the briefest of seconds, an intense overwhelming agony came through our bond and he shut down our minds. He cleared his throat and turned to Jair. "You want to talk about why you shielded Winter's general from my shadows?"

Jair leaned his head against the worn seat back, dark circles entrenched his eyes. He fluttered them closed. "No."

The air grew tense for a minute before Kade huffed and shuffled out from the booth and my side. "I'm going to get us food from the kitchen."

"I'll take first watch," Jair said, eyes still closed, and I looked on in awe. I could barely move, and he was volunteering to head back out.

I wanted to say something to Teal. She'd known Sloane from before all this, and even her blue skin was paler in mourning. But when the words came to mind to say, 'I'm sorry' something else bubbled up. Something stronger inside me wanted to say, 'He will pay for this.'

And I didn't understand yet just how I felt so confident. I was angry. There were a lot more powerful fae across the island letting him get away with it. Like Lord Grigory, like Lord Ohrem, Kaderyn . . . Cillian. And I did not know what Lady Fede of Spring Court was up to in Scarlotta, but she must have known about Blackwater and chose to let a demigod take care of it.

So I laid my head on the table, saying nothing to Teal as the realization hit me. I was running from a fire pit into an ice cage.

The smell of food pulled me out as Kade set down a bowl between us filled with warm meat and potatoes. He brought one for Jair and a small plate of raw meat for Teal.

"There was enough for two bowls. Jair's taking first watch so he gets the bigger portion," Kade explained, tossing down forks for us all before crashing back beside me into the booth.

He and I shared the meal. I ate the vegetables, which were much more agreeable for my stomach, and he scarfed down the meat.

I tasted nothing but regret and morbid anger.

7

VALENTINA

BY THE MIDDLE OF THAT NIGHT, I had a plan.

Sometime in the hours I'd been asleep next to Kade, because when it came time to find beds for the night, I found myself in his, I'd woken with overwhelming dread.

There was a familiarity between us, and even though we weren't tied together, we still moved as one. And I craved his closeness. I chalked it up to my fear of being alone, and we both refused to talk about it because there was no room for rest. So, in the middle of the night, I sat by the window staring out toward my future.

I would go back to Elaria, like I had promised, to make sure they were all right, but I was no longer staying there. I was going to head to Hawrenthia, Summer's capital. I would *make* Lord Grigory do something about these tyrants. Summer Court had an army, I knew they did, and they were holding idle.

But after a few hours of restless sleep later, I awoke as a different feeling hit me—a feeling I hated. My fingers were met with cold sheets as I reached across the vast bed to where Kade used to be.

I was alone.

My heart, as though someone else controlled it, started racing as my feet moved due to the building anxiety. Kaderyn was supposed to wake me when it was our turn to watch the town lines. But he hadn't, and now I didn't know where he was.

A part of me knew he wanted me to sleep, but that ugly voice in my head connected it with the way Cillian would always leave me in Otti Theater. It took far longer to shake *that* anxiety and I found myself in the tavern's kitchen, sifting through the cold cellar for food to make us.

I wasn't allowed to cook in Otti's theater due to an incident when I was eighteen when I blew a hole right out the side of the clay oven trying to heat a pot of water. Someone wrote *'Val's hole'* next to it in indelible magic and up until the day I was taken, it was there, taunting me as I scrubbed the dishes. I would bet dimas it was Petri.

So, as I cooked, I pretended I was in Elaria's kitchens. I found some chickpeas and yeast and made some hummus and pitas, throwing things together until they tasted palpable. It wasn't filling food the males were used to, but it was the best I was capable of. Nothing like Avika could do, but it would get us through until she returned. Teal, Jair, Kade, and I all funneled into the booth shortly after the sun peaked high in the sky.

"The male with the feet of frost
Is thankful for your assistance.
Thanks to you, his legs are not lost
Though to touch, they're showing resistance," Teal
said, clacking her tongue to the roof of her mouth
between mouthfuls of bread.

Pitas and hummus must have been a far cry from a regular pixie's staple diet. Though she was looking more like herself, a sadness lingered in the air. I wondered if that male I saved would ever be able to walk again.

I mumbled something incoherent in answer.

An awkward pause lingered before Jair decided he'd had enough, apparently. "We're going to discuss this exactly once, Valentina," Jair said with a hefty weight to it.

I froze, pita halfway to my mouth, but I held his eye.

"You can take away another fae's pain?"

I nodded.

"And this was something you knew before Blackwater?"

I nodded again and chewed the bite I had lined up, wishing Kaderyn's Solanci was nearby for what was coming.

He nodded along with me as if things made sense. "And when I was lying on the ground in the Narrows, a holly arrow in my gut, you did it then? You took that pain from me?"

Terror shook me still. Too many people were finding out. This was what Cillian, damn him, and Daria were worried about. What Mohr exploited. But I nodded anyway because I was so far into court lines, I had no one else to trust.

Kaderyn rubbed a hand across his face and said, "By my fucking hounds, Valentina." His voice was rough with frustration.

Jair reached across the table in a startling move, bumped his enormous chest into it, and dragged me into a hug. "Don't you ever do that again," he said into my ear. His voice was muffled by my hair. "You hear me?"

We need to talk about this, Kaderyn said via mindspeak as Jair sat back down.

Eat your hummus, I said back.

Valentina, he pressed.

"No, we don't," I said, turning to him sharply.

Teal and Jair looked up from their food and stared at us. Jair's eyes narrowed. "What's happening here?"

Kade cleared his throat. "Fuck, sorry, Jair. In everything that happened, I forgot to tell you. It seems that when I used my shadow magic in the nuckelavee cave"—Teal's mouth flopped open from where she sat on the table gnawing on a pita—"it allowed us to mindspeak."

"You absolute *BRUTE*,
It could have sealed your fates
Weaved them together like the mangrove root
Dropping you to your death on her fateful date," Teal
seethed, balling up the pita in a tight fist.

"There was no way around it," Kaderyn answered, taking the brunt of Teal's fuming anger.

But I looked at him because there was another way. He could have severed my arm, dropped me to the nuckelavees below. And suddenly his leg was too hot on mine. His presence, too close. The way his hair fell and the way he looked at me, eyes wide, almost vulnerable, then back to squinting at Jair and Teal, guarded.

"I knew something was askew
When I saw that icy dew.
I should have pried sooner
We could have bypassed Blackwater altogether.
Left Adrian to his devices
And his disciples—
No matter how misguided," Teal tutted, shaking her
head, but handed Kaderyn one of her small mugs filled
with an earthy, cinnamon-smelling liquid.

"You'd had a run-in with Winter before?" Kaderyn asked, taking a sip of the drink.

And this was the question, wasn't it? My body froze, my mind replaying that day so long ago. And what was I to do now but tell him?

So I told them everything, what I did in Elaria to warn Cillian and why Mohr was trailing us.

But more importantly, I told them about the death of my town when I was a faeling.

"Winter blew in like a rolling storm full of hail and wild things on a gale." I thought of the first time I saw their telltale eyebrows and eyelashes and their bronze armor inlaid with blue. "They did not ask questions when they funneled all the faeless to the middle of town. They did not hesitate, no matter the age, when they sent their frost magic crawling up their limbs. Winter did not stop when their victims' screams stretched far across Summer's open meadows. Not until it was over."

"You got away?" Jair asked, his nostrils flaring.

I shrugged. "Faeless and fae lived together. I could use water magic." I swallowed, because now I knew I was just siphoning it from those around me. "I blended in."

"But how?" he pressed. "You were a faeling."

"I fell into the Robinswallow River and floated in its current until it took me to the docks in Elaria. Daria, the theater's owner, took me in from there."

"Why not get out sooner? Hawrenthia was the opposite way," Kaderyn reasoned.

Teal pulled the map out from wherever she kept it and slapped it down before us, pushing bowls of hummus to teeter precariously on the edge of the table.

"I couldn't—" I started, a ball in my throat.

"Couldn't swim?" Jair asked.

"She's still Summer
Born and raised.
As all faelings are
Taught the ways of the water
Before her home was razed."

And they bickered back and forth.

"Because I—I took my father's pain. As he was stuck frozen with frost climbing up his legs with Winter's spears at his throat. He was faeless, and I took it from him." They stared, and my nerves sent me rambling. "I stumbled backward into the river, and I couldn't get out. I clung to a chunk of driftwood until dock hands pulled me out in Elaria."

"Why did you do that?" Kade gritted out.

And would they ever understand? This innate need to be helpful? But I was aware of how this last part sounded, so I mumbled into my hummus, "He asked it of me."

Teal's little face changed three shades of blue. Her cheeks puffed up and spit flew out of her mouth as she screamed and curled the map into a tight fist.

"YOU SAY NO!" She foamed at the mouth as she
leaned over the table, now on all fours.

I winced as her body shook.

"She was a faeling, Teal," Kade said in my defense.

Teal peppered me with more insults, blue sparks flying as she zoomed around the tavern, pulled a small mug from what magical place she kept it, and dunked it into a patron's drink at the bar. Liquid sloshed over its sides and on him. He shouted some obscenities, but she was already on her way back, full mug in hand, and plopped herself down straight onto the map.

We ate the rest in silence, giving Teal time to calm down.

Jair had finished his food and, with a last look at me, said he was going back out to patrol for other courts. I looked at Kade, who was still sipping something from his own mug.

"What are you drinking?" I asked as he stilled before chugging the rest and handing it back to Teal.

"It's a tonic we make in Auris
Gathered plants from Gillies Forest
The mushrooms, though unpleasant some say
Help to take the pain away," Teal answered, not looking at me. Her fury had wracked her with exhaustion.

I sat straight, furrowing a brow at Kaderyn. "What pain?"

My eyes traced his body, drifting to his forearms, where he leaned on the table, the muscles pulsing beneath and the . . . the bandage?

I gasped, reached across him, and tugged his sleeve up. "What happened?"

But he pulled out of my hands, and my spirits fell. My stupid heart caved in on itself.

His black eyes drove into mine as he raised his glass of Solanci to his mouth to wash down whatever was in Teal's medicine. "Got a little too close with Winter's blade. I'll be fine."

I stilled in the seat beside him. I had just shared my worst memories. I told him of my past, and I told him my fears, and he hadn't felt it necessary to tell me he was hurt when I possessed the very magic that could help him.

Don't you even dare, came his warning through mindspeak with a growl.

And I shut it down so hard I recoiled; I pushed him out of my head so fast I heard him suck in a breath. Why wouldn't he let me help him? It was the one thing I was good at.

I dropped the pita to the table and pushed away my wooden bowl of hummus.

"I'm going to go see if I can help around town. Excuse me, Kaderyn," I said, careful not to look at his eyes. But he was blocking my way, and I was close to climbing across the table just to escape this moment.

His mouth twitched as if he wanted to say something, but eventually he relented and scooted out of the booth, holding out a hand to help me that I promptly ignored. Because *I* was the help.

"Want me to come with you?" he asked, and my face heated.

I mumbled a no and hurried out the tavern door.

And in walking the streets of Blackwater Junction, helping reattach rain gutters and hang laundry on clotheslines to dry, I realized I was spreading myself too thin. I couldn't possibly reach Elaria, whose safety I had originally promised myself to, and help Kaderyn reach the last shadow chest, save the people of Blackwater Junction from Winter's wrath, and keep away from General Mohr and the firefae he controlled. I told Roshan I would make it back. I had made a commitment to Elaria, to Daria and Sisaria and Petri. I missed the honey mead of Summer, the fleshy peaches, and the soft silks.

But Blackwater's ruin would be on our hands, so here I stayed, anxious to get going. Anxious I was going to feel the fire-fueling anger again.

The shadows trailed in my wake like the satin aerial ribbons of Sisaria's dance, looping between my feet as I worked folding fabric with Glynnera. She told me the villagers had moved the fallen soldiers' bodies, and burned them in a ceremony last night, Winter and faeless together. Because for the faeless at least, she told me, dead was dead, no matter the court. They spread the ashes atop the tallest peak, scattering them into the wind for Spring Court's god, Daina. Which was Spring Court's way.

In Summer, ashes flowed on the sea's waves or in the winding rivers. In Autumn, they buried them. I didn't know what they did in Winter, and it wasn't the right time to ask Glynnera, who'd just spent her days hiding from them. And I didn't want to think about the Courtless or The Court of Shadows at all.

A memorial of flowers for Sloane was set up on the fountain's edge. A bouquet of yellow field daisies and white meadowsweet. It hurt my heart every time I looked at it.

Eventually, it was time to head back to the tavern. We were losing the sun, and I was preparing to take up guard duty for the night.

I met Kaderyn in our room, the one we shared back when we were tied together. My wrist still felt bare.

"Hey," he said, looking up at me as he sat on the edge of the bed.

Teal zipped around and around like a flashing blue light, wrapping a new bandage around his forearm.

"Hi." I sucked in a breath, watching the deep cut of a blade be covered by Teal's wrapping. "I'm getting ready to take the night's watch. Could one of you show me where the town's blind spots are before settling in for the night?"

"I'll be with you," Kaderyn said, pulling his sleeve down as Teal tied it off.

"What?"

"Teal, give us a minute," Kaderyn said, moving toward the door.

She mumbled something unintelligible before fluttering out, and the door shut behind her with a click.

I tried to swallow, but a lump in my throat threatened to choke me. He was hesitating too as he walked back toward me and grabbed my hand. His rough callouses and burn scar scratched at my skin as he led us to the edge of the bed. We sank down together.

"Listen, I know you're mad I didn't tell you about Angus's daggers—" he said, pausing. "I was just getting comfortable with gods' daggers in my gut. Thought I would miss it if you left."

But I wasn't listening because something bigger was stirring my anger. "I'm mad because you don't want me to help you," I blurted out.

He stopped talking and leaned back.

"You hid your cut from me. You knew I could take away your pain, and you didn't let me," I continued, feeling smaller than Teal's drinking mug.

His hands found my face, urging me to look at him. Even as my vision blurred with tears, I could see his brows were furrowed together in distress. "As best as I've been able to tell, I'm as immortal as any fae. This wound won't fester like the faeless or the Courtless. Valentina, my pain is not yours to carry."

He wasn't letting me help him and there was too much on my mind. I had to get to Elaria; I had to go to Hawrenthia and get Lord Grigory to *do something*; *anything*. But sitting here, staring back into desperate black eyes, some frantic part of me ached for him to tell me he needed me. Wished he would say I could help him, almost to give me an excuse to see his journey to the end; travel north with him to the last chest in Winter's Isles.

And before I could speak, before I could let my mouth run away with my desire to stay with this party, the soft pitter-patter against the wood-shingled roof startled me. Along with it came the smell of the sea and . . . something else, something godly.

I looked up to the wooden beams of the roof as the downpour grew in fervor. I turned to the window, hearing the faeless outside. Some yelped and ran to pull in clothing off lines, others rejoiced as they twirled outside in Adrian's rain.

The demigod was back. Avika was successful.

And my things were tucked together at the base of the bed.

I looked to Kaderyn.

His face was a wreck of emotion I didn't know how to unpack. He kept the bonds—the mindspeak—between us closed for reasons only he knew.

So, I pulled free from his grasp and got up from the bed.

Blackwater was protected again, and we were no longer leashed together. He was free to return to his search for his shadows. And I was free to return to Elaria. Where they needed me.

"Valentina," he started.

But I could hear loud talking downstairs, and I hoped it was Avika and Breena. There was no need to stay here any longer. So I looked back to him, his beautiful face, his dark body outlined in the room we shared, the bed in which he'd confessed he'd do nothing for this island I was becoming desperate to save. "We are on different paths, Kaderyn. Yours—to your shadows. Mine to—"

My chair.

I choked. "Elaria."

We got tangled, quite literally, in each other's problems but that was over now. I turned and walked to the hallway and down the stairs. Avika's gray eyes found me instantly and her smile faltered.

"I think it's safe to say any further welcome will not be heeded," she said, throwing down some packs she'd brought inside from the wagon.

Her daughter, Cillian's daughter, sat on a stool near the bar, guzzling what looked like fruit juice. Her green eyes watched me with an intelligence ages older than her stature indicated. No, there was nothing faeless about Breena.

I shuffled the bag onto my back.

Jair, his jaw set, stepped out from the crowd surrounding Avika with Teal on his shoulder.

Avika turned to him before he had time to say anything. "You lot as well. You've done enough here."

I knew she meant Sloane and the three other faeless who had died because we antagonized Adrian. And there was no arguing with her. Not just because she was right, but because Avika carried herself like any lord I'd ever met. Poised with intelligence and confidence, and I felt so stupid next to her as I slid my way around the faeless surrounding her and headed out the tavern door.

Rain coated my skin.

I vaguely registered the door opening behind me, and through the sound of the falling drizzle, Jairek's voice broke out. "What is it you're so determined to go back there for?" he shouted, rain dripping against his face.

Kaderyn appeared beside them and leaned sorrowfully against a wooden post that supported the tavern's awning.

"It's where . . ." I trailed off because it wasn't truly where I was from. "It's all I know," I settled on, shouting over sudden, resounding thunder.

Jair used the sleeve of his shirt to wipe the rain from his face. "The sun shines on us in the Courtless the same as Summer."

Oh gods, I sobbed as my tears mixed with Adrian's rain.

"I can guarantee
I make better tea
Than any you'll find in Summer's cities," Teal said as
her little hat sagged down with the weight of the
downpour.

"You could stay with us," Kade said, loud and strong as rain dripping onto his lips.

You could stay with me, he said through mindspeak and oh, did I want to.

But could I live with myself knowing I left Elaria to Mohr's wrath? And would I ever know the difference? Between someone wanting me for me instead of what I could do for them?

"I have to go," was all I could manage as the tears flowed freely down my face. I turned on my heel and made my way through the southern streets of Blackwater Junction. On my way back to Summer Court.

Back to the Otti Theater in Elaria.

8

KADERYN

S HE WAS THE CLOSEST thing to goodness I'd ever known. A vision of pureness walking away from me. I'd spent a century sorting out the details to get my shadows back and, within weeks, this small Summerfae was melting my resolve. And not just because she was more than fae, more than any creature of Eadha, but because the very thought of not having her by my side sent my heart into convulsions I couldn't explain. She'd mentioned once the island was beautiful, and I was sure the only way I saw any of it—the only way I *wanted* to see any of it—was through her eyes.

The list of things I wouldn't do for her had grown so short I was terrified I'd leave my shadows behind and follow her to Elaria.

I felt her walking farther away. Our mindspeak allowed me a small connection to the fae who made my palms sweat more than any beast or enemy we encountered so far. And she was leaving me.

That's far enough, Valentina. Any farther and I can't feel you, I told her through mindspeak, careful to keep the panic that I didn't understand hidden.

The connection was so thin, a wisp between us, but I felt her hesitate at my words. I held my breath and wished I could tell her to come back. Wished I could tell her I wanted her help —needed her help. But when my shadows exploded across lower Eadha, I swore I would never call out for help again and now I didn't have the words to tell her.

I felt her take that one last step, stepping farther away from me, and the connection fizzled to nothingness.

She was going to Elaria, and I didn't know what I had to do to get her to stay with me.

9

VALENTINA

FAT BUMBLEBEES TRACED intricate patterns through the sky as I hiked across Spring Court's vast meadows of yellow yarrow and pink wildflowers. It'd been a day since I left Blackwater, left Jair and Teal and Kaderyn in its soggy mist. The rain stopped almost as soon as I passed its village boundaries, the smell of the sea leaving with it. And the noise of the crickets filled the space Teal had kept—her incessant chatting in my ear about anything and everything. I missed it. I missed her Nightale tea. And Jair's tranquil music, and his sly, confident smile, and the way I felt brave when he came near. I missed Kade's wit, his determination, and his perseverance. Because with every step I took, I found myself floundering.

And I knew what I would find in Elaria, a basin to wash dishes and a chair with one broken leg. I hadn't had to siphon anyone's pain since Jair's in the Narrows, and that was of my own accord. But I would find pain in Elaria. I'd be sent back to the sidelines of the theater as Daria drove her parlor tricks on in full force.

But my feet carried me on. Because I said I would return. And what was I, if not helpful? But as I passed the skinny rows of corn, cobs still young on their stalks, I thought about all I'd been through. About Terna in the Fortress where I had my first look at what the females of Autumn Court went through. At what they'd overcome and where their courage was going to lead them.

I thought about the faeless, Jassa, and The Dented Spoon Inn in Kyrrahalyn, and how much she missed her sister but carried on. How they made bargains with Winter to survive. How cruel it was and how brave it was. And I thought about the basement I was heading back to and the basin to wash the evening audience's dinner plates.

I thought about Blackwater Junction. Oh gods, so much about Blackwater. They were stuck, unable to leave or rebuild with Winter breathing down their necks, having to trust in the unknown motives of a trickster god to keep them safe.

And so, I stilled in a meadow of amaranth stalks, ducking to avoid the notice of the farmers nearby. What was I doing while all these other fae and faeless were risking life and limb every single day?

I looked to the west, and I knew Summer Court's capital was there, over the hills of neatly packed rows of grain, over the canyon that separated Summer from Spring. I almost imagined him, Lord Grigory, though I did not know what he looked like, hiding in his chambers while these horrors were being committed. And what did that say? If I knew the dimples and freckles of the rest of the lords on Eadha except my own?

I wondered how Roshan fared with him. Would he have listened to the poor fae from Elaria? *But maybe he will listen to the one with Angus's daggers,* I thought as they lay heavy on my back in the new holster Glynnera had given me.

Was I being brave? Was I going to be able to leave all that

alone? Could I go back to washing dishes and being Daria's . . . what was I? A puppet? Bending to the wants of others regardless of my own will. Exploited for my need to be helpful on an island so good at manipulation and coercion. My pace slowed. What was waiting for me in Elaria? The same sandy sun, a bed smelling of Cillian and deceit, a chair so damn designed to cause me pain and all for Daria's theater and others' entertainment. I wasn't helping at all, at least not those who needed it.

I was in a constant state of falling. Falling into despair, out of wagons, off horses, boats, and falling to the fallacies of Eadha. And Kaderyn, oh gods Kaderyn, he was an entirely different sort of falling.

I steeled my bravery—the small bit inside me that had nothing to do with brave-hearted Jair. I would go to Elaria because I said I would. I had made a commitment to a theater outside a dusty desert. But I wouldn't find myself in that splintered chair with the broken leg ever again. I couldn't sit by and do nothing. I needed to see to an absent lord.

So, I sucked in a deep breath of sweet-smelling air and carried on until the chill of spring rains pounded the allium fields, drawing up the pungent scents of garlic. I hid under an old beech tree, wondering how Kaderyn was. Missing him at my side. But if Terna could stay brave, if Jassa could find hope and if the faeless could smile another day, then I could do this on my own.

Once the rain cleared, I continued on, sticking to the tall crop fields. Because there was a war to consider, or at least there was one brewing, and a firefae was hunting me down. The wind whipped from seemingly nothing into a ferocious tunnel storm, flinging debris throughout the air. My hair wrapped around my face with a life of its own, blinding me.

The clouds moved so fast, chasing each other like Kaderyn's shadow horses, changing from one shape to another across a baby-blue sky. My instincts started screaming because it felt the same way it did when Cillian would trail me down the halls of the theater. I dove for the stalks of corn, looking to hide in their cover, but a strong wind, massive in its unnaturalness, blew me back and I landed hard on my butt.

"Female, are you dense? Did you miss the ringing of the bells? There's a curfew present."

I scrambled to my feet and drew my daggers in one go. Which was my downfall as the three Springfae soldiers went for their own weapons, and they braced their stance. I realized too late my mistake. Dressed in Spring's cottons, and wandering their fields, they thought I was one of their own.

"Sorry," I began and plastered a smile on my face, "you startled me. I'll be on my way. It won't happen again."

But now they were squinting, eyes flicking over my clothes to the lack of silver streaks in my hair, and over the waterdrop tattoo on my clavicle. My heart pounded in my chest. Every second I was losing the ability to convince them, and some part of me knew I should withdraw my daggers. But I'd been through an auction at Autumn's Fortress, shot at by Winter's general, dropped into nuckelavee sludge, and I'd defended a town from Lord Aborys's attack. I relaxed my stance, but the red and yellow daggers would be pried from my hands when I was dead.

I could tell who their leader was, as he stood a foot in front of the others, and they glanced at him every few breaths, waiting for a command. The larger one behind had small beady eyes I'd recognize anywhere. I'd seen him ogle Sisaria in Otti Theater enough.

"Using water magic against soldiers of Spring Court in our own borders is a punishable offense. I suggest you hold yourself in check," the leader said.

I flinched, as it felt like salt in my wounds. I couldn't if I wanted to. But a stirring—like a tornado in my chest—rose up, and I realized I'd felt this a thousand times before, this breathlessness and headiness when Cillian was around. I looked down at my hands as the dirt stirred around my feet. Was this wind magic? This feeling I always got when the two of us were alone. The stirring in my belly that I mistook for love or lust was really just me siphoning his wind magic. A pained laugh bubbled from my gut.

I tried to remember what Roshan had said to the soldiers he met up with and the words sputtered out. "I'm trying to get to Elaria. I am employed at the Otti Theater," I said quickly as the stirring continued. My blood was singing from the wind magic that I was siphoning from them.

The beady-eyed fae cocked his head and looked me up and down as bile rose in my throat before he shook his head. "I know all the dancers in Otti Theater, and I know you're"—he jabbed his long bronze sword toward me and I backed up— "not one of them."

"I w-work—" I was stuttering as the fluttering in my stomach picked up, and I realized I'd never been around *just* Springfae before. Even with Cillian, Summerfae were always in the rooms next door. There was always water magic around to quell this inner turmoil. "I work backstage."

The leader grunted. "Regardless of where you work, you're across court lines. You are not accompanied by a soldier of our guard and, therefore, are trespassing."

"It was never a crime to cross court lines. You do it all the time coming to the theater."

"That's different."

"Because it's for your pleasure?"

He took a step forward. "Because we have a lady who will do something about trespassers. As such, you are charged with traversing court lines and must come pay tithe to Lady Fede in Scarlotta."

"I will go nowhere with you." I was seething, mad as a summer storm. I got in a ready stance. I couldn't go to Scarlotta.

The big fae laughed, but his body stilled as his eyes turned dark, and a breathlessness consumed me like the air was being sucked straight out of my lungs.

"Easy, Jacques," the leader warned as I grasped at my chest with one hand and put both daggers in the other.

I was stammering, trying to suck in a deep breath, to get any air at all into my lungs.

"Do you see those daggers she has? I'm not letting up until they are properly on the ground," said Jacques, the one I'd recognized.

"Drop the daggers and we'll go easy," the leader said.

The third stayed behind, watching nervously toward Lady of the Woods.

Something grew in me stronger than their wind magic. A fury was building. *Drop the daggers,* he'd asked. *Take my pain,* Mohr had commanded. *Pay a tithe with the female,* Lord Ohrem demanded. *Stay out of the island's affairs,* Cillian warned.

Something in me snapped as I sucked in a deep, shuddering breath, focusing on the wind magic coursing through me. The wind magic that I had always attributed to Cillian. My muscles clenched just thinking about him. These were his soldiers. And where was he? Before I could think again, I leaned into the anger and attacked the fat, arrogant soldier named Jacques. I plowed into his long sword with my daggers.

Both fae, spurred by my attack, came at me, and I swung out a dagger at Jacques again, causing him to stumble back. But the leader blocked my next blow aimed at Jacques's neck. I sucked in a deep breath again as they tried to use wind magic on me. The sand stirred around us on the dirt path, tunneling around us.

"Is she one of ours?" the one on lookout shouted as he took an uneasy step toward us. He fumbled in his steps, unsure if he should hold still or come to their aid.

I held tight to the daggers like Kaderyn taught me as the Spring leader slashed at me with his sword.

And when I dodged it and attacked with my own, he said, "Easy, female, she'll just want to talk." His eyes traced over me again, no doubt looking for the streak of silver hair they all had, but his eyes fell on the watermark tattoo and his eyes narrowed. "What are you?"

And a deprecating laugh rose from my lips because wasn't *that* ever the question.

But before he could ask any more, I attacked again, only vaguely aware of a voice shouting.

"Jacques, look at me! Jacques! What's happening? Torrance, look at this."

"Little busy," the leader retorted, blocking my blow with a grunt. I just needed to get inside his arms, just like with Petri, just like with Kaderyn . . .

"Get away from her! She's a monster!" came a shout from a soldier behind me.

I stumbled, freezing mid-attack. *What did he call me?* I turned to look as he knelt overtop Jacques's body—Jacques's lifeless body—a small cut bleeding from his bicep.

"What-t . . . what are those blades?" Torrance, their leader, asked, stepping away from me. "Did a witch enchant them?"

But I stayed immobile because Jacques lay dead. His lifeless eyes stared up at the frothy blue sky. I'd been called many things: whore, Siphon, dishwasher, but not monster. Never monster.

I was the *help*.

Another soldier clad in Spring's regalia ran up from beyond the cornfield. "We have to go. Autumnfae are beyond the tree line. There's seven of them—what happened to Jacques?" His eyes shifted from them to me.

I needed to run. I needed to get out of here.

"You killed a Spring Court soldier in our own court lines. Drop your daggers," Torrance said. To his comrades, he shouted, "Put his body in the carriage."

"Kill her, Torrance!" the soldier yelled.

"We're taking her with us. Lady Fede will want to know of this." Torrance twirled his sword in his hand, mounting an attack.

Could I kill them all? Physically, I might be able to. But inside, I was reeling from one fae dead at my hand.

A sword sliced at my arm, and I lost a dagger in the dust. The air, once again, was pulled from my lungs, but stronger and all at once—like they were all working together. I wasn't prepared this time. I couldn't think over my grief. The other dagger fell to the gravel as my face, gasping for air, fell next to it.

"Get the daggers. Careful, they're cursed."

The last thing I heard was boots grinding in gravel next to my face as everything went black.

10

KADERYN

A DAY PRIOR

WE PASSED A SMALL RAVINE lit with fireflies atop a lily pad–infested pond, and I wished Valentina was here to see it. I knew she'd find the beauty in it. They looked like little stars, and I wanted to tell her it was the same in The Court of Shadows. It was delicate and soft and I'd never appreciated either quality until her.

We'd made it almost to Arnprior, a two-day trip north of Blackwater Junction. Spring Court's winds brought change, blowing fates across the lands like a coming tide, ominous and unrelenting. For the thousandth time in the short journey, I saw something that I knew Valentina would be in awe of. But we were dragging; Teal wanted to stop for tea about four times a day, and Jair decided every break was time for a small cat nap. Me? I'd pulled Malvasia off the path, hopped down, and paced for hours with no excuse coming from my lips.

Valentina was consuming me. I wished to experience this with her, but her entire life was being used by those who should have known better, exploiting her deep-seated desire to help. The theater's owner, and that fucking monster and Spring Court's weapon, Cillian. An absolute fucking meathead during any interaction I'd had with him. My hunting hounds had a better sense of control than him. Which was saying a lot as Dormar, my main hound, often spent half his afternoons in Auris's courtyard licking himself.

Needing Valentina scared me, but knowing she was traveling the island alone made me want to hack through this court's countryside with my bare hands.

"Kade?"

I swiveled my head toward Jair's voice, pulling my attention away from the ponds. He sat atop the mare, and it was clear he had been saying something.

"Sorry," I mumbled. "I missed what you said." I looked back at the lily pads and the glowing fireflies dancing above them like stars out of orbit. Valentina would have loved this. I needed her to see *it*. I needed to see *her*.

"He said it's a keen thing
Dangers not near
With your head stuck so far up your rear.
You've ignored us now, thrice
Staring off at bug lights
If I had less control
I'd gnaw off an ear," Teal said from where she sat
lounging on Jair's shoulder, half draped on his head.

"And how would that help?" I retorted, feeling worse off. I gave a slight apologetic nod to Jair.

"I said we should spend an extra night in Arnprior." His

eyes didn't meet mine, and it seemed for my benefit. "Gather lost supplies. It will give me a chance to signal for Rhett in a court that's not actively hunting me down."

Rhett was Jairek's second-in-command—a hawkshifter from the Courtless. His moods were as spiky as his hair, which mattered not to me, as I had no patience for small talk, anyway.

But I let out a sigh of relief I didn't know I was holding. I was eager to hear how Shadow Court was faring, eager to know everyone was all right, and eager to delay the distance between myself and Valentina.

I searched for the bonds between us again, wishing I could see—if just for a second—that she was safe in Elaria. But what was I going to say to her? That I was miserable before I'd met her but impossibly devastated without her?

Nothing came back through the weird bond created when I used my magic in the nuckelavee cave. She was either too far or I didn't have enough of my shadows back yet. I couldn't be sure which.

She was going back home, being chased by a ruthless general, and I was here, watching fireflies and getting called out by a pixie that I could stuff into my pocket.

I could call Lord Grigory of Summer Court a coward until the moon fell from the sky, but the only coward here was me. If only I'd told her I wanted her to come with me. If only I'd told her I *needed* her with me.

If only I'd asked her for help.

". . . and then we roll through thistle weeds, bare skin on pointed needles while Teal blasts pixie magic at our backs."

My attention shot back to Jair's low voice marked with laughter, whose teasing eyes had my heart sinking. I did it again. "Agh, for fuck's sake, Jair. I can't seem to find my bearings. My body is beside you, but I fear my mind is—"

"You know, I've never seen a performance at Summer's

theater," Jair said as if I wasn't about to rip my heart out of my chest and confess my need for her.

I watched the lionshifter beside me, who was careful not to meet my eyes, again, for my benefit. I was dragging them on this trek, and we'd pissed off enough foreign courts already. What was one more?

"You up for a slight detour?" I asked, but it was so close to begging. Jair and Teal had already faced so much because of me.

Jair cut right through the bullshit. "I'm up for getting Valentina back. Can you keep shadows on her?"

"Not without pulling from elsewhere."

If I got my shadows first from the chest in the northern islands, I would have to hope she'd stay out of Mohr's clutches until I could shadowfade, use my shadows to transport us anywhere, to her side. But could I risk the wait?

We swiveled the horses around, back the way we'd come, and spurred them onward. Our meetup with Rhett was going to have to wait.

We were going to Elaria.

We were going to get Valentina back.

11

VALENTINA

I WOKE WITH AN awful buzzing in my head that wanted to consume me. My head pounded like it was receiving blood for the first time—every vessel pulsed with my heartbeat. Did it always beat so loud?

I righted myself, but a dizzy spell had me vomiting onto the light-wooden floor of what looked like another damn carriage. But more noises trickled in over my obnoxious heartbeat, and I righted myself faster than I had back in the cabin in the Glenora Desert.

A hauntingly beautiful sound called me to the one barred window with a curiosity of anything I'd experienced in Eadha before. I dragged myself against the bronze bars and pressed my cheek into the smooth aspen-wooded wall, breathing in the salty air outside.

Three massive wooden reeds—flutes, like the ones I'd seen Teal and Jair play—were embedded vertically in the ground near the edges of a cliffside, with various holes carved into them. The wind whipped across them, sending out a soul-piercing sound. I'd heard about these. This was the Aeolian Cliffs, and those were the Aeolian Flutes.

My skin prickled as sheer nostalgia rose in me and tears dotted my eyes. I desperately wanted to be back leashed to Kaderyn, traveling the island, and listening to Teal and Jair play a similar sound.

"That's good. Stop here," came a voice that stilled my heart in my chest before he came into view, blocking out the Aeolian Flutes.

"Gods, Valentina, what were you thinking?" Cillian was fuming as he ran his hands through his hair.

This was the greeting he had for me.

I hadn't seen him since I warned him of the threat against one of his cities, since I'd been taken across court lines, and *this* was what he welcomed me with. I was stunned, and a pain in my chest bloomed so fast it brought tears to my eyes; I couldn't form a cohesive thought. What was I thinking about what? Warning him of Autumn's plans? Tying myself to Kaderyn? Protecting Blackwater and a family he didn't tell me about? So much had happened since I last saw this beast of a fae before me.

He unlocked the carriage door and seemingly held out a hand to help me down to the soft ground marked with tufts of crabgrass. I batted his hand away and stabilized myself against the door. Cillian wasn't the help.

"Killing a Springfae guard? Lady Fede charges that with a death sentence. Do you know how much she enjoys throwing fae off the Aeolian Cliffs?" he said to my back as I watched the wind whip across the Flutes.

It wasn't a structured song like those created by fae, but a dance between air and earth. Nonetheless, it was music, and I wished it could drown out the scowling general before me.

"Did you even go looking for me?" I asked as he continued to criticize. My voice came out small.

At my words, he froze, and his face blanched.

So, with a shake of my head, I continued, "I was trying to save you."

"I don't need saving! Fuck, Valentina! I told you to stay in Elaria." He swung his arms to the sides and grimaced as his skin rippled, mottled even, like bugs were running under it. He was fighting the beast inside.

I dropped my heavy head back and rolled my shoulders. "Well, General Mohr had a different opinion on that." I could sense the other guards now. Wind magic coursed through me so fast I felt transparent. I looked around. At least a dozen surrounded us.

"I gave you my daggers to protect yourself. I don't even want to know what you did to coerce Angus to give you his. Where are mine?"

I snapped my eyes to his. "In a fucking nuckelavee cave, Cillian. Feel free to go get them."

His gaze was intense as he stared at me in his pressed-clean cotton uniform. I'd never felt dirtier.

A silence stretched on between us that I almost preferred because I could hear the beautiful Flutes playing again, but I needed answers.

"I met Avika," I said. The words seemed to echo around the cliff edge, repeating themselves across the churning waters below. The waves roared here just like they did across the island near the Fortress in Autumn Court, but I knew seamutts lived in these parts, and I wanted nowhere near their teeth.

He sucked in a breath and bowed his head, promptly ignoring me. "I'll talk to Lady Fede, try to get her to see reason. She wants you thrown off these cliffs, Val."

"Is that why we're here?"

"We're here to give her time to calm down. Our Ostara Festival is starting, and she doesn't much care for distractions on a good day, let alone during our biggest celebration of the year."

I said nothing. The wind blew the smell of spring flowers and Cillian to me, and my heart stayed steady. I couldn't believe that what I'd thought was love was just me siphoning Cillian's magic. An ugly laugh bubbled in my throat that he shook his head at and went to walk away.

"I saw your daughter," I said, and he spun back to face me.

A muscle in his jaw twitched. But still, he said nothing. Silence greeted me like a slap in the face. He still wouldn't tell me the truth.

"Damn it, Cillian! Why didn't you tell me about them?" I was screaming now for all the times he'd come to my rooms behind Otti Theater; all the times I'd drawn his pain from him. He had an entire world I knew nothing about.

"It was never supposed to be like this," he shouted back, running his hands through his hair. Out of the corner of my eye, I saw his guards move away a step. "Avika and I met a long time ago. Far before Adrian took an interest in protecting them. She and I—Valentina, you have to know . . . it wasn't an ongoing thing, at least not at the end. But then Breena—"

"Looks exactly like you," I said.

He stared at me with wide eyes—with far more vulnerability than I'd ever seen from him—and I looked away. I refused to feel sorry for him.

"I used to check on them more, but Lady Fede's kept me busy. When you told me Blackwater Junction was being targeted—" he stopped. Like he didn't want to tell me he cared for their safety more than mine. Which would have been *fine* if I had known about them from the beginning. "Adrian had been dousing that town for a century, maybe longer, but . . . it's

Adrian. He could pull it all away on a whim"—didn't I damn well know it—"that's what got him shunned from the Otherworld to begin with. Adrian . . ." Cillian said, then shrugged. "He does whatever he wants."

The Otherworld was the opposite of the Underworld. Kaderyn ran the Underworld—at least he did when he led the Hunt. But the gods, those we worshipped, ruled, and lived in the Otherworld.

Angus; the God of Love in Summer Court, Gael; the God of Forging in Autumn, Daina; the God of Fertility and Air in Spring, and Winter had a goddess of their own. I hoped to never find out her name.

There were other gods—of the seas and earth—and those I supposed Jair and those from the Courtless held in high regard. But a common thread here was that no one knew *why* Adrian protected Blackwater Junction. Not even Cillian. But he must have known what I was.

"Cillian, did you know I'm something called a Siphon?"

He tilted his head to the side. "Val . . ."

For fuck's sake. I scoffed. "I cannot believe I placed you on such a high pedestal."

His pride showed itself; he pulled back his shoulders, and his eyes grew dark.

So, I gave him my back as I swayed to the cabin door and climbed inside. "Let's get this over with."

Prying information he was reluctant to give was a waste of my time. Wherever my fate lay, it wasn't with Cillian.

WE CAME UPON SCARLOTTA QUICKLY; THE HORSES knew the way well. It was a sprawling city built both wide and high. A castle vaulted high in the middle and was surrounded by shorter houses and shops with curved roofs. Kites of pale colors blew in a never-ending breeze. The white-bricked castle looked entirely made of breeze walls, and the peaks of the castle were lost in the white, billowing clouds above. I thought, at first, that this would make an entirely vulnerable stronghold. Any well-shot arrow would soar straight through a window and out the other side, piercing whoever was in between. But because their magic is air and wind, I supposed it benefitted them to allow the east-flowing breeze to charge through its massive corridors.

Cillian led the way through a small nondescript door while two guards held my arms, one at each side. He looked back once, and I ignored him completely. A musty smell blocked out the floral scent of Springfae. Wherever he was leading us was damp, and it figured we'd be going some place the sun never reached.

Finally, he stopped and held open a bronze cell door. "In here, Valentina."

I blinked at him. He was putting me in jail. After everything . . .

"Angus's daggers will be in my rooms. Safe. I took them when my soldiers grabbed you." Though his voice stayed quiet, it echoed around the dingy, crude cell. "I'll be back soon to try—"

"You're leaving me here?" My eyebrows shot up. "You know what? Fuck you, Cillian."

I was never crass before, and Cillian winced at my words. An ugliness inside me reveled in this.

"Where am I supposed to put you, Val?"

"Don't call me that. Gods will damn you, Cillian." I looked away as the wind magic—the magic I mistook for love—

coursed through me. I looked out the small, barred window to the streets on the other side, and a tiny dust tornado curled into existence at my command. Small and useless, but there, none-theless.

Out of the corner of my eye, Cillian's skin rippled across his bones as the beast underneath took notice of my words. His words were soft as he said, "They already have."

And he showed me his back as he left me locked in his court's cells.

Alone, again.

HOURS LATER, SPIDER WEBS TICKLED MY FACE AS I craned my neck for a view of the world outside the two-foot window. Above the gutters, through stone-clad streets, I could —though faintly—still see the Aeolian Flutes. Which was an attestation to their size as their sound fluttered across the city.

Springfae mingled in the streets laughing and carrying on, smelling of Cillian and new flowers. Which, I was learning, was just a smell of Spring Court and had nothing to do with him. And it now numbed me. The very thought of asking for him—shouting for him—made my mouth clamp shut, and run as dry as the Glenora Desert.

So, I closed my eyes and pressed myself into the dark corner of the cell, finding solace in the shadows.

I wondered if I'd secured my passage to the Underworld by killing Jacques. Had I done it? Had I corrupted my soul? I hoped Kaderyn was on his way to his shadows because maybe that was the only way I was going to see him again.

The clang of metal jarred me awake, and a rush of a breeze

danced across my skin. It curled around my insides, telling me that the soldier in front of me was Springfae before I could see him clearly out of the shadows.

"Food," he said bluntly, squinting into the darkness, laying a tray on the floor.

"I wasn't expecting food," I said, rubbing my eyes.

"The general demanded it."

And for a brief moment, I felt bad for swearing at Cillian. At least before it hit me that food does not have to equal forgiveness.

I looked down at the tray and the sparkling purple liquid in the cup that smelled like cinnamon. But no amount of concentration could distract me from the fact that I was stuck here in Spring's prison.

I brought the drink to my nose and frowned. Why was this smell familiar to me? There was no orange and vanilla of Solanci and no floral scent of Teal's Nightale tea. It was good, if a little strong, and I was so thirsty.

The buttered vegetables and candied nuts went down quickly as Spring Court's food was closer to that of what I grew up with back in Summer. I licked clean my fingers after the honey rolls, but it took two tries to trace my tongue up my pinky finger. I must have become delirious with want over memories of my old home. I leaned back against the only wooden bench in the small, hollow jail cell and chugged the rest of the cup, grimacing at the grittiness in the bottom. I pulled it away as my hand grew heavy and watched with curiosity as the cup tumbled to the floor.

I tried rubbing my eyes, but even moving my arms made me unbalanced, and I toppled over to the dirt floor. And from my spot on the cold dusty ground, I looked up at the window—to the only light source in the cell. Were there always twelve bars on the little window?

My body wasn't listening to me. A heat entered my bloodstream as my eyelids grew heavy. I struggled to keep my traitorous eyes open, because that heat wasn't one of panic. My blood was screaming, stoking a roaring, angry fire inside that I knew better now than to attribute to anything other than Autumnfae.

And pieces were coming into place. Why were the southern towns in Spring on a curfew? Who was it that the guard had warned Torrance about coming out of Lady of the Woods?

Thick brown boots came into focus. Though now not coated in a layer of sand and clay, I'd have recognized that gait anywhere. It was the slow clomp-clomp of a fae with a chronic spine wound favoring a leg. Tears rolled down my cheeks as Mohr's scruffy face leaned down into view.

"I told you. You are mine, Valentina."

12

VALENTINA

"**YOU'RE NOT SUPPOSED TO BE HERE**," I mumbled as spit dripped from my mouth. I tried to get to my knees, to feel my fingers—feel anything—but I was no better off than a bumblebee in winter, slow and drugged.

"There isn't a corner on Eadha you can hide where I won't find you," Mohr said, adjusting his posture. I could tell it hurt him to crouch down the way he was.

"You're not supposed to be welcome in Spring," I said again, and thought of the feuds between the two. Though not safe, I never imagined fire could reach me here in Spring's jail.

Mohr frowned. "It's really quite fascinating what Spring would bargain with to ensure that their festivals run smoothly. They are truly devoted to their god. And a rather large bonfire south of their borders may have helped, too."

My heart stopped. "What?" I slurred. Oh gods, he wouldn't have, would he?

"I told you what would happen if you left me, Valentina. You knew what the price was and who would pay it."

No. A sob left my lips.

"I reduced it to ash and dust. I reduced it to nothing. There is nowhere on this island for you to go except with me."

"You lie." I sobbed into the cold dirt as memories of Otti Theater flashed across my mind. I cried harder at the thought of Sisaria, beautiful golden Sisaria and the burn mark on her neck from Mohr's hand, and Petri, my graceful friend. The poor faelings next door.

His voice grew sharp. "I am not faeless, Valentina. I cannot lie." But with reverence, he added, "By Gael, I think it burned hotter than the Glenora Desert."

Fury pumped through my veins, hot and deep; I wanted to kill him. I wanted to gouge out his eyes with my fingernails, but I could barely blink, let alone make idle threats. "What have you done to me?" I moaned.

He leaned closer and picked up the cup, letting out an ugly groan as the move made his spine stretch out. "It's a spice from The Court of Shadows."

The very mention of it made my heart skip a beat.

"Though I admit, I may have given you a fair bit too much." He dropped the cup back to the dirt floor. "Too much is a sedative. I wasn't sure the Springfae guard would deliver it at all, so I had to take risks. It used to be the only thing that would numb the pain. Until you, that is."

My brain whirled. The fae who delivered the food. He'd said Cillian, hadn't he?

No, he'd said 'general'. He didn't say *which* general.

I focused the fire magic into my hands, and we both looked down when small licks of flames appeared at my fingertips. I was going to burn him alive. Just like he did to Elaria.

Mohr frowned. "Tsk, tsk, tsk. None of that now."

And with a dismissive pass of his hand, he snuffled the fire out. Just like that, my last ounce of strength. Gone.

"Take my pain, Valentina," he demanded.

Snot bubbled from my nose as I sobbed into the dirt. I tried to shake my head, but nothing moved. There was no way this was happening again. "No."

He sucked in a breath and looked around the cell. "You know, I tracked you all the way to Kyrrahalyn. To a small inn off the main road. And you are right, Spring was quite put off having Autumnfae in its cities. I had to make a bargain to ensure our passage to regain"—he raised his eyebrows at me— "my property. And in return, we would honor their god by volunteering for their festivals. I didn't just bring myself to Scarlotta." He placed a large, dry hand, like fire-dried kindling, on my arm. "Take my pain away, Valentina, or I drag that innkeeper's daughter down here. Pretty little thing. I'll burn her alive in front of you. And I can promise you, I won't lose sleep over it."

I ground my teeth. It was Jassa. He was talking about Jassa. "You're a monster. She's one of your own."

"She's faeless. There's always more of them. Take . . . my. . . pain. . . away."

"I will kill you, Mohr." And even though I couldn't feel my fingertips, I could feel the stirring power beneath my bones. I could sense my power to siphon, waiting and ready. Did it have no shame? Did it not understand the pain it put me in when I unleashed it?

My body felt traitorous, putting evil, murderous fae like Mohr before its own. And this was my curse, my ingrained need to help, to save the hurting. And this was why I couldn't have him hurt Jassa. "You'll leave Jassa alone?"

"I won't harm her."

I tried to shake my head. "Not good enough. You'll make sure no harm comes to her."

His mouth twitched, and he looked up at the crude stone roof. "It took great negotiations with Lady Fede to allow us entry into Scarlotta without starting the War of Many. Tensions are high, to say the least."

"What did they want?"

"Weapons, mostly. And participation in their festivals."

"You'd renounce Gael for permission to find me in Spring Court?"

"That's what we've brought ones like Jassa for."

The ones like Jassa. The faeless. "But Spring won't care about the lives of a warring court's faeless." They didn't care about their own in Blackwater.

Mohr shrugged. "Courage will carry her through."

I squeezed my eyes shut.

He dragged his thumb against my jaw and brushed saliva from the corner of my mouth. Bile rose to my throat at his touch as he lifted my limp hand and placed it on his. "I would give Spring all our faeless if it meant bringing you back with me," he said in a whisper.

There was nothing I had to bargain with. There was nothing I could do but save Jassa from dying in these cells. I relaxed my hold on my abilities and took his pain away. I sucked in any air I could as sparks of pain pushed through the drugged drink and shot down my back before my vision blacked out entirely.

But I heard him bolt up to his feet, quickly and purposefully. I heard him let out a sigh and crack his neck. "I don't need you to like me. But you will obey me."

And quieter—more like a lover—he said, "You're mine."

The gate to the cell closed with a bang that echoed around the dank room.

"Lady Fede is proving difficult in moving you to my rooms. She enjoys flexing her control. But once this blasted fertility festival is over, we go home to Autumn Court." His steps thudded down the hallway without so much as gratitude or a goodbye.

And I was alone, again.

It was hours before I could control my body again, and even then, I was limited to just my neck. But by gods, Spring Court sounded divine. The beautiful melody of the Aeolian Flutes lulled me softly into a calm I hadn't felt since Elaria.

Poor Elaria.

And there, sitting on the edge of the small, barred window, I saw the silhouette of a bird. Its red breast was alight in Spring's morning air. It chirped and eyed me sideways as a bird ought to. My breathing rattled hoarsely in my chest as the robin sang a song for both of us. I fluttered my eyes closed.

And I wished I'd seen more of Spring Court than one soggy village and a castle's holding cell. But as I drowned in self-pity, still, the robin sang. As I vomited the rest of the drugged drink, still, the robin sang. In the soft lulling of the Aeolian Flutes and the song of the robin, I wished for Kaderyn. I wished I was laughing with him over his awful songs. I wished I was curled up tight by his side.

He had to be across the island by now.

But I'd killed that soldier, Jacques, and Lady Fede—for good reason—seemed reluctant to pardon my crime. The cliff edge beyond the Flutes seemed a more peaceful death than anything I'd find in Autumn Court.

I didn't know how I was going to get myself out of this one.

Mohr was here and Cillian was showing me just how much he could let me down.

But still—through my misery—the robin stayed.

Even when faelings flung stones at the bars and shouted wildly through to me without inhibition. The robin fitted itself between the bars and jumped to the bench below before fluttering to the dirty stone floor in front of me. The delicate bird hopped around inside the grimy cell.

When it chirped again, singing its song, the sounds echoed around the cell, bouncing against the walls, pushing away damning thoughts that threatened to swallow me whole. It stayed curious. It pecked at some grasses growing through the cracks in the floor before flying back to the wooden bench, fidgeting atop it and eyeing me askance. It stared at me with the intensity of a challenge, almost like a dare. That here in this filthy cell sat a delicate fluffy bird, like a ripe dandelion moments before a wind carried its seeds away, *still* singing. It was staying true to what it was: a song-maker. My circumstances may have changed, but I was still *me*. I still cared for the faeless. I still wanted to see them rise.

I tried to flex my wrists. Eventually, I would regain movement and would have to petition on my own for Lady Fede to release me. I was the Siphon of pain and magic, and I would not give up.

I was the help.

Whether this little bird knew it or not, it was filling me with hope. Or at least the urge to keep going, despite it all. So, I thought of the honey cakes in Summer, the majestic Autumn forests, the sounds of Spring, and the bravery of the faeless. I could be a coward like Cillian and be afraid of what I was or, curse or not, accept that this was me. I had to keep going—no matter the stones or where my fate lay. I had to tuck my head down like the little robin until I saw this through.

The robin was here bringing change and new beginnings.

I lay limp, listening to the Flutes, when a figure blocked the light from the one window to the cell, casting me in darkness. Though they kept their face out of sight, I saw the silver streak running through their long blonde hair. Wind magic stirred at my fingertips—she was fae, too. Her hand moved out suddenly as she tossed something into my cell. It bounced three times before rolling a foot away from my face. The heavy scent of cooked yeast flooded my nose. It was a mouth-watering chunk of freshly baked bread. A scattering sound, like pebbles against a rock wall, followed shortly after and I squinted to see seeds covering the ground between me and the door. The robin chirped twice and began hopping around, snapping them up with its beak. The kind Springfae quickly stood, and light streamed into the cell again as she hurried off, humming a tune I would never forget.

I sucked in a deep breath, the pain on its way out, and I could tell by the stirring in my gut that more Springfae were close. But a hardening film coated my chest like a caterpillar's cocoon, and I knew someone else was closer. I would recognize Jairek Sanguis, heir to the King of the Courtless, across any court in Eadha, and the trailing shadows that slunk through the bars in front of him.

I blinked twice and fluttered my eyes shut in relief once I saw the comforting sight of the golden lion on the other side.

"Here kitty, kitty," I whispered.

But then, tall and dark, he rounded the corner, eyes so full of worry and pure rage that tears instantly wetted my eyes again. Kaderyn was here.

"Kaderyn," I sobbed as he lifted his shadowsword above his head and smashed it down onto the bronze lock holding me hostage.

"Kade," I whispered again, trying to get up, but the drink was still sucking me into its hold.

He took two giant strides toward me. "Shh, I'm here now," he said, his voice calming and strong. Which just sent me further over the edge as he scooped me into his arms, into the embrace where I wished I could stay. "By my hounds, Valentina. Hold on. Jair, clear the way. Let's get Teal and—"

I felt her before I saw her. There was no other way to describe the sheer change in air pressure. Almost like being around Cillian, but stronger. Like the air we breathed was for rent and Lady Fede was its landlord.

"The Lord of Shadow Court and the heir of the Courtless in my dungeons. Well, I'll be," came her melodic voice from where she stood blocking the exit. "Festival guests are usually required to use the main gates."

Kade tucked me in close to his chest, and I lolled my head to the side to see her better. "Lady Fede, we were just leaving."

"With my prisoner, Kaderyn? You really must not know me at all." A scoff left her lips that sounded like musical notes I wanted to sway to.

"She was one of my riding companions far before your prisoner."

"And yet I have a general—who, by the way, entered through the main gates—who tells me she belongs to him." Her narrow eyes pierced me still.

"A bargain was struck. I traded his soldiers' lives for her until I was through with her." I could feel Kade's eyes on my face. "And it just seems I am not quite through with her. Besides, I am merely following up on an invitation to Spring Court you extended."

Lady Fede's face froze. "One hundred and seventeen years ago, Lord Kaderyn. And though Lord Ohrem might not care for tardiness, that invitation was revoked when it went unanswered the very next day. This . . . fae"—her cold eyes went to me—"has killed in my court. She must, and she will be held accountable, though Cillian has convinced me to spare her a sharp shove off the Aeolian Cliffs."

Kade's shadows licked around us, and his voice dropped low. "You forget what I am."

"You may be a fallen soul Hunter, Kaderyn, but the lionshifter at your side and the bumbling pixie somewhere in my castle are not. They are in my court uninvited. She doesn't go until I say so. Follow me."

She had the mannerisms of a bird, cocking her head like the songbird in my cell. A coldness rolled off her, and despite Kaderyn's calm demeanor, I knew he was on edge. My head flopped to the side, and the movement drew her gaze back to me.

Kaderyn said something about leaving the way they came, but they smelt like ash smoke, and I wasn't entirely sure he was talking about a door. We followed her down a wide hallway marked with breeze windows every six feet or so on both sides. The sweet smell of spring blew past us before the breeze windows were replaced by sets of doors.

Lady Fede stopped before one with the turn of her heel. Her flowing, sandy blonde hair, with a streak of silver near her forehead, swayed across her back. Her guards, all four of them, stood stiff at her sides.

"Leave her in here to . . . feel more like herself. It will be a bit more comfortable than my cellars and wildly more appropriate than my general's chambers. Jairek, I encourage you to change forms. I am entertaining Autumnfae, and I am afraid your lion form"—her eyes flashed—"as glorious as it is, is distracting to both my court and them."

I couldn't see Jairek, but I could feel the quick pulse of magic in the air I'd grown accustomed to recognizing as a shifter changing.

Lady Fede continued, presumably staring at Jair off to Kaderyn's side, "Though for vastly different reasons."

One guard opened the door in front of us, and Kaderyn walked us in. The room was grand but carried a soft elegance to it—like a field of dainty, wild forget-me-nots in a sea of mid-morning sunshine. Everything was pale yellow and soft blue. The small cobalt flowers were etched or painted into every piece of furniture. It was a far better upgrade from the cell. The wind blew in from the tall windows, curing my nausea from being jostled.

Kaderyn laid me down onto the softest down-filled four-post bed I'd ever been in. "Jairek can stay with Valentina while we negotiate her release," he said.

"Jairek and yourself will come with me. To discuss what you could offer my court in repayment for letting the Summerfae live," Lady Fede countered.

Kaderyn stilled once before surprising us all as he bent to press his lips to my temple, soft and sweet. It was a lingering kiss that sent my sluggish heart racing. "Stay in here, no matter what. I'll come back for you."

I could hear Jairek's voice from the doorway as he answered Lady Fede's tuneful questioning. But as Kade turned his back to the bed and walked away, tears rushed to my eyes. It was irrational, but here I was, being left alone again as I mourned the burning of Elaria.

I blinked the tears away as something moved against the white sheets, curling and unfurling with a will of its own. The shadows danced along the bed, dipped into crevices, and floated up to surround me. They covered me in a dense fog I could hardly see through, like half-closed blinds on a summer's morning. Kaderyn was keeping shadows with me.

I sucked in a shaky breath. They smelt so completely of Kade that not long after the room emptied, I fell into a deep sleep. Lulled again by the steady sound of the Aeolian Flutes.

Not alone.

13

KADERYN

I COULD SMELL the Virtusa Tonic on Valentina's breath, and guilt raked its sharp claws through me. Because it was a medicine developed in The Court of Shadows of my own creation. I knew of only one fae who would have needed that amount. And even just thinking of him near her made me want to rip the castle to shreds.

Mohr.

Autumn Court was here. Lady Fede confirmed as much. So, even if it made Jair and me more vulnerable, I left half my shadows by Valentina's side so she didn't have to be alone.

By the time we had reached the castle grounds earlier in the day, I could feel Valentina was here, but she wasn't responding to my mindspeak, and it was difficult to tell which way she was. All Jairek could smell was smoke and fumes from our earlier detour. We lost sight of Teal after she had gone through one of the many pixie-sized vents in Scarlotta's castle when we'd split up looking for Valentina.

Lady Fede hired quite a few pixies as helping hands to have

around for the festival, though I had a feeling the word 'servant' fit far better. I also had a worse feeling that they were stuck in this fucking castle full time—no longer allowed to live in the woods around Spring Court. Which was why Lady Fede had the castle outfitted with pixie vents to begin with.

Leaving Valentina alone in one of Lady Fede's rooms had me struggling for control. So, I counted the doorways and memorized the twists and turns as we followed her down the many hallways. I sent my shadows out farther from my body as we trailed her, pushing them to tickle the bottom of the long train of her dress. Enough so that I caught her guards watching them. They bounced glances off each other. But she was pulling at the air, exerting her dominance, and I didn't traipse across a damn court just to have a pissing contest with another fae in control. I sighed, letting my shoulders drop. Since I lost Teal in the mess trying to get in, and until we could regroup with an able-bodied Valentina, I was going to have to play lord.

I looked up to the stone ceiling as one of those vents led the entire way down to the hallway, joined with others, and then dipped off around the corners and into other rooms. What a mighty fine way for a fae who could control wind magic to access every room all at once.

By my fucking hounds, I grumbled, following on.

The castle was in a flurry of activity as Spring's Ostara festival was steadily underway. The sweetly nauseating smell of daffodils made me want to dunk my head in nuckelavee sludge. We passed tables in the main hall full of desserts I knew Valentina would go wide-eyed for. They looked tooth-achingly sweet with small blue flowers pressed into their flakey tops. I knew she'd find them pretty, and fuck, if I wasn't doing it again.

We passed rooms along both corridors full of Springfae chattering wildly. There were drawing rooms set up with easels facing a naked female fae splayed out across a softly lit stage. A constant wind came from nowhere in particular and blew her hair back off her shoulders. Spring's fertility festival had started, and unfortunately, we now found ourselves in the middle of it.

"Stay close," I murmured to Jair at my side as Springfae's nostrils flared, and eyes—both male and female—sparked at the sight of a Shifterfae in their midst.

Spring Court was far enough away from our courts, and the Courtless never ventured off their lands, that there laid a reveled curiosity about him that had me on edge. Jair grunted in answer, but it couldn't be helped. Confident swagger poured off him. It was his nature.

"I feel you might be safer under lock and key, my friend," I whispered to him when the next group of females we passed felt it necessary to let their hands linger across his chest.

"I won't ever go into a cage again, Kaderyn," Jair said, eyes hard.

Damn, I forgot how long he was trapped in Bran's illusion until I freed him two decades ago.

We made our way to a large throne room with a bulky back platform raised higher than the rest of the floor. There upon it sat one massive chair carved out of the trunk of a tree. My eyes caught on a smaller throne chair turned backward against the wall covered in spiderwebs far to the right. In traditional fae custom, the head of each court was supposed to have a male lord rule. Spring was the only court where a lady ruled in her husband's stead.

I knew he'd been sick. Which was almost unheard of for fae. It happened shortly after I'd been turned fae when my shadows exploded across lower Eadha. For a long time, the courts blamed me for the missing fae and for Lord Brexton of Spring's untimely illness. For a long time, they came for revenge through Gillies Forest. That was before I charged out my shadows in cloud cover above.

Now any intruders through Gillies Forest never left my darkness.

Lady Fede grabbed my arm and pulled me close to the throne chair. I could feel Jair move behind and face the door in a defensive position, protecting our backs. She danced her long, pointed fingernails up my arm and across my shoulders. What the fuck had I gotten us into?

Her palms slowly fanned down my chest, but this close to her and a sparkle in her rosy-amber eyes had me wrapping my hands around her wrists, halting their descent.

I squinted at her, trying to place where I'd seen eyes like that before. I was sure I'd never met Lady Fede in my nearly two hundred years stuck on this island. She sent Cillian to trade and bargain back in the early days when she heard of the medicines we could produce. An alliance that came and went with every fae who went missing.

But fuck if there wasn't something familiar about her. I scanned her round dewy face, her small forehead, immaculate skin, and button nose.

She ran her pink tongue over her white teeth. "It is desirable, joining shadows with wind. We could—"

"Why are you familiar to me?" I challenged softly, squeezing her wrists. I wouldn't be surprised if any fae held grudges for what I was—what I used to be, what I was responsible for. "How many of your loved ones have I pulled to my darkness?"

She surprised me as she scoffed and settled down into her chair, writhing her wrists from my hands. "Love is for Summer Court and weak hearts." A sudden apprehension had her ducking her small face away from my shadows, but not before I saw the fear in her eyes.

I stepped back off the throne steps, half turning away from her. This was about the end of my patience. "What do you want, Fede?" I asked, dropping her title before looking for my friend. "Stop with the games. And where's Jairek?"

Her mouth twitched, but her voice grew sharp. "I sent him off for a private dinner. He's safe. And what I wanted stopped mattering the minute I had, not one, but two lords in my court during our single most important festival."

I grimaced. I knew Lord Ohrem was around here somewhere, and I'd face him when the time came. But I had Jairek—a type of lord in his own right—with me and she wasn't considering him. That sparked anger in my gut. Jairek was the heir to the throne of the Courtless. He deserved her respect.

"You forget Jairek," I growled.

She stood and stalked toward a table that held Spring's desserts. "He forgets himself," she seethed before throwing a small round pastry covered in white sugar into her mouth. "I will not cause quarrels with the Courtless, but until he rises to his rightful place, he'll entertain my court in the watching box."

My shadows snapped in the air, and I stepped toward her, a clear threat.

Her eyes flicked to my shadows once before she turned and faced me head-on. "Ah, ah, ah careful or he'll be next in line for the artists down the hall."

Ah, I was beginning to understand just how ruthless she was. I had mistaken this viper for a vixen. My body was vibrating; I wished to end this now. Fuck being diplomatic. But that would be a death sentence for Shadow Court's fae, and we weren't ready.

My shadows spread out further, slinking through the room. "He will not be harmed in this court. Do you hear me? None of them will."

Lady Fede let out a sigh and waved a hand at me like what she had to say was regular talk of the weather. "If I cannot send the little female off the Aeolian Cliffs without a war with

Autumn, nor fearing your wrath or my general's dissent, then she will participate in my festivals, where her fate will be decided by the gods. She dies? You leave my court for good.

"Besides, Lord Grigory has sent word that another Summerfae has gone missing. Taken from her bed, the family says. Almost accused Spring Court of it, and Daina knows I was going to send his messenger back footless if I wasn't so preoccupied with the festival. I'm surprised you hadn't gotten a similar accusation in Shadow Court from him."

"Shadow Court doesn't give a fuck about the rest of Eadha. That I can promise you."

She flinched, but she could fish for information all she wanted. All *I* wanted was to leave with my friends.

She walked toward me, and I braced myself; I didn't know what she was capable of. But the air grew thin like it did at the top of the Anduat Mountains. "Perhaps, and that's why I enjoy having a court between us. Though I think I would enjoy the feeling of your shadows when there is *nothing* between us," she said as she looked down at where they curled around me.

I cocked my head. "And how is Lord Brexton of Spring these days?"

She sighed. "Diminishing. My husband's mind is lost, scattered to the four winds."

"What a tragedy. And yet you've never sent trades for anything that could help him."

"Hmm," she purred, raising her eyebrow. "He leaves my bed open." Which was the only truth she was willing to give up.

"Where've you sent Jairek off to?"

"Relax, we are not Autumn. We never get the privilege of seeing a Shifterfae up close, let alone the majestic lion, Jairek Sanguis. No harm will come to him."

"Why do I have a feeling you and I have different definitions of harm?"

"You're the one who brought the Shifterfae into my city, Kaderyn. My females will take good care of him."

I turned on my heel, pivoting toward the door. That was enough of that. A chill ran down my spine. Valentina was drugged by my court's medicines, Jairek was in danger of his consent, and Teal was . . . fuck if I knew where.

I reached the doors before I heard the melodic tune of Spring Court's lady a final time. "I expect you both to be present for our festival celebration tonight. A ball, of sorts. You'll find appropriate clothes in your rooms. Then, tomorrow, she will take part in our games when the sun welcomes us, Kaderyn."

I slammed the door back against its hinges. I was going to have to find them all and get us out of this court before then.

14

VALENTINA

I HALTED MY PACING at the sound of the door clicking open. I had regained the feeling in my legs an hour ago and fought the urge to race through the hallways searching for Teal, Jair, and Kade. To run from this place, Mohr, and the memory of what he'd done. But I wasn't yet steady on my feet, though I had wicked cramps in my legs. I had to move.

Kaderyn came through the door and closed it behind him. I let out the breath I'd been holding. Though, he looked as annoyed as ever. I continued walking from the bed to the chair and back again, shaking alive sleepy nerve endings. I didn't know where his head was at or if he'd welcome me running to him like I desperately wanted to.

"Where's Jair?" I asked, stopping briefly to shake out a lazy leg.

"Stop pacing, Valentina," Kade growled as his dark eyes tracked my movements.

I stopped so abruptly that my hair fell forward over my shoulders. "Is Teal all right?"

He moved into the room, working on the buckles of his shirt. His normally clean black clothes were stained with gray ash. I frowned. "Why are you filthy?"

He continued working on the many buckles that fastened his shirt to his body. "I have shadows out searching for Teal and Jairek." And he told me what Lady Fede said; that Jair was in danger of a curious court, and though Lady Fede would spare me from falling into the western seas, I would participate in their trials.

"What are the events?"

"It doesn't matter." His eyes found mine. "How are you doing?"

Like a charging hurricane, I broke down as the tears came. He rushed for me as some semblance of sound came from my mouth. "They died, Kade. They're all dead because of me."

"I'm so sorry, Valentina. I'm sorry I didn't figure things out sooner," he said, cupping my face to his chest, and I cried.

Oh gods, did I ever cry in Kaderyn's arms. I grieved my town, my theater, and my friends. I cried for the fae, the neighbors, and the others who died that had nothing to do with the mess I started. We sunk to the floor. My shoulders shook into the strong, capable Lord of Shadows as he consoled me with soft words and gentle touches, soothing my aching soul.

And eventually, sometime in my misery, my grief morphed into anger. "Mohr will pay for what he'd done."

"I know," he promised. He pulled my face away from his chest. "But first, we're going to get Teal and Jair and be out of here by dawn."

He looked down at his hands, equally stained with black smudges, then up into my eyes and held me still. "I need to wash. Come with me to the baths, Valentina. Now that I have you, I will not lose you again," he said as his shadows licked down my calves.

My heartbeat skittered in my chest as we stood, and if he didn't look so emotionally pained, I would have wrapped my arms around him.

He started toward the adjoining bathroom, throwing his shirt onto a chair near the fire on the way. I watched the strong muscles of his shoulders flex. The sight of his skin sent warmth through my body.

He placed a curled fist on the doorjamb of the bathroom and—when I hadn't moved—he turned his head. His broad, firm jaw was outlined in the light of the setting sun. "Come, Valentina."

By the time I entered the bathing room, his back was to me, and his hands were working on the ties of his pants. Abruptly, I turned to the open-air breeze walls, counting the ornate latticework of the breeze windows. He let out a throaty chuckle before the sloshing of water echoed around the equally yellow and blue room.

I felt his shadows, soft and caressing, before their inky darkness trickled into view. They smoothed over my body, pressing my loose shirt and pants to my skin like tickling tendrils sifting leisurely. My cheeks flushed as I ever so slowly turned to face him. He was leaning back in the massive white porcelain tub in the center of the room, looking at me through hooded eyes. His head leaned against its curved frame, jutting his chiseled jaw into the sky. I wanted to lick along its edges.

I won't stop you, came his voice in my head, light and careless. Like we weren't in Spring Court, and I wasn't being forced to take part in Lady Fede's festivals. Whatever that meant. He peeked at me headily through thick lashes, and desire ran down our mindspeak.

"We're in the court of a fae holding us hostage," I reminded him, swallowing thickly, not knowing what to say because *here he was.*

Kaderyn came to Spring Court's capital for me. And I was standing there, intoxicated by a flood of emotions whipping through my body. The only constant was Kaderyn. It was only ever Kaderyn.

"That won't change until we're back in Shadows."

And he was right. There was nothing we could do now but play her games. Not with Jair and Teal loose somewhere.

The shadows became solid and gently nudged against my back, pushing me closer to the edge of the tub. I felt a smile curve my mouth as I sank down beside it, letting my hand dip into the water by his knees.

It brought up memories of us bathing in the warm springs outside the nuckelavee cave. It reminded me of the feeling of his hands through my hair, his eyes piercing mine, and all that we'd been through. Through Autumn's auctions, getting the key in the Narrows, opening the first chest of his shadows in a sea monster den, saving Blackwater from Winter, and now this. I blocked our mindspeak as thickly as I could before the memory of killing the Spring guard took over and the deaths of everyone in Elaria, burned by Mohr. All because of me.

Water dripped from my fingertips as I stood. I wanted him closer; I needed his skin on mine. I needed something constant to hold on to when so much of what I loved was being taken away. I took a step back and worked on the buttons of my shirt until it floated loose against my breasts. I wanted peace with him again. My fingers looped through the ties on the loose Spring pants I got in Blackwater, filthy now from laying on the cell floor. I wanted to tell Kade just how much I needed him.

Shadows danced up, dark and flowing, covering my skin where I shucked off my shirt and shimmied my pants down over my butt. They blanketed me in modesty as his lazy eyes stayed on my face.

"You don't want to see me?" I asked, suddenly feeling weak in the knees.

One eyebrow quirked up, and he opened his mindspeak to me, flooding me with images of his mouth trailing down my body as his hands held me still. I gasped and gained the courage to pull at his shadow magic, thrusting the shadows away altogether.

He leaned his head forward, his black eyes steady, as the shadows I dispersed froze in midair. I let him see all of me. I swayed to the bath, resisting the urge to run and sink into its comforting bubbles. I was only just regaining my balance, and I was going to have to go slow.

And only when I leaned over and dipped a leg in did his eyes ravish my body, searching. He watched the waterline as my torso slowly sank into the bath's comfortable depths like he was desperate to drink as much of me in before the water hid my naked body. I hoisted my knees under me and held on to the bathtub's edges when I learned the hard way that it was too deep for me to sit.

I dipped my mouth under the surface, relishing the water's comfortable hold while I tried to think of what I wanted to say. It also stopped me from saying something stupid. Stopped the flood of tears again because *I was the water, the river ran through me*. Once. Long ago.

"I appreciate you coming," I finally settled on, which felt empty.

There were a thousand places I needed to be, though one fewer now that Elaria was gone. In Hawrenthia, getting Lord Grigory to rally the lords and lady against Winter's attacks. And getting the Summer lord to do something, anything to prevent Autumn's increasing pressure. But for right now, even if Kaderyn had no interest in saving Eadha, he'd saved me.

Quieter, I said, "I'm glad you're here, Kaderyn."

The intensity of his matte black eyes drew me in. A vein twitched in his jaw, and I worried I'd said the wrong thing when he let an impossibly long silence run on.

I almost considered breaking it to discuss if he'd seen food on his travels when he spoke. "Come with me, Valentina."

I froze. Hesitation bubbled in my gut, and I didn't know where it was coming from because I wanted to stay by his side. Oh gods, did I ever want that. But I couldn't go back to ignoring the plights of those across the island. Not after what I'd seen. Not after what had been done to me and those I loved.

I opened my mouth to speak, but he continued, "Come with me across Winter's plains. Come with me, and I'll join any war you want me to."

I gasped. "You'd do that for Eadha?"

"No," he said, his voice low and deep, echoing across the water between us and into my very bones. "For you, Valentina. I'd do that for you."

I was choking, fully imploding on this inconceivable idea that he might want me as much as I wanted him.

He pulled me across the tub, nestling me between his legs. His thumb stroked my cheek as his suddenly wide eyes watched mine, intense and devouring, but with a vulnerability that always made my heart skip a beat. "I need your help, Valentina."

I blinked at him, at the shadows by his side, and at the thought of his very deadly shadowsword that could reappear whenever he wanted. "What could you possibly need me for?"

"If there was any good on this island, it's because of you. If there was any reason to save it, any reason at all, it would be because you are here. You are gold in a sea of crassness."

But my brain was stuttering. "I barely know how to siphon much of any other—"

And he cut me off, pulling me tighter to him through the

warm water, to his hard body until our faces were inches away. "I need *you*." He brushed a hand along my cheek in a tenderness I'd never seen from him before. "Not the Siphon, of magic or pain. Just you."

I leaned my head into his, our foreheads touching, breathless and hearts wild, as my lashes brushed his cheek. He closed the space between our mouths as I ran my fingers through his black hair, desperately drinking him in. With a moan, he pulled my body down against him, groaning when we met, skin to skin. Our tongues danced as I pulled him tighter, wishing to never let go. Wishing to forget we were in Spring.

My hips rocked instinctively against him, spurred by his strong hands roaming my body. His arms wrapped around me in a locked embrace I couldn't get enough of.

I want more, I want . . .

His mouth stilled against mine, and his hands froze against my lower back. I pulled back, searching his thoughts, worried about which of mine went through to him, but he kept the barrier closed between us.

Let me in, I implored via mindspeak, though it carried more anxiety than I meant.

"It's Jair. I found him," he said as his eyes fogged over.

He opened his mind to show me exactly what that meant. I recoiled as it hit me all at once, but his strong arms around me held still.

My vision fogged over into a gray-clouded mist as I was seeing what Kaderyn's shadows could see. Jair was in a room. Though still elegant, it was much simpler than ours, but there was screaming—

So much screaming.

My heart raced, urging Kaderyn's shadows on as they trailed the room, slinking across furniture, searching for the Shifterfae they sensed so clearly. Kaderyn and I sat still as death, both too scared to move or even breathe, embracing each other in the lukewarm water as the shadows touched the naked foot of our friend. My breathing hitched.

Faster! I urged.

Jair sat in a large high-backed chair with his hands tied behind him with pale cotton ties. His disheveled clothing was half undone, but thank the gods, still on. The shadows reached his face, and I breathed a sigh of relief as he looked, perhaps unkempt, but not harmed. He cocked his eyebrow at Kaderyn's shadows in a greeting that softened my worry. But what was the screaming?

Kaderyn swiveled his shadows around to find its source when we saw six Springfae females being chased out the open door. Chased by a slow creeping frost that made its way across the stone floor and up the yellow daisy-covered wallpaper that surrounded the thick-wooded doorframe. The frost weaved itself together across the doorway, lacing through to make a blockade of its own, barring the females from entering again. One such female, who had ice chunks in her hair, had good enough sense to slam shut the door against the sparkling ice.

Their pattering footsteps and shrieking echoed down the hall. We heard the muffled voice of one utter, "It touched me! Did you see that? It touched me."

The three of us watched—Jair; tied in the chair, and Kaderyn and I; through his shadows as the frost consumed the door handle and the bronze lock. It coated itself into a thick, white web of ice that caused the wood to groan under its pressure.

Jair was effectively trapped in his room. Which, right now, seemed to be of benefit to him. "Little help here," Jair said in his lighthearted tone.

Kade's shadows twisted into the ties and got to work. But the untimely interruption was a stark reminder we were separated in Spring's castle and despite the look Kaderyn gave me, I pushed myself off him and moved to the far side of the bath, clearing my vision.

"Any idea what just happened?" I asked.

"Any *good* idea? No. Many, many bad ideas about why ice magic would follow Jairek around," Kade answered, dunking his head briefly under the water.

Whatever the ice was, it was going to keep Jair out of Spring's clutches for the night. I thought back to our battle in Blackwater when Helle, Lord Aborys's daughter, licked his lion snout. But I didn't think Winter, or one lone female, would be so bold.

I cleared my throat when Kaderyn's head popped back up, and he shook the water out of his hair. "And Teal?"

He sighed. "I'm still searching. There're quite a few pixies around the castle and quite a few more places for a pixie to hide."

I nodded. "Will she be all right?"

"If she can keep her mouth shut in Lady Fede's presence, she'll be fine." But I felt Kaderyn's shadows moving quicker through the hallways.

I let out a yawn.

"How are you feeling?" he asked with such passion that I focused my tired eyes back on him.

"Dizzy. Mohr had . . ." I cleared my throat as even his name sent nausea through me, and I didn't want to focus on it. "Mohr had me drink something that smelled familiar."

"It was Virtusa." Kaderyn grew angry as he ducked his eyes and cleared his throat. "We make it in Shadow; traded it with Autumn for weapons when we had none. Numbs the body, but too much and it can cause delirium and paralysis. Seems Mohr was not in short supply."

I nodded, not meeting his eyes.

"Come on," he said, stepping out of the tub. "We have a ball to get ready for. It'll allow my shadows to search the far side of the castle for Teal."

"As long as there's food," I said as my stomach growled. Which wasn't the entire truth—as long as Kaderyn stayed by my side, would I risk a dance in our enemies' clutches.

15

VALENTINA

I SEARCHED IN A WHITE-WOODED dresser that reached from floor to ceiling for something to wear. Inside, I found a floor-length dress the color of pale sea glass, made of cotton and chiffon. A folded partition stood off to one side, and I stepped behind it, though I was not sure why since Kaderyn had just seen me completely naked.

Something in the air had changed; we couldn't relax now.

The dress slid over my curves, just big enough to cover my chest before it plunged low and tumbled to the floor. It was light and airy, like butterfly wings kissing my skin. I closed the dainty gold clasp around the back of my neck and grabbed the equally gold-detailed waistband that would cinch around my middle. I had to give it to Spring; they made beautiful clothes in this court. But by the third try, I couldn't reach behind to clip the belt properly.

"Kaderyn?" I asked, quickly moving around the partition. "Can you—"

He turned to me so sharply that his black hair flopped to his shoulders. His jaw fell open as he looked me over, wide-eyed, with that vulnerability he only showed to me.

"What?" I asked, suddenly self-conscious. I was far more covered now than in the fur outfit I'd been wearing in the Fortress in Autumn Court.

"You look beautiful."

My face heated, and the air sparked between us like lightning between charged clouds. How I wished we were still in the bath and had time to finish what we started. But my stomach growled again. "And you're"—I looked him over—"still filthy?"

He tugged at the collar of his obsidian Shadow Court shirt; the gray dirt was still deeply embedded in it. "I much prefer my own clothes."

We stared at each other for a healthy minute before I cleared my throat. "Can you fasten this, please?" I turned to show him the struggle I had going on with the waistband.

His firm hands laced through mine as he grabbed the gold corset and tugged me gently to him. The shadows that clung to him reached out and embraced me to him as he worked on the clasps. I lifted my arm and watched as they twirled around my forearm like playthings. Soft fingertips traced my spine, up and down, up and down; I closed my eyes as I felt Kaderyn's wandering fingertips and truly considered forgoing food.

"Done," he whispered into the curve of my ear.

I fluttered my eyes open to see him making his way to the door, and a jolt of panic shot through me. "Kade," I said with more urgency than I'd planned.

His dark eyes narrowed and watched me slowly. "What's wrong?"

"You won't leave me, right? You'll stay by my side out there at the festival?" I twisted my stupid, anxious hands together.

His face went unreadable, and I regretted everything I said, every moment of weakness I showed. His eyes traced the contours of my face as he sauntered back to my side with careful steps that were far too slow for my rising anxiety. He gathered one of my hands into his and I watched as shadows swirled down his shoulders, twirling around and around. They reached where we clasped hands and did not hesitate to stop as they twirled up mine, rising further until they kissed my own shoulder. There was no pulling out of them as they linked us together in a grip I knew nothing could break, much like the Caterina del Aamod ties had.

He was promising to stay.

"Ready?" he asked as we stood side by side, hands linked, bound by shadows.

I sniffled, shrinking back from the heaviness I carried in my chest. I didn't know its meaning. "I hope they have honey pastries."

A guard led us down the castle's winding hallways to a large banquet hall overflowing with Springfae. Crystal chandeliers hung from the vaulted ceilings and green vines trailed up the surrounding walls, twirling through the breeze walls, leaving gaps big enough for an ever-blowing wind to find its way in. The smell of food pushed its way past the heavy floral scent, and my mouth watered.

Kade led us along the center of the room to tables and chairs near the base of Lady Fede's large throne chair.

"Welcome," Lady Fede said, greeting us from the largest of chairs. The one carved out of a large trunk of a tree.

She was dressed in a soft yellow billowing gown whose bottom touched the chairs of the Autumnfae to her right and Cillian's to her left.

"So glad you found your way, even if you forgot to change. Sit and enjoy our festivities." She gestured to two chairs stationed beside Cillian.

Oh gods, please no.

"If it's all the same, we'll find a spot with a wall at our backs," Kaderyn said, pulling me away from the stares I was receiving from the lot of them.

Lady Fede rose her shoulders in the most graceful shrug I'd ever seen. "Suit yourselves. Enjoy the food and the dance. This is night one of our celebrations as we shower Daina with our love, and I implore you to act accordingly."

Kaderyn didn't grace her with an answer as we moved out of the swarms of Springfae ready to curtsy, greet and give praise to the lady of their court. I pulled Kade to an open table that already had trays of food splayed out on it.

Large, sharp yellow crystals sat on glass plates and rose up from the table like stalagmites on a cave floor. We dove into the roasted duck and sweet watercress salad rolls wrapped in thin rice paper. The nutty bite of nasturtium flowers lit up my taste-buds. Kade could have my duck if I got to eat these forever.

I passed a lingering gaze toward the dance floor as globes filled with what looked like stardust floated overhead. Springfae, all in pale dresses and tunics, moved to the soft symphonious sounds of an orchestra in a choreographed dance. They smiled wistfully at each other as they twirled as one beat, one heart, one court.

Along the walls of the hall were large glass cloches that held spiraling, gray tornados; it was contained chaos. And above all, even overtop the beautiful thrum of the band playing, I could still hear the Flutes from across the court. My mouth fell open. It was magical. They put much time and care into their festivals.

Like the vast Autumn Forests, I didn't want to *like* this court. I wanted out, or to be a simple passerby traveling through, experiencing all I'd missed out on, all it had to offer.

"Want to dance?" came the voice of a Springfae male before me.

His brown eyes flicked to Kade, then back to me. His boldness surprised me. He braved a seething member of the Wild Hunt to ask it.

"Yes," I blurted, because though I was a Siphon, something unique, I still could not lie. I *did* want to dance. I looked quickly at Kade because I knew how it sounded. "I mean, no."

Kaderyn had danced with me in the Fortress to get me away from that Autumnfae who danced so strangely. But he had refused to dance with me in the clearing in Spring when we were on our way to get his shadows. He looked at me now with careful thoughtfulness and stood. The surrounding shadows drowned out the Springfae male; I didn't want to be rude, but he wasn't the male I wanted to dance with. I wanted Kaderyn. I was becoming afraid I would always want Kaderyn.

I curled into Kade's side, hands tied together by shadows, as we moved as one to a foreign court's dance floor. Kaderyn's shadows parted the crowds of pale-clothed Springfae like death through a meadow. I placed my hand on his shoulder as his went to my waist and he pulled me tightly to him.

We swayed, apart from everyone else, to Spring Court's beautiful music. Our hands, tied by his shadows, our fingers locked together, sat on his chest near my head. Safe and comfortable.

His hand curved to my hips and pulled me tighter to him, pulling our bodies together to dance as one with the music. I turned my face up to him as the friction between us grew, heating my body straight through my core. Kaderyn did his best not to look at me and kept his focus on the plethora of dangers around us. But his strong chiseled jaw lay bare, open for my curiosity, and I sent my tongue along its edges from chin to ear.

I was searing hot from Solanci and *him*.

His black eyes flicked down to mine with careful control that vexed me. But his hand scooped through my hair as the other pulled me closer, if even possible, half lifting me as he swayed us to the music with grinding passion.

And I thought it was what I wanted. I thought I wanted to be up and moving with the rest of them. But now everyone was staring, and what was worse, I was siphoning their magic.

Spring wind curled in my gut, and the fire from Mohr—and his stares—burned through my veins. It sent me into turmoil that made me want to run for cover under a table. At least Cillian, sometime during our dinner, had left. But dancing was a mistake. I should never have wanted to do something so silly.

Pull harder on my shadows, Valentina. I can take it, Kade said through our mindspeak.

I just wanted to do something . . . normal, for once. I'm sorry, Kade. I tried to pull away. I tried to return us to the corner of the room, but he repeated what he said.

Use my shadows until you can control them.

In the theater, I always had water magic around me to quell the stirring in my chest that wind magic brought. I sighed and leaned my heavy head on him. But maybe he was right. Maybe I could pull on his shadows now until one day I could learn to be *okay* around them all.

I focused on the twirling shadows clinging to us and urged them to me—to follow and listen. They snapped the air like tiny whips before settling in around us, thicker than before, blocking us. Until all I felt was Kaderyn and the safety that he provided.

"Better?" he asked.

"Better." I smiled.

A long while later, when my feet ached and my lips were swollen from Kaderyn, when my hair clung greedily to my sweaty neck, we returned to our table and chairs, I curled my knees in his lap as we—or I, rather—munched on the very needed desserts.

The boldness of the Springfae females surprised me as they walked right up to start a conversation with Kaderyn like I wasn't sitting half in his lap.

Maybe it would have bothered me, but they didn't know what we'd been through. They didn't know the secrets we kept. They didn't know our travels. So I licked the honey off my fingers from my pastry desserts and mindspoke—or mindsang —that awful song about the virgin on the cliffside. But a new version.

> *Once upon a time there was a lover on a cliffside*
> *Who searched the night stars for her Hunter on the high tide*
> *She waited by the shores for the sea to bring him back*
> *Searching through the darkness for those eyes of shadows, black*

I watched, victorious, as his mouth curved up with a small smile, and those vulnerable eyes turned to me, ignoring what the female before him said. But we both heard her bring up the trials tomorrow in that beautiful Spring Court dialect. It sunk my spirits.

So Kaderyn quickly cut her off as he said, "Sorry, but we must be leaving."

We stood and moved through the now-drunk festival guests to the door.

"Does Auris have celebrations?" I asked, yawning against the back of my hand as we were about to leave the large hall.

But before Kade could answer, a gruff voice called him back. "Kaderyn!"

Kade snapped all his shadows back to him, which I relinquished easily as we turned. General Mohr stood a few meters away, his hand on the hilt of his sword.

"I don't think you realize what you've started, Kaderyn," Mohr said. "I don't think you realize just how far I'm willing to go."

Kade's shadowsword materialized in his hand as he hefted the massive thing up to rest on his shoulder. "Why don't you come and try to pry her out of my fingers, General?"

Mohr's eyes flicked pensively to the shadows that locked us tight. And if he had another minute, if just one more second lapsed, I thought it was all going to come crashing down right there.

"I expect generals to have better manners!" Lady Fede snapped as she and Lord Ohrem hurried to the standoff between Mohr and Kade. To Ohrem, she sneered, "I wonder at the strength of your army if even your general can't control himself."

"Mohr!" Lord Ohrem warned with a quick bark, no doubt insulted by Lady Fede's words.

Mohr's gaze bore into Kaderyn's, who stood tall and defiant between us before he rolled his shoulder once and turned to trudge away. Lady Fede scurried after him as they returned to the festival.

Lord Ohrem watched them go until they were out of earshot. He looked at me once, like he was trying to figure me out, before turning to Kade. "I don't think this is going to end how you want it to, soul Hunter," he said.

But I couldn't tell if it was a threat or an idle warning.

Kaderyn must not have cared how he meant it as he said, "I know how it ends, Ohrem. Or at least, I know your ending. Keep your general away from Valentina, or I'll have my hounds rip your flesh from your bones twice a day when you're in my halls."

"You're not reunited with the Hunt yet; you should do well to remember that."

"I'm one court away from what I need, and we both know where your soul is headed once I find my way back."

Lord Ohrem's eyes flicked down to the shawl of feathers on his shoulders, sniffled once before jutting his shoulders out, and turned away. Something gross bubbled up in my stomach, and I wished I hadn't had all those sweets or seen the way Lord Ohrem looked at the cloak he wore.

We returned to our room only after checking on Jair. Making sure he was okay behind the door, tightly locked with ice. Kade turned to the night stars as they shone through the open windows while I fished through the white-wooded dresser for clothes more comfortable for sleeping. Kade released the shadows from my wrist, allowing me privacy to change. Privacy I didn't exactly want, but I didn't know how to say it.

Kade took one look at the soft pale blues of the cotton clothing I now wore and, with a huff, went back to the bathroom. A short while later, he came out with a towel wrapped around his waist and his Shadow Court clothes dripping wet in his hands.

I had crawled into the soft bed while he was gone and now wore a fresh pair of Spring's pants and a small shirt that hit just below my waist. I watched him sling his obsidian shirt and pants over a beautiful high-backed chair near the windows. My attention was pulled from the fat water drops that were falling onto the velour seat when Kaderyn slid into the bed beside me. Without hesitation, he pulled me close to his hard body, and the shadows swallowed us in a safe embrace.

He kissed my hairline before settling himself in. "Get some sleep."

16

VALENTINA

I WOKE TO KADERYN'S voice saying my name, and I couldn't think of a better place to be, but lying in bed facing each other, tucked—curled even—against his warm chest. His pulse in the nape of his neck beat steady and strong against my forehead.

I'd woken twice in the night by the sounds of my own crying, mourning the town the firefae burned down. My chest ached, and my eyes were swollen. I sighed deeper, wishing to drift back to sleep. To forget.

"Valentina," he said again, and the tone of his voice had my eyes fly open. "I found Teal. It's time to get out of here."

I jolted up, pushing the down-filled comforter off us both. Right. We weren't out of the clutches of the courts just yet.

I scrambled into clothes better meant for traveling, and Kade threw on his now-dry shadow clothes. The chair below it held black marks that I didn't think would come out without a housekeeper's magic.

"Teal's down the far hallway on the other side of the courtyard. We're going to stay in the shadows, out of the rays of the rising sun," Kade said.

We opened the door quietly, looking for spring guards before stepping out into the stone hallway. I held Kaderyn's hand, wishing I had my daggers when, six rooms down, shadows trickled out of the bottom of a frost-covered door. We stopped in front of it and looked up at it together. I thought about asking Kade what it meant, but I was a prisoner of Spring Court being chased by Autumnfae, and I couldn't wrap my head around what Winter would want Jair for.

"Brute force it is then," Kade murmured, leaning to kick in the large wooden door covered in a lattice of ice.

But I grabbed his forearm to stop him. "We'd wake half the castle," I warned. Now was not the time to draw attention.

He swore as his mouth moved to form a straight line, but before he could argue with me, a soft sound like running water had us turning toward the ice-covered bronze lock. Slowly, specks of water melted through the cracked ice and dripped down to the floor. The handle jiggled, and after testing it a few times, the door heaved open from the inside, shattering ice all over the hallway floor.

There stood Jair—in all his golden glory with smiling, easy-going eyes—holding a steaming kettle.

"Subtle," Kade said with a raised eyebrow.

Jairek tossed the bronzed kettle over his shoulder, where it clanged unceremoniously to the floor, the sound muffled by the same yellow and blue carpet. "Let's go," he said, moving out into the hallway.

We rushed down the stone corridor with hushed footsteps, following a slinking, faint trail of shadows leading us to Teal. Kaderyn never let go of my hand and, if Jair noticed, he never said a word about it.

We stilled against an outside wall, the courtyard in sight to our left, and the hallway that the shadows trailed down veered straight ahead. We were almost free. But the courtyard was busy as Springfae cooks and decorators finished up some final touches for a festival we wanted nothing to do with. The murmur of a crowd trickled down from the far side. Was it starting already? I siphoned the shadows to me. I desperately clung to them as the strong wind magic insisted on flowing through my veins. It was a light, fast magic that sent my pulse racing.

"On the count of three, we turn the corner and walk like we own the place. We get Teal and put behind us this entire fucking detour . . . one . . . two . . . thr—"

"Ah, how wonderful! You're up. Just in time for first light's meal," Lady Fede said, gliding over to us from a different hallway.

Alongside her stood a pleased-looking Lord Ohrem with Mohr just behind. The anxiety and determination rolled off him in bouts of obsessive frustration.

"I do hope your rooms were satisfactory," Lady Fede continued.

"It wasn't really my color," Kade said, blockading his shoulder in front of me.

A move Lady Fede noticed. "Follow me, please."

I felt myself being tucked closer into Kaderyn's side as we followed behind them. *Deep breaths, Valentina. He won't touch you again,* he said via mindspeak.

I looked behind us, back to where the shadows gathered outside a plain door. We were walking farther from Teal, farther into the clutches of Spring Court's festival.

AND SO WE SAT AT A MADDENINGLY AWKWARD breakfast table. Lade Fede was at the head of it in a large curving chair that was twice the size of any other. Mohr stared daggers at me I couldn't duck from, and Jair batted off the hands of the waitstaff who felt the constant need to touch him.

Pixies like Teal flew around lugging jugs of too-sweet tea. They plunked small wooden stir sticks with decorative bronze kites on one end—like an upside-down spoon—into the steaming mugs. A wind blew through the breeze windows and pushed the little concave kites, turning, spinning in the mugs. A particularly narrow-faced pixie poured a dab of cream from a small pitcher into Lady Fede's, and it smoothed out within a few self-stirring strokes of the little bronze kites. Quail eggs in dainty egg cups and freshly picked arugula appeared on our plates, and I stifled a laugh when Jair just looked at the meal. How much of this would he need to eat to keep up his Shifterfae strength?

Lord Ohrem droned on about something I had no desire to listen to. He continued at some length about peace in trades and of something else I tuned out entirely.

You've stopped listening, Kade mindspoke, with a warm chuckle. I risked a glance at him. He was nodding along, and his mouth was answering something Lady Fede had said, but the sparkle in his eye was all for me.

It's drivel, I said back. *She wants me dead.*

"And look at us now," Lady Fede said, and my eyes shot to her. "All drawn together because of Valentina. Who hasn't been listening to a thing we've been saying." She pouted. "Pity."

My heart raced in my chest as magic from their courts tried to consume me. This exhilaration that I always mistook for excitement back in Otti Theater was just me siphoning their magic. "Well, my lord, my lady," I said, looking to Lady Fede and Lord Ohrem, but was careful to keep my eyes well away from Mohr.

They are no lords of yours, Kade growled, his voice so low it bounced around inside my head.

I continued, "It seems we have something more in common than just me. The faeless are being hunted by Winter right under your noses." I looked back and forth amongst them, but their interest had waned the second they heard "faeless."

Lord Ohrem signaled for more wine, and Lady Fede's nose twitched.

Both of their power-hungry gazes found somewhere else to land, but no one stopped me, so I went on, "We could discuss what could be done against it instead of talking about Borage Tea and hunting season, which is so very far away." It was March, the time of Spring. Summer came long before Autumn's months and any talk of hunts would start.

Kade pushed pears onto my plate, and I knocked the egg onto his, sending it rolling.

Lord Ohrem surprised me when he spoke first with a loud snort. "Winter will never rule Autumn's lands. This I can ease your mind about. But the faeless seem a fine distraction for him."

"Oh, and had you not heard, dearest Valentina? Autumn's hunts have been included in our ceremonies." Lady Fede's smile shriveled my insides so much my throat closed.

What does this mean, Kade? I asked silently.

But he sighed inside my head, and his voice was rough as he said, *We'll be finding out soon enough.*

My head was spinning with a fit of anger that wanted to

erupt. Not because of the firefae across from me but from the indifference of the lord and lady. I gripped the edge of the table, looking for stability because I wasn't done. "Do you know why a demigod protects Blackwater Junction?"

Lady Fede's eyebrows rose by a fraction.

"Blackwater Junction," I repeated. "The town Lord Ohrem sent soldiers to just over a month ago. You know? When you were *at war*."

I pulled shadows and fire and air into a churning tornado that sent the pixies clamoring away. The wild flames spun and got snuffed out by shadows just to be lit again.

Lord Ohrem leaned back in his chair, crinkling the impossibly long bird feathers of his cloak. Mohr stayed where he was, resting his chin on his hand like he'd seen my temper all before.

But doing this took courage because I was being *seen*.

I pulled harder on the lion-heart resolve—the strength from Jair—and pressed my hands harder onto the table.

"And look at this ceasefire that came in the form of a Summer Court female. Watch yourself in my banquets, Valentina," Lade Fede warned, pulling the air from the room.

Kade snapped up to stand at my side and sent shadows around us like a transparent box. "Those who ride with me will not be harmed," he snarled as the shadows turned threatening.

A crunching sound came from my hands, and I was too busy to look down, but I felt the table give way under my fingers.

"She dares threaten me in my court!" Lady Fede wailed as a twisting tornado scooped up a panel of sheer cotton drapes and it whooshed into flames.

"By Gael, I swear—" Lord Ohrem gritted out. "Kaderyn!"

"She's redecorating," Kade answered, and sent shadows out to the firefae, holding them down, forcing them to remain in their seats. But he had shifted his body toward me.

Easy, little lion. Since when did I become the reasonable one? he said through my mind.

"I am the ruler, not my ill-fated husband. Not fire, not shadows, and definitely not a theater rat from Summer Court. You will behave yourselves!" Lade Fede's voice grew dark—far darker than I'd heard her before.

A high-pitched ringing started, at first faint, but grew louder and louder until it rumbled the table I clung to. Dishes clacked together; pixies flew off squealing, covering their ears, and I wanted to do the same as it became painful.

My gaze shot toward the open window. The Aeolian Flutes were vibrating, shaking, from where they stood embedded in the earth. I covered my ears and dropped to the ground. Kaderyn leaned over me, shouting something at Lady Fede, trying to be heard above the noise. Jair ducked his head down beside mine as glass shelving along the wall started exploding.

I was sure my brain was rattling inside my skull. It became clear how Lady Fede controlled Springfae. The Aeolian Flutes, though mesmerizing in their beauty and sound, could be turned into a weapon.

Slowly the rattling died down, and I pulled my hands from my ears. Gods, I didn't think the ringing would leave anytime soon. But when I went to look at Lady Fede, who stood poised as ever in front of her chair, my eyes snagged on the table in front of me. The wood was crumbled in, crushed and splintering, and claw marks dug into its surface where fingernails would have—should have—been. My eyes shot to Jair, who was looking at it, too.

Through a grimace of pain, he gave me a quick smile. "Well done, Valentina."

"Could have been anyone," I muttered low enough for just him.

"I don't lack control," he whispered with a wink as he

straightened to his full height. He grabbed a napkin and nonchalantly placed it on the spot my nails had broken through the table.

Drawing on Jair's shifter magic felt more invasive than any of the others.

You'd make a magnificent lioness, but deep breaths. These fae are not worth it, Kade said, mind to mind.

Could I shift? I didn't have time to think about it as Lady Fede was still peppering off insults at me.

"Valentina will participate in today's festivals or join my guards on a sightseeing tour to the edges of the Aeolian Cliffs and keep . . . on . . . walking," Lady Fede seethed.

Within the blink of an eye, the table was clear of food and plates as if we weren't in the middle of a meal. Guards came to both our sides and stood at the ready.

A false confidence surged through me, almost like annoyance, and I wondered if I was feeling it through Kade's mind. I thought of the robin in the jail cell, continuing on no matter what. So, I pulled my shoulders back and was the first to move toward the door.

Let's get this over with.

17

VALENTINA

WE WALKED ON through large, ornate, white-wooded doors into a giant, humid dome. But Spring was known for fertility, music, and wind, and I didn't know what to expect. My fingers brushed against Kades. "Will I have to dance naked around a roaring fire?" I asked half joking, and saw a small smirk grace Lady Fede's face.

"No, Valentina," Kade said solemnly.

"Will I have to play an instrument?"

But Kade turned to Jairek and whispered, "Stay sharp, Jair. We might have to cause a scene."

Recognition of something dawned on Jair as his nostrils flared. "Kade, I smell citrine."

Kade's body grew stiff beside me as we followed Lady Fede to where a group of fae waited.

"What's citrine?" I asked, searching the faces for any I recognized.

"Citrine Tonic is a drink," Kade mumbled. "Made from a yellow crystal found in Spring's western Yegevani Mountains.

It's harvested by those willing to brave a nuckelavee den. One you might remember." He gave me a knowing look. "Then crushed under strong wind magic and mixed into a drink."

But I thought back to the Virtusa in the cells, and my stomach heaved. "I don't want to drink anything else."

"I have a feeling it won't be for you." His eyes darkened, and his shadows flicked around us, regardless of the strong wind that threatened to scatter them.

I could hear the Aeolian Flutes now in the open air but couldn't see them over the high walls of the auditorium seating, which were half-filled with Springfae. More filed in every second.

Lady Fede turned to address us as we stood halfway up the benches where, ahead, sat six large chairs meant for her and her guests. Her guards stopped still at her sides, and a dozen servants flocked over. "Well, Jairek, my esteemed guest. You have a special seat to view the festival. If you would be so kind as to follow my servants, they can show you where you can be . . . hmm . . . more comfortable." Kaderyn went to move in front of Jair, but Lady Fede's voice challenged him as she continued, "Watch yourself, Hunter."

"It's all right, Kade," Jair said, following the servant down the seating and across the large staging floor, and up into the stands on the other side. He drew the attention of nearby fae, who whispered and craned their necks to get a better view of the Shifterfae in their midst.

She led him to a large glass box carved with holes the size of my hand. One chair sat squarely in the middle. But as the servant went to shut the glass door, Jair thrust out an arm, leaned close to her ear, and said something low only for her.

The servant's wide eyes turned to Lady Fede in a panic. Jair must have been refusing to be shut into the glass box. Lady Fede waved a hand, which seemed to signal to the servant to not press the issue. Lady Fede was putting Jair on display, and the entire crowd pulsed with excitement to see him better.

It made my blood boil.

He was not some prize to be groped and prodded because of what he was or his reputation. But I wondered what happened to him when he was stuck with that giant before Kade saved him. I wondered if it gave him that guarded look in his eye.

The blow of a horned instrument—one I didn't recognize —sounded, and the crowd hushed.

"It is a pleasure to honor our goddess, Daina, in this spectacular fashion. We welcome Lord Ohrem and his general from Autumn Court, who have so graciously joined to help admire her. They've brought us tradables and, as such, we've extended our festival to include some of their rituals. It is Spring's nature to show gratitude when it is extended, after all." Lady Fede's voice boomed as if amplified by the wind over the crowd.

Movement to our left down on the stage floor caught my attention, and I watched as a fae I used to care for sauntered out with his green eyes locked on me. Cillian led the way as six males followed closely behind. I could feel wind magic roll off them all.

"Lord Ohrem has graciously volunteered some participants for our annual Ostara Festival," Lady Fede continued.

A sarcastic laugh echoed around the massive stadium from somewhere across from the hallway the males had come out of. I squinted through the darkened corridor to see another group of fae being led out. Except in this group, all five of them were females.

Out Jassa, the innkeeper's faeless daughter from Kyrrahalyn, was dragged with a Spring guard's arm wrapped around her upper body and his other hand clamped over her mouth. I didn't have to guess who had laughed at Lady Fede just a moment ago.

I breathed a sigh of relief that she was still alive, but Lady Fede was still drawling on, ". . . and as a gesture of good faith, I've incorporated his Autumnal hunt into our fertility ceremony."

The crowd began whispering to each other like a group of drone bees near a hive, and I had a feeling this spectacle was being forced on them more than I'd realized.

Spring and Autumn had been at odds with each other for as long as I could remember. The only thing that brought them together was . . . *ah*, I groaned, the theater in Elaria. And this was suddenly feeling much like that.

Lady Fede cleared her throat pointedly at the crowd, and they exploded in an uproar of forced applause. "With a song on its wings and life at its feet, wind guides us all!" she shouted. It was the Spring Court mantra.

The crowd erupted in a choir of nods as they said, 'May the wind guide you' to the fae beside them.

"It also appears we've been lucky enough to have Lord Kaderyn of The Court of Shadows and the very exotic, very noble heir of the Courtless, Jairek Sanguis, here to witness our love for Daina."

The audience reacted accordingly in whispers and tittering. Many pointed to Jair, who sat on display in the center of the left side of the benches. Fae clamored on top of each other to get a better look.

For Kaderyn, they stared cautiously and watched the shadows swirl around him and me. Some Springfae had that glint of curiosity in their eyes; others looked on wide-eyed. They saw the swirling shadows and saw all their misdeeds. They searched the folding shadows at our sides like doing so could tell them if they'd be thrust down to the Underworld when they moved on past this life—like the shadows could tell them their fate. I swallowed. I knew this because I did it too, when Kade wasn't looking.

With shark-like features, Lady Fede spoke, but her voice was barely above a whisper, "They're afraid of you."

"They are afraid the next time they see me I'll have my hand around their throats, leading the way to their judgment." Kade's voice was full of impatience.

My eyes met his. I had killed that Springfae, Jacques. I nicked his skin with Angus's dagger. My mouth ran dry. Had I solidified my place in the Underworld?

"Kaderyn, I had to go from making my court hide in their homes at night to allowing Autumn into my festivals. All for a doe-eyed fae from neither of our courts. So do not pretend you're the only one inconvenienced here," Lady Fede said. "Now, please go take your seat up next to mine. It is a far better view while I chat with Valentina here for a moment."

"I'll first be checking on Jairek. Wouldn't want him losing air in that . . . box you've graced him with," Kade answered.

"Watch your accusations. It is for his protection."

Kaderyn glared at her before turning to me. "Teal's in the corridor waiting. She followed my shadows out. I'm going to lead her to safety with Jair and be right back." And in a move that had all lords, ladies, and generals staring, he leaned down and pressed our lips together, hard, before heading toward the corridor we almost found Teal down.

I ignored Cillian as his stare bore into the side of my head from where he stood down in the middle of the stadium with the other males. His skin was rippling as the muscles underneath protested what he just saw.

Lady Fede sent Lord Ohrem and General Mohr up to her thrones. My body was buzzing from wind and fire magic as she and I stood there, halfway up the stadium, alone.

"It's curious to me how a dishwasher has garnered so much attention," she said.

I pressed my lips together. I wasn't going to give her any information.

Her long, flowing dress swirled in the wind around us. She cocked her head, taking my silence as a cue to keep going. "It's too bad what happened to Elaria. Burned to nothing but ashes. Be a pity if a dust storm blew in and pushed what was left of your home into the desert beside it."

Tears pricked my eyes. Fae couldn't lie, and I knew Mohr wouldn't ever need to lie about what he did to my home, but hearing it confirmed by someone else made me feel like I was losing my footing.

Tell her to get fucked. Your home is with me, came Kade's voice via mindspeak.

I searched for him in the packed stadium. I watched how he moved to the shadows of the darkened corridor, then trudged through the crowd with a blue blob under his hood like an ink blot against pale clothing.

The fae scrambled to get out of his way.

When Kade was close enough, Teal burst from his hood and perched herself on Jair's glass cage. Her little face and hands smooshed to the sides of the glass, distorting her features. Jair let out a loud laugh that made me heavy with need. I wanted out of here and all of us together again.

"If I wasn't in the middle of Spring's single biggest festival, I'd invite you to stay." She looked me up and down. "See what all the fuss is about. But really, there's only room for one powerful female in Spring," Lady Fede said as her face turned severe, "and it's me."

Lady Fede nodded to a guard and, with a singsong voice, purred close to my ear, "Almost time. Follow me, Valentina."

She led me down the stairs to the center of the stadium near the five females. Three of them had huddled together. The fourth, a tall blonde with a silver streak in her hair, was blowing kisses to the males across from her. The fifth was Jassa, who apparently couldn't be trusted without a guard next to her. Her short bangs were scattered across her forehead, where she'd fought to get out of the guard's tight grasp.

I risked a glance up to Mohr. That asshole really brought Autumn faeless into Spring Court, but Lord Ohrem's expression beside him had me fidgeting. He had his eyes locked on Jairek so tightly that bile rose to my throat.

Cillian stood near the males, who all had silver streaks in their hair, but his eyes were on me in shock. The males stoked the crowd, pumping their fists in the air, riling the crowd into a moving force. The crowd erupted in cheers, and small dust storms kicked off from the arena floor.

Movement beside me snagged my attention as a scared female tried to make a break for it back toward the corridor she'd been led from. Ten steps into her retreat, she dropped to her knees as her hands flew to her throat.

Lady Fede's fingers twitched beside me, and her voice was saccharine sweet as she said, "Don't think I won't do it to you."

Before I could say anything, Cillian bolted from his post near the males. "Lady Fede, Valentina cannot take part in this ceremony."

My eyes shot to his, and my heart hammered in my chest at the attention this drew to me. Kaderyn was making his way back through the crowd and I could see his concerned eyes.

"She can and she will. She owes her service to our court for murdering one of our own. You'll remember your place and your purpose, Cillian. Valentina, you either join the other females of your own accord. Or I break both your legs and you're dragged through the ceremony by my guards," she said.

But Cillian didn't give up. "Put her in the kitchens. She can be on clean up. It's what she used to do."

Fury flushed through me from head to toe as I let the nearby fire magic take control. What I used to do? How *fucking* dare him. I used to pine for him for weeks. Just for him to come, have sex, and then ask me to take his pain away before leaving again at a moment's notice. His eyes flicked to me, and I wished to drive my daggers straight through them.

"I have pixies for that, and besides, washing dishes is not a proper place for a female during Ostara." Lady Fede gave a wave of her hand.

I worked to quell the raging fire that I let build.

Easy, Valentina, Kaderyn cooed in my head.

Cillian moved beside us, and I balled my hands into fists, hiding the fire that I was sure was licking my fingers. My hair stirred wildly around my face as the wind picked up. It was causing chaos with the flags in the skies.

"Not this one, Lady Fede," Cillian said, his voice low.

I was suddenly shoved and dragged across the arena floor. I dug my nails into the ground trying to slow the rolling. My arms scraped against the sandy dirt by an errant wind before I landed at Jassa's feet. Her shining golden eyes looked down at me as I grimaced and stood up next to her, dusting the sand off my face. The guard said a warning low in her ear that Jassa snarled at before he let her go.

The pressure of the crowd's stares threatened to drive me into the ground. I wasn't used to this attention, not at the theater and not now. Only once I was shoved in line by Lady Fede's wind magic did I realize the Autumnfae from the podium had come down.

Where are you, Kaderyn? I mindspoke. I had lost him in the crowd.

I'm coming, he said, but it was laced with worry.

Lord Ohrem cleared his throat from where he and Mohr stood not far off from me. "Lady Fede, remember why Autumn is here. She must come back in one piece."

"And I must remind you this is my court which she is found prisoner in. She will participate. Her fate is in Daina's hands."

"I'll join," came Kaderyn's voice as he stalked out of the crowd, black eyes locked on Lady Fede.

Her mouth turned up at the corners, but it was a fake smile. "How generous to offer. Our God, Daina, would be pleased, but alas, there is already the proper number of males." The crowd erupted in cheers that caused her to waver. "There would be no room for you."

My eyes stayed on Kade, even when there was a commotion in the male lineup. *What is it? What do I have to do?* I asked, but his dark eyes just bore through mine, filled with a desperate determination.

I could see his mind working over a thousand different ways to get us out of this. Yet every idea was falling short. There was no getting us *out* of this, just *through* it. Fear drove his muscles to tighten, drove his feet to act, but fear had pinned me still. I couldn't get out, let alone save Teal and make sure Jair didn't become Lord Ohrem's trophy.

"Uh, L-Lady Fede. My apologies . . ."

We all turned to look at who was speaking.

It was a guard who brought out the females, but he was now standing next to the male lineup. "It seems we have a problem," he said, pointing to one of the Springfae males prone on the ground, eyes open.

Dead.

Lady Fede whipped around violently. "Who is responsible for this?" Her voice reverberated around the stadium so loud I winced. "Interfering with a ceremony is punishable by death off the Aeolian Cliffs and to the seamutts below. Kaderyn?!"

Kade walked up to the dead male and leaned over his body. His chest had concaved in on itself. "No steam rising to indicate firefae, and it was no shadows of mine."

Kade didn't have to say it: one of her own killed him. And if she admitted it, she'd admit to losing control in her court.

"Prepare another participant!" she shrieked, and I saw for a second the veil drop as her careful control was threatened. The crowd had grown silent. Lady Fede's normally soft round features were now sharp and jagged. Her glamor was shaking. A dull ringing sounded from the Aeolian Flutes.

Oh, no.

"I'm right here," Kade said, leaning up and unbuckling the neckline of his shirt. The crowd erupted in cheers as he moved to take the place of the dead male. A guard was distributing small white cups into the rest of the males' hands.

Lady Fede was sputtering, and her voice was pitched, "He doesn't have—"

"Here," Cillian said as he moved forward, handing Kaderyn a cup. "It's Citrine Tonic. You'll temporarily lose your magic. And logic." They gave each other a knowing look.

"Kaderyn! Your death in my court cannot be challenged by any successors," Lady Fede said.

"Then it's a good thing I don't plan on dying," Kade answered, never looking down at the cup he held.

"No one from your court can come—"

"Oh, for fuck's sake, Fede. Let's get this over with." Kaderyn chugged the cup in one go before tossing it into the sandy ground.

"Oh, ah, well then, males . . . toast to the one true goddess, Daina! You may now drink your tonic." Lady Fede was flustered —blustering even—as she tried to regain some of her posture. She turned to the crowd and said, "The Citrine Tonic will absolve them of their magic, evening out the hunt. Allowing them to follow their very basic of instincts."

Jassa jostled beside me as one of Lady Fede's servants dipped her fingers in sparkling silver paint and smeared it on Jassa's cheek. I looked at the rest of the females, who now all had the same marking.

"It marks us ready for the fertility ceremony," a blonde Spring faeless said from beside Jassa. She stared at Kaderyn, and was grinning from ear to ear.

"This is fucked up, Arden," Jassa answered.

The servant turned to me, fingers coated in silver paint ready to lift them to my face and mark me ready for the hunt when shadows snaked up to her wrist and held tight. Her mouth fell open and out came a strangled gasp.

"Don't touch her," Kade growled for all to hear. Shadows curled into the forms of massive black hounds at his sides, snarling and spitting.

The entire arena held their breath.

"No matter. She enters the arena all the same," Lady Fede said, shooing the servant away once Kade released his shadow hold on her. Large doors opened into the rest of the arena. "Let the hunt begin!" she shrieked with one last look at Kaderyn's dissipating shadows before lifting her skirts into her hands and scurrying out of the arena.

I moved closer to Jassa, who looked as angry as a roaring fire. This was a hunt? I braced my footing, thinking about the moose we saw in Autumn Court or the birch hounds that trailed us in Spring.

What are we hunting? I asked Kaderyn, whose midnight black eyes stayed fixed on me, penetrating my very core.

You, Valentina. I'll be hunting you.

And it all clicked. They were mixing a fertility ceremony with a hunt. A clashing of Spring and Autumn.

The groaning of the doors stopped as moist air billowed out. Inside was a lush green jungle cordoned off with trees and vines as moist air billowed out. The sky seemed to stretch and morph far above the stadium. I heard a bubbling stream come from inside, and I knew it was much bigger than it looked on the outside. It was an illusion.

I looked at the females around me; the Springfae who taunted the males with the streak of silver through her blonde hair, Arden, still had her eyes set on Kaderyn from across the arena. She winked at him and thrust out her chest, pushing her breasts up in her shirt. Beside me, Jassa rolled her eyes.

"Look at them. They're likely to kill us once they're through with us," someone behind Jassa said, her voice shaking. She was Springfae too, but no magic rolled off her.

"Not if you do it right," Arden said, brushing her hair off her shoulders.

Though Kaderyn stayed deathly still with his eyes locked on me, something was happening to the other males. Their limbs grew agitated as they bounced on the balls of their feet, and a slick sheen of sweat glossed over their skin.

"Well, Arden, you win for most sadistic court," Jassa said.

Don't run, Valentina. It will spark the chase in me, Kaderyn said through my mind. *Hide.*

His eyes were now glazed over, and a sightless appearance rested on them all. *Kaderyn? Kade!* I tried, but whatever the Citrine Tonic was, it had taken him under.

Hide. Hide until I come for you, was the last thing I heard before our connection became clogged with a gross stench that muddied our mindspeak completely.

18

VALENTINA

THE SUN ROSE BEHIND us in the courtyard, flashing everyone in red hues. I grabbed Jassa's hand, and her golden eyes shot to mine.

"Stay with me," I murmured.

She nodded, and though her eyes were wide, no fear flowed off her.

"Where do we go?" someone asked from behind us.

"We find a nice soft pile of fallen leaves and wait for a male to start the fertility ceremony," Arden said, winking in Kade's direction.

"With everyone watching?"

"They make a big deal about sex in this court," Jassa spat. "Like it's something sacred."

"They don't seem to hold those values when they visit Otti Theater's back rooms," I said, and we exchanged glances.

"The leader of the Wild Hunt will find me. I just know it. His shadows will dance across my skin," Arden said.

An ugliness bubbled up, and I wanted to shove her face in

the dirt. But a blow of a horn and a rough push from the Spring guards told us we were supposed to be moving.

"Oh, put a lid on it," Jassa said as we moved past her into the bushes.

Kade's black, menacing eyes tracked my every movement, every stretch of my legs, every sway of my arms. "Come on," I said, moving at a jog, pulling Jassa and one more female who followed us into the thickest part of the vines.

"Ah, *by all Gael's graces*," Jassa swore, tripping on a thick branch as we made our way out of sight of the large doors. "Valentina, I'm fast, but not when tangled in Spring Court's vines."

"We aren't running." I looked back at their scared faces. "We're hiding."

Before they could say anything more, a second horn blew, and my heart stopped entirely. The males were coming.

"Please, Jassa," I urged, searching for any magic I could siphon.

But she nodded once and clamped her mouth shut tight as if to say she'd sit and have a glass of whiskey and argue about it if we weren't running for our dignity.

We stayed low, crawling through thick ferns and strangling vines with only the sound of the crows answering our heavy breathing. We ducked down under a giant elephant hosta, skittering beetles from their homes. The hosta's leaves were larger than my entire body. I turned to the other females, pulling them under further when a scream rang out, followed by cheering. Jassa's hand squeezed mine.

"We're going to the river. It will distort our—" I started, but all of a sudden Jassa was ripped from my hands.

She screamed a guttural scream worthy of only firefae as I scrambled to catch her as she was dragged out from our hiding spot by her waist. Shit! Shit! Shit! I dove for her.

"Valentina!" Jassa shouted as her body left the cover of the hosta completely.

I had no weapon, no way to defend myself, and I had a scared faeless behind me and no magic to siphon from any of them. But I wasn't leaving Jassa to fend for herself.

"Stay here," I told the brown-haired faeless who I had to pry off my arm.

I bolted, following the sounds of heavy panting and snapping branches. Whoever had her was crashing through the jungle with very little care, but they were moving quickly, and I forced myself to keep up. I followed until my feet ached and my thighs burned, curving around the riverbed through hanging vines that tripped me. I followed until I heard nothing but the damn crows again.

"Jassa!" I whispered to the trees.

Nothing came back.

An eerie quiet condensed around me as the blackbirds hopped from tree to tree behind me. The jungle became a weight pushing in on all sides. But I wasn't the same as I was in Elaria, and I'd felt this before, walking with Kaderyn.

Something was stalking me.

I needed to hide. I slowly, silently, moved to the river's edge, sinking into its waist-high depths. Along the far bank was a massive, uprooted tree that had half its roots still covering the water's edge and a recess far enough in that I couldn't see the end. I tucked into the twisting roots, forcing myself back against the shore bed.

Then I waited, because it would not do Jassa any good if we both got caught. A shudder ran through me as something slithered against my leg. Footsteps on the fallen trunk had me holding my breath, but I didn't dare move. Not even as something, again, slithered around my ankle and fastened it in a tight grip. The footsteps thudded away before disappearing altogether. I sucked in a deep breath and reached down to pull the snake off my ankle. I couldn't just sit by and allow—

A massive body jumped into the water, and was to me in seconds. A shriek got stuck in my throat as a hand smoothed against my mouth. Heavy and strong. His black eyes pinned me still as he pressed us back against the root bed of the shoreline. His body vibrated against mine, and I didn't dare look away from his pitch-black stare.

Kaderyn removed his hand, and his mouth crashed into mine in a grinding passion that sent shivers down my spine. His hands greedily took to my body.

"Kaderyn," I panted, pulling as far back as I could, trying to see his face.

His mouth moved to my neck, nipping and sucking on my pebbled skin.

"Kaderyn, please," I said, trying again as his hands pulled and stretched my clothing.

He froze, clutching me to him, and I didn't know if he heard me at all until he pulled back to face me. His head flinched back slightly as he tried to blink away the confusion.

I rubbed my wet fingertips down his cheekbone, wishing he wouldn't look at me like that. Like he didn't know me. "Kaderyn, Jassa needs help. Please, I beg you, go help her."

His eyebrows furrowed once before his mouth dove back on mine. His strong fingers tilted my head to move his mouth deeper, but frustration was building like a force I couldn't control, and I pushed hard at his chest and hands.

Mohr dragged Jassa here because of me. If something happened to her . . .

"Kaderyn," I said into his mouth. I rubbed the sides of his face again with my thumbs. "Please save Jassa. For me," I pleaded as tears rolled down my cheeks because whatever that Citrine drink was, it had taken away *my* Kaderyn.

His eyes traced my tears before he reached up his fingers and brushed them away. He stared at his wet fingers, blinking hard. His nostrils flared as he sucked in a hard breath, and his jaw twitched. I watched the determination push away the lust in his eyes, and he disappeared as fast as he came.

And a part of me worried that I just sent him out to another female. To Arden.

But I couldn't have any more blood on my hands, so I counted one hundred chirps of a cricket before wading out of the water. Hiding was no longer an option.

The crowd cheered and groaned with whatever was happening out there, and I prayed to Angus it had nothing to do with Jassa. My clothes stuck to me as I climbed the embankment, cringing at the sound of the water sloshing to the ground. Ducking under strangling vines, I stayed low, stepping over broken twigs, and stayed parallel to the path.

Every moment felt too long, every second was too much. Anxiety was rising like a boiling kettle, distorting time. Had it been a minute or an hour? I couldn't be sure.

There was a clearing up ahead, and I knew from traveling the island now that when something didn't feel right, I should dodge it entirely. Intuition was building inside me, something I had been robbed of experiencing for so long.

I heard whimpering to one side and froze, adjusting my sight to see Jassa's golden, wide eyes and matching freckles sparkling through the moss green of the bushes. She sat low, crouched in front of the brown-haired faeless I had tried to hide under the hostas. Her clothes sat askew and disheveled against her frail body, and she sobbed into Jassa's back.

Jassa stared at me, and everything her sister said in the backroom at the Fortress, which felt like ages ago, came flooding back. *When it's done. When it's finally quiet, their ashes will line our roadways.*

The faeless needed to stop being shoved around like cattle, moving any which way it pleased the fae. Me dying in Spring's fertility games would not change that. I wanted to hug the crying faeless, but it would not do us any good right now, so I balled my hands into fists. We had to survive this.

I looked back to the clearing and realized why I had such a bad feeling. There on the far side, half covered in brush was a dead male.

Jassa held a small broken tree trunk; its mess of roots created a ball on one side. "Did Kaderyn find you two?" I whispered, ducking down.

She nodded to the dead fae in the clearing.

I tried to bridge the connection between Kade and I, but the mindspeak was still muddled.

But we were fae—we were stealthy—and I didn't hear the footsteps until they were upon us.

"Stay hidden," I mouthed as I backed up into the clearing.

The male whose footsteps I heard watched me like a cat stalks a mouse. He straightened his posture out and rolled his shoulders back, ready to pounce. He was the largest one, the one enticing the crowd earlier. A chorus of shouts roared from the far end of the arena, and it gave me an idea of where some of the others were.

The crowd near us cheered as we circled each other. His eyes explored my body as I noticed the scratch marks puckering against his neck. He'd been busy. But if he was distracted by me, he wouldn't be after the two I had hidden.

I glared at him, and I wished I had my daggers.

A deafening roar, like a warning, sounded out from the crowd nearest us as they noticed what I should have. The male before me braced on the balls of his feet and leapt, closing the distance between us.

"Valentina, here!" Jassa shouted, launching the root ball to me.

I caught it in a vice grip and swung high and hard just in time. It clipped the side of his head with a sickening smack.

But his hand snagged my arm, and I toppled backward to the ground. His hands gripped my neck in a matter of seconds as his weight pressed down on me. Desperate for air, I dug my nails into his back, matching the scratch marks on his neck. One of his hands left my throat to paw at my clothes as the other squeezed my windpipe. Oh gods, I wasn't strong enough. I twisted, trying to bring my knees to my chest and push him off.

"Hey!" I heard Jassa growl and tipped my eyes up in time to see her connect a massive log across the Springfae's temple.

His hands left my throat, and I gasped for air, scrambling backward.

"Keep your ogre hands off her!" Jassa screamed, smashing the log down on the male again and again. "Screw you! Screw the fae! And screw this stupid festival!" Each declaration was marked with a blow to his body.

But Jassa, though mighty, was small—and faeless. Blood dripped down both temples as his eyes bloomed with an anger to rival any Autumnfae's. He righted himself and smoothed his hands back through his hair, smearing crimson blood through the silver streak. Whatever this Citrine Tonic was, it helped him recover quickly.

"We need to run," Jassa panted, holding the stump higher.

"No more running, Jassa. Keep him distracted," I said, slowly moving for the root ball I had dropped.

"Oh, sure," she replied, stepping the opposite way.

He seemed to latch onto movement, so I stilled until Jassa distracted him enough to give me his back.

I was done running.

I leapt onto his back in the only way I knew how—with one

foot on his calf, the other on his back, I hooked my weapon around his neck and pulled. Hard.

His hands flew to his neck and my arms, and I grimaced at the touch.

But Jassa wasted no time. With a shriek, she charged, smacking the log into the male under me. Her fury fueled me, and I pulled harder on the woody root matter around his neck until my muscles screamed.

We were feral and savage, screaming and shrieking—wild beings, and I'd never felt more a part of the War of Many than now. We were angry at this fae before us. Angry at this court. Angry at this entire island.

But the great tragedy, the truth, was that we would never be stronger than the fae. Not Jassa, who would always be faeless, nor me; without magic to siphon. He flipped me upside down over top of him, and I crashed into Jassa. Together, we fell to the ground.

He panted, sweaty and bloody above us.

But before I could jump as fast as I could track him, a shirtless Kaderyn pummeled the fae to the ground. Jassa bolted for the other faeless hiding in the brush and stood as her guard. I kept my weapon high—should Kaderyn need help.

They were equally matched in strength and stature. But within moments, Kade had the upper hand with the Springfae's throat in his grip. Kade's black eyes bore into mine as the male squirmed at his mercy. It was the same maneuver I'd seen Jairek do the first time I met him in Autumn Court.

Kade stared at me, not in an asking but in a promise as he twisted and snapped the male's neck with a crack that echoed through the clearing, echoed around Scarlotta and, I was sure, the entire island. The fae dropped to the ground in a heap, and the crowd hushed into a stunned silence as Kade and I stared at each other. He was going to protect me, and I, him.

19

VALENTINA

ARDEN TRIPPED OUT of the brush into the clearing to my left, and I looked her over. Her clothing was ripped and torn as if the jungle had tried to have a piece of her. But she had come out of the same path Kaderyn had, and I blinked back at him. Why was he shirtless?

Kaderyn stepped a massive boot over the dead fae and pulled me into his chest.

The crowd slowly erupted in shouts and cheers. Whatever this messed up Ostara hunt was, it was now ending.

Slowly, a groaning, grinding rang out on the far side of the trees as the doors opened. Jassa pulled the hurt faeless out of the bushes, and we made our way to the exit.

Kade, in my arms, kept blinking and shaking his head, trying to clear it. The Citrine Tunic was fading. Much to my disappointment, the first person I saw outside of this stupid game was Cillian. He stood, fists clenched, on the other side of the large doors as his green eyes glared at us.

But Kaderyn was having none of it, and without formality, he pulled me around Spring's general entirely.

"Did you have to hunt them all down?" Cillian snapped at our backs.

"They stood between me and Valentina," Kaderyn said, his voice intense and strong, like crashing swords.

The crowd was roaring, but it didn't feel like any sort of victory. We searched the stands for Jair and Teal.

Lady Fede swayed into view, her dress billowed still in an unnatural wind. "We haven't seen such a reaction before. It's intoxicating, knowing that I gave that to them," she said, twirling for the crowd like they were cheering for her.

The kites flared in the skies, moving in concise patterns, and the Flutes chimed deeper, fuller.

"She has participated. She is free to go," Kaderyn growled.

"Oh! What is the *rush*, Lord of Shadows? Stay for a few days," Lady Fede said over her shoulder.

"Respectfully, Fede, but not a fucking chance." Kade coughed as the rest of the Citrine left his system.

"Well." She turned to face us, giving us her full attention. "I've cleared the north passage to aid in your travels," Lady Fede said with a smile I knew not to trust.

Kade stilled beside me before he gave a curt nod and guided us to the far corridor. I saw golden-haired Jair and a ball of blue push their way through the stands. We walked down the far hallway as Jairek and Teal made their way over.

Jair clapped Kaderyn on the back. "Time to go?"

"Time to go," Kade confirmed.

I spun around, searching wildly for Jassa through the heavy crowd that now made their way down the stands to the arena floor, but I couldn't see her. Had Mohr taken her back? Had she hidden in the mass of fae? Could her golden eyes ever hide?

"What about Jassa?" I stepped out of Kade's arms.

He carefully turned to face me, and I noticed how exhausted he looked. Cillian had said he'd killed the other males, and here I was, asking more from him. He seemed to pause before answering. "Fede has agreed to let you go, Valentina, but I'm not sure the Autumnfae will settle for it. If we stay to find out and if I have to kill them all," he said as he brushed his forehead against mine, "because, for you, I will. I will have two courts coming for Shadows, wanting blood."

I would be asking him to risk his court to stay and find Jassa. Bile rose in my throat at the thought of leaving her alone here.

"Valentina," Jair said, stealing my attention.

Kade and I both looked to where Jair nodded down the far corridor and saw a flash of wide, gold eyes sparkle off the chandelier overhead.

Jassa was pushing the brown-haired faeless forward with quick steps. I wanted to tell them of Blackwater Junction. Maybe they could go there until we were done our quest. Jassa paused in the doorway and gave me a small wave before hurrying onwards with a quick glance behind her shoulder. The bravery of the faeless never ceased to amaze me.

Within minutes, and after many smooshed-face kisses by Teal, we were at the stables. Malvasia and the mare were happily munching oats and grains, looking no worse for wear. Kaderyn kissed me quickly and left to check if the way out was clear as Teal and Jair stole gear from the adjoining stalls when we were unable to find ours.

The west wind came in through the open windows.

I hopped up on a saddled Malvasia after giving her a few nose rubs.

The breeze increased down the stable hall with a scent I longed to forget, and I froze my hand on her mane. "Cillian," I said without turning around.

"Val," he answered, rounding to the front of Malvasia.

She snorted.

And all I could do was stare. How dare he call me that. I was so far from the same Valentina back in Elaria. I quickly said, "Don't you dare tell Mohr—"

"I won't. Of course, I won't. I just wanted to talk to you." He shrugged.

"It's not necessary."

His green eyes stared at me longingly, but I still carried an anger that made me want to reach out and punch him in the nose.

"I just wanted to give these back," Cillian said as he held out Angus's red and yellow daggers, which sat safely in their dark brown holster. The red one glinted in the afternoon sun.

I leaned down and grabbed them out of his hands as a sigh of relief left my lips. I thought I lost them for good.

"Listen, I know you're mad at me," Cillian started, rubbing the back of his neck.

I sucked in a deep breath and snapped the holster around my shoulder blades. "I'm not."

But he continued as if I had said nothing, "I didn't want to hurt you. I'm sorry you didn't know about Avika and Breena—"

My eye twitched. He was sorry *I didn't know* about Avika and Breena. He wasn't sorry that *he didn't tell me* about them. He very well knew I had no way of finding out stuck in Otti Theater.

"You should have told me," I said, adjusting my seating on Malvasia, trying to let go of my irritation.

We were going to need food and warmer clothes. I'd have to ask Kade where we could stop when he returned.

"I was afraid you wouldn't want to see me anymore," he said.

I stilled. Because back then, I would have begged for some company. I would have begged for him to return to me. But I looked at Cillian now, tormented by what he was, and the anger I carried dissipated into the breeze he controlled. And nothing replaced it. Not sadness or regret.

I looked at Cillian now, and I felt nothing.

"I went to our libraries south of the castle. I went asking about what you are." Cillian's eyes flicked down my body. He shook his head. "There was nothing there regarding a Siphon. Nothing in the records of a fae—or faeless—being able to take another's magic," he said, pausing briefly, "or pain."

I squared my shoulders.

"But you've always been from Summer. At least as far as Daria told me. And they might have records that Spring doesn't."

In Hawrenthia. Yet another reason to see Lord Grigory.

"I know you have Kaderyn now—" he said, but I cut him off quickly because any talk like that was sure to bring my daggers out.

"I'm not afraid of what I am, Cillian. Regardless of who I'm with," I snapped.

"Just be careful he doesn't—" he tried again.

But I wasn't giving this male the time of day. "Use me? Lie to me?" I pulled his wind magic to me and tugged at Kade's shadows I felt from down the hall, twisting them together into a miniature obsidian tornado in my palm like I did at breakfast, but on a much smaller scale. Much less destructive.

"Remember what I said, Val, being a part of someone else's war is not my idea of being helpful."

"Time's up, windbag," Kaderyn said, darkening the hallway.

Cillian cleared his throat and backed up a step. "You're

bringing her into the danger of the North. There's no safety for her up there."

"What do you know of safety? She told me you left her in the cell. I know you took out that ceremony participant, and that's the only reason your throat isn't at my sword right now."

Cillian's eyes narrowed. "Don't forget you're still in my court, Kaderyn."

"And you're at the very end of my patience," Kade growled.

Cillian's mouth twitched. "You'll take care of her?"

"You have no idea what that means."

"She was safe at the theater with Daria. Safer than she could ever have been with me."

"It doesn't matter." Kade climbed up onto Malvasia behind me. "Come near her again, and I will rip your broken fucking soul so far down into the Underworld. I'll give you a real Berserker to be afraid of."

And we left Cillian gapping at us there in the stables as we followed Jair on the mare out into the streets, stolen boots tucked under his arms.

"We won't take the north passage?" I asked as we followed a well-worn road heading east out of Scarlotta.

"Nope," Kade answered.

"Go on," I implored when he didn't elaborate. I looked over my shoulder and caught sight of that small dimple when he smiled, and I sucked in a quick breath.

"Lady Fede said she cleared the north passage. Of what? Brush? Tree litter? And what did she put in its place? Soldiers? Mohr? No thanks, it's a two-day trip to Arnprior. We'll get what we need there, then take the southern passage up through the north."

Jair trotted beside us on the mare as Teal kept his shoulder warm. We were all together now, and nothing was going to get in the way of Kaderyn's shadows.

I looked back at Scarlotta, but I wished I could have made sure the faeless who were wrapped up in their games were leaving with me, too.

"Did Arden find you?" I whipped around to face Kade.

He looked through his lashes at me. "Yes."

My heart skipped a beat, and my stomach launched into my throat. I wanted to jump off the horse. I wanted to—

"Quiet your thoughts, little lion," Kade said. "Citrine Tonic or not, I was not away from you for nearly enough time." His lips traced the curve of my pointed ear, and his arm flexed tight around my waist. "And when I bring you to bed, you can be sure we won't see daylight for hours."

20

KADERYN

I WOULD HAVE.

I would have killed them all for her.

I had been stuck so heavily in my own plight that I lost all careful consideration of what life had to offer. It took her dancing at my fingertips to be able to see it. I dared a glance at Val, who, in all her beauty, was sure to see straight through me. I followed her hand where it hooked around her pointed ear, pushing her black hair from her face. A stirring in my chest at her smile drew my gaze away to the trees of Kinswood Forest.

Without my shadows, I was stuck at a clear disadvantage, and before I pissed off more lords of Eadha Island, I was going to need to get them back.

There was just one problem—the urge to race the Wild Hunt, to lead them through the lands, purging the earth of trapped souls, might be too great a force to hold back long enough to get the ones I cared about home to The Court of Shadows. I would be leaving them.

My heart did wild things in my chest every time I thought

about leaving her. So I held her tighter to me as we rode Malvasia east through Kinswood Forest to Arnprior.

The northern borderlands between Spring and Winter were not as diverse as the Lady of the Woods. Sprawling silver pines met with strong, white-wooded aspens as they battled each other for space, and, as we were currently on Spring Court's side, the aspens were winning.

It was a slower trek. The ground was either a sheet of ice or brown mushy topsoil that threatened to steal our boots right off our feet anytime we gave the horses a rest. But as we trudged on, the quaking leaves of the aspens were becoming a noisy roar inside my head as the souls of the dead decided this was a great fucking time to speak up. I wondered if Valentina heard them now, too.

"Does Malvasia lead the Wild Hunt?" Valentina asked, rubbing her forehead as dark settled over us.

It took me a moment to realize what she was talking about. My head was stuck so far into the mess I was dragging us into. "Malvasia is a noble and brave mare, but if we had Deathmarch we'd be across the Dahlin Tundra by now."

A small gasp left her soft mouth as I pulled Malvasia to a stop and hopped down. "He's that fast?"

My mouth twitched thinking of Deathmarch, my lead mare of the Wild Hunt, and as much a part of the Underworld as I was. "He's a *she*, and she's incorrigible."

"Where is she now?" Valentina asked, and it took force to focus on her instead of that damn whisper, faint but urgent, that was threading its way through the rustling leaves.

"Paying off a bargain. My hounds and I entered the cave that day I was forced to become fae some two hundred years ago. The only smart one to stay out was the horse."

"So she's still Shadows?"

I nodded, finding a proper spot to dig my hands into the

ground through the heavy root beds of the trees. Fuck it, I was going to get dirty.

"And the hounds?" she asked from atop Malvasia.

"Back in Auris in Shadow Court. They're mischievous pups who get into far too much trouble."

"What is it like in Auris?"

"It rains a fair bit," I said without thinking, cursing myself when she paused, no doubt thinking of Autumn's frigid rain. I wanted to bite off my tongue for being too honest, so I quickly sputtered out, "But it's warm."

"I can't wait to see it," she said softly before whipping her head around. "What is that noise? It sounds like we're surrounded."

A chill north wind blew the leaves at my feet; the voices grew louder. I dug my hands deep into the mucky humus, the nutrient-dense layer of the earth. The ground pulsed through my fingers. "Aspens hold the voices of the dead."

"What are they saying?"

"They're trapped, stuck neither on this plane nor the next." The rumbling grew louder—into a roar—as I laced shadows through to them, controlling them all. Then, almost at once, all became silent.

"What did you say back?" she whispered.

"I promised them that they would not like where I was going to take them."

BY OUR SECOND DAY OF TRAVELING, WE RODE INTO Arnprior as the sun was setting. Jair and Teal rode up ahead to get a feel for how the locals would greet us. Which was good because something was off with Valentina. She sat atop Malvasia as I walked, reins in hand, alongside.

"You sit there pouting any longer, and you'll have made a perch big enough for even Teal to land on," I said with a chuckle, trying to lighten the air. I tried gently to ask via our mindspeak what the matter was, but she had blocked me out the minute I noticed her thoughts had turned dark. I glanced up at her, and if looks could kill, she'd have just dragged my own soul to the Underworld.

I gave her calf a squeeze and wondered if Mohr was on her mind. Yesterday she was in good spirits, but today her color had paled, her expression muddied, and my anger at Mohr for whatever pain he'd caused her sent my mind spinning.

"Kaderyn?" she whispered.

"Yeah," I answered, but I kept my eyes on the streets, devising an entirely too gruesome death for Autumn's general.

My mind was off somewhere, thinking of my sword in his throat or his head at my feet, when she spoke again.

"Kade."

I turned my face up to her and tightened my hands on the reins. "What's wrong?"

"Am I—what I did in Spring Court's fields . . ." but her voice trailed off as my eyes searched her wrecked face. "Did killing Jacques with Angus's daggers solidify my place in the Underworld?"

I stilled Malvasia with a hand on her nose, then locked my eyes on Valentina's, holding her hostage. "Valentina," I started, but her name on my tongue sent tears running down her cheeks.

She had killed a guard. I had found out enough during the festival.

I leaned up and rubbed away the tears before holding her face still in front of mine. "Valentina," I said, trying again, "if ever there is an option between your neck or theirs—you choose yours. For the love of my hounds, please save yourself."

"Am I going to the Underworld?"

I shook my head. "Monsters don't worry about being monsters, little lion. There are no worlds where your soul would be taken by the Wild Hunt. But if you ever find yourself in its path . . ."

"Don't run." She sniffed with a slight nod.

"Don't run," I repeated.

WE STOPPED AT A SHOP NEAREST THE MAIN ROAD TO resupply. We were unsure how the fae would react to the festival we'd just been forced to take part in. But by the second nod of a head from a local fae, we felt comfortable staying in Arnprior for the night. By this point, they had either heard of the ceremony games or had seen them firsthand, and they did little to deter our movements through the city. Most faeless had moved to Blackwater once Adrian had taken it under his protection, and as such, this city was all fae. No one here knew why he did so, either.

"Will I need lined mittens or a hat?" Val asked, wide-eyed inside the large, elegant shop. I frowned.

I didn't want to drag her across a frozen tundra, but I was too selfish to tell her to wait for me here in Arnprior.

She could see the look on my face as she plopped it all down on the counter. "We'll take it all and the smallest coat you have." She thought for a moment. "One perhaps for a faeling. And some needle and thread."

My heart stuttered in my chest because, for fuck's sake, she was still looking out for Teal.

This city's food had far more variety than in Blackwater, as they could rely on magic to help them. The lack of a constant rain drowning their fields helped too. We found an inn on our second go after trying a nicer place first.

The first guesthouse was immaculate. Pale blue breeze walls lined the far west wall, allowing a strong breeze in and keeping the wildlife out. A group of well-mannered fae had their heads down, focused on their instruments as they played soft concerto music that seemed to lift the air entirely. The smell of roasted lamb made our mouths water, but we didn't let the main door fully close before we took off back out of it, looking for a corner booth in a shady bar to tuck ourselves down in.

I'd bring Valentina to Auris if I wanted her to have an enjoyable meal.

We fell into the booth in a tavern called Salmon Run Inn in good spirits listening to Teal tell us about her adventures in Scarlotta. It was something about her cousin's friend's brother's adventures. She was going on about a pixie named Bean, who dressed in a sock.

"His head popped right out through a hole in the toe.
Stark naked underneath
His clothes—dragging in tow.
Said a witch cursed him to wear no clothes that
would fit.
So we'd all see his bellflowers
Every time that he'd sit," Teal said, her voice pitched
high.

Valentina's laugh at my side dropped me into a comfortable slope that let my thoughts trail away. I wanted her on me, feeling her chest rise, sucking on her neck, hearing her breath hitch in my ear.

The Citrine Tonic's effects wore off as fast as they came on, but a part of me wondered if I needed to apologize for my behavior during that fucking festival.

I shifted in the seat, and her eyes shot to me, in surprise. But I couldn't feign my desire for her, so when the waitress came, Jair ignored us both and ordered one of each of everything—enough for the table.

Because all I wanted to do was get her upstairs.

"What creatures live in the North?" Valentina asked as she fidgeted beside me, ignoring the very clear thoughts I was sending her via mindspeak.

"None I want to meet less than the lord's daughter," I answered, pulling out a bottle of Solanci Ipsum from my pocket.

We all looked at Jair, who quite busied himself with a turkey leg. Val dove into the jams with bread. Teal had her hands on a bloody chunk of venison and growled at anyone who came near it.

"You get on all right back there?" I asked Jair, narrowing my eyes. I still had no clue what the ice was about. Well, I had one idea. And I hoped she was very far away by now.

He threw a greasy chunk of meat into his mouth. "Nothing I couldn't handle."

I grunted, staring at my friend, the one I was dragging all over this damn island. All because I saved him that day in Bran's lair up past the northern pass. My chest ached with affection toward them and the beautiful fae sitting next to me. Finally, back where she belonged.

We weren't out of the dangers yet, but Cillian promised to hold Mohr up in Scarlotta for the last leg of their ceremonies, and it should give us enough time to cross into Winter. Political bullshit meant I couldn't kill Mohr on any lands not my own—being a lord and all—but I'd never wanted to take a soul from the living as much as I did with him. And I knew one way to quench this anger that was building, and it was having Valentina safely by my side.

"All I can say is that if there are any other towns rumored to be drenched in an unnatural downpour," Jair said with raised eyebrows, "we're going around them."

"Typical, the first god I meet is deceiving and untrustworthy," Valentina said through mouthfuls of food. "I thought them as noble."

Teal let out a loud, 'Pahhh!' of sarcastic derision.

I turned to Val. "That wasn't the first god you met."

"What?" Her face blanched.

"In Autumn's Fortress. That fucking male that danced like a chicken. Remember him? Though I don't know why Gael spends his time on Eadha."

"Gael, the God of Forging? Autumn Court's god danced with me?" she asked. "Wait, he'd said he'd been demoted. Not allowed to leave the Fortress. That he had to stay behind while the others had their fun."

I turned quickly to her. "Why?" *These fucking gods, I swear...*

"I don't know. I thought at the time he meant he couldn't go off with other Autumnfae soldiers while they dragged me half dead through the desert."

"Can Gael not return to the Otherworld?" Jair asked, and I caught his eye.

"What could he have done to be shunned by the other gods?" I added, pushing my empty plate away with my elbow. "Valentina and I seem to be attracting the attention of the gods. And that's never a good thing."

"Was this before or after you did all the kissing?
I almost cuffed your ear for losing track of our mission,"
Teal said, with her big eyes on me.

Valentina stilled beside me. *That's right. Why did you kiss me then?*

Gael was too close to you, and I protect those who ride with me, I answered in her mind. *And . . . your lips looked delectable.*

She hesitated. *And would you consider doing it again?*

I cleared my throat. "Well." I yawned or at least went through the motions. "We'd better be—"

"Just go." Jair waved a hand in our direction. No doubt he'd realized we'd gone silent.

"Right." I tapped the table once before hoisting myself out of the booth.

Teal, wide-eyed, looked on.

"But my tale of Bean and the sock
There's a saga about a ribbon around his—"

I shot Teal a stare, raised my eyebrows, and watched as her small cheeks wrinkled around a wide, pointed-tooth smile.

I held my hand out for Val; that was enough for tonight. I sucked in a breath as I walked ahead of her into a room in Salmon Run Inn's upper hallway. I wished we were in Auris walking into my bedrooms where I didn't have to enter a room first to make sure it was safe. Where I didn't have to send my shadows out to the room's darkest corners searching for witches or traps or fae hunting her down.

I tangled her fingers in mine and pulled her in close behind me. Once the room was clear, I moved to the side of the bed to light the lamp.

"Leave it off," she whispered, her voice shaky enough that I whipped around to her, opening our mindspeak further for any indication of where her head was at. But she stayed closed to me, reluctant to let me in.

I sank down on the edge of the large bed and laid my palms open to her. Maybe she just needed me close for tonight. Whatever she needed, I was here.

She moved in, hesitantly, like a doe unsure of its surroundings. And the Hunter in me held back a growl something fierce.

I soaked her in, her body tight and small between my knees, her hair cascading down her back and over her shoulders, her pink lips and depths-deep blue eyes. So desperately like the sea in the Underworld.

The silver light of the moon—the only light—shone on her face, and fuck if I didn't think she was going to look absolutely breathtaking in the black linens of Shadow Court.

I clenched my jaw, trying to be patient. Hunters of the Wild Hunt never needed to be patient as we chased the souls to the Underworld.

No one could ever outrun us.

And right now, I wanted to strip her bare, rip Spring's clothes right off her, drench her in shadows as they pressed close to her skin. But some intuitive part of me knew she needed to do this, to slow it down and take her time. So I let her undo the many buckles on my shirt, but *by my fucking hounds*, did I wish I was in nothing at all already.

The cool spring air met my skin as I lifted the shirt over my body and tossed it to the ground. Her eyes traced the swirling shadows across my chest, and I risked tugging her closer to me by the waist of her pants.

I'd let her control how far we went, but I didn't have the patience to keep her mouth from mine.

Our lips crashed together in a desperate ache I could never get used to. And when a small sigh escaped her, I pulled her thighs up around me and wrapped my bare arms around her small back.

Her tongue dancing along mine was driving me insane, challenging any self-control I carried. And only when she sucked on my tongue, slow and seductive, did I reach my hands under her shirt and pull it up over her head between us. Desperate for her soft skin on mine.

Her hips rolled into me, and as I kissed up her neck, her breathing turned sharp in my ear. Her skin tasted sweet like I'd imagined those honey things she always talked about were.

I couldn't get enough of her hands around my shoulders, holding on as our bodies crashed together. My patience lasted maybe five minutes more before I flipped us over and laid her gently on the soft cotton bedding below me.

My mouth left hers long enough for me to look back and trace my hands down her legs, taking her pants with me as I went.

And there she lay, naked before me, with half-lidded eyes glowing in the moonlight. Her body was open to me, and she was mine, trusting me, and I was never going to break that.

I ran my hands up her smooth legs, rubbing my thumbs up the inside of her thighs. Her body arched off the bed so temptingly that I leaned down to press my mouth to her breast, but she halted me with small hands on my chest before dipping them down to the buckles of my pants.

Seems impatience was in full force tonight.

And I couldn't talk. I didn't trust myself to speak. I was sure I'd sound like a baffling idiot.

Or worse, tell her I loved her.

Tell her I'd break apart the skies to stay with her.

So, I stayed quiet and let her undo the onyx buckles, only helping her by kicking them off when she was done. She reached for me, and I closed the distance between us, my mouth finding hers. My shadows swirled, dipping us in and out of darkness.

She lay there in the most angelic state I'd ever seen. This beautiful being couldn't possibly have been meant for me. But here she was, and I worried I was too selfish to ever let her go. "You sure?" I muttered reluctantly into her throat. Pressing my lips to her neck, feeling her heartbeat through my body.

And with swiftness of practice, she opened her mind up to me, breaking the barrier she held between us.

I love you Kaderyn, she mindspoke. *All your darkness and the light you show only to me.*

I stilled. My throat choking, my body pressed against hers. And she'd just said the most dauntingly beautiful thing I'd ever heard.

Angus was a damn fool for putting her in my path.

"I love you, Valentina," I said, brushing my lips against the curve of her neck, and thrust myself into her. Her hands spurred me on. With her under me, she was safe. With her in my arms, nothing was going to get her.

And by my side, we'd find my shadows together.

I propped myself up. This wasn't enough to show her, and so I pulled out, retreated from her warmth, ignoring her pout, and licked my way down her summer-kissed skin. Savoring the body I'd been tied to for over a month.

The sweetest gasp left her mouth as I reached the apex of her thighs.

Her fingers found my hair and didn't let up on their hold until she was screaming my name, coming apart on my fingers and mouth.

Her gentle hands coaxed me up, and I thrust in again, groaning at the sheer tightness of her. She wrapped her legs around me as I thrust harder.

"Valentina," I panted, and before I could give her fair warning, she grabbed my face and pressed her soft, warm lips to mine.

I grabbed her hands in one of mine above her head and held her butt still with the other as I pumped faster until I couldn't fucking see straight, and we were both gasping for air. Until finally, stars dotted my vision, and I came apart in her with a passion I knew was going to live on forever.

Sweat glistened off both of us as I kissed her cheeks and the tip of her nose. Finally, understanding what vulnerability was and trusting it only with her.

I tucked her close to my chest, and we fell asleep not long after. I'd let the shadows do the spying for me for the night. A part of me didn't want to leave for the north at all because here she was, laying beside me, and she was warm. Not just her body heat, but in the way she made me feel. Lighter, like it was safe to care about something. And I did. I cared a whole damn lot about things I didn't before. And if this place created things like her, then it couldn't all be bad. And maybe they were worth saving.

Maybe I could care enough to save them all.

Maybe I could do that.

21

VALENTINA

HIS BREATHING WAS RHYTHMIC and relaxing, and he looked serene laying beside me in the soft bed of the inn. Seeing the Hunter beside me snore gently was peaceful, and it was easy to pretend we weren't in a foreign court with a firefae chasing me down. I wished to capture this moment forever. I'd put it up there with Autumn's forests, Spring's music, and Summer's flowers.

I brushed a lock of black hair from his forehead. He held no anger at the world here—not when he was forced to sleep like the rest of us. And I wondered if he'd ever been young. I wondered if he left a love behind in the Underworld before his shadows were split. Did Teal say something about this?

He stirred, rolled a heavy arm over that slung me down, and pulled me back closer to him.

"You're noisy," Kade mumbled into my hair.

"I haven't said a word," I said, kissing his fingers.

He pulled his hand away and tapped my temple. "Up here."

And I stilled because I'd been careless and left the mind-speak open.

"Sleep, Valentina. There's no one for me but you."

And this noisy part of me wanted to perk up and say I'd heard it all before. It was a scared part that had nothing to do with Kaderyn and everything to do with me putting my self-worth in those who so easily took what they wanted.

But I looked at him—*really* looked at him—laying beside me. Dark hair framed his strong face marked with battle wounds and scars. He'd dropped his glamor for me again. How could it not be him? How could I have found happiness in anyone else?

Kaderyn, the fallen Hunter of the Wild Hunt, could see darkness better than anyone. He saw mine and still loved me. Even with his shadows swirling around him, he was a beacon, a shining light on forever that I wanted to cling to with Jair and Teal by our side. I promised myself I would close my eyes for another hour or two, but then I had things to do.

I watched Kade's shadows dance above him as he slept. My needle moved faster and faster as I raced the rising sun. I had bought a small faeling-sized coat down at the shop and was in the process of stitching leg holes and buttons onto it. Once the sun rose completely, we'd be off, and I needed to have this coat done for Teal before then.

I sighed, holding up the thick off-white material. It still might be a bit big, but it would have to do. We were running from fire's embers into ice's hail and couldn't spare any time.

Kade woke shortly after I finished and bolted straight up in bed. His black eyes searched for me. I smiled at him—his messy hair and grumpy scowl. I felt that steadiness in my chest, and I knew Jair and Teal were somewhere close.

It was time to go.

Kade seemed to think as much, and we found ourselves downstairs not twenty minutes later. After we woke each other up once more properly.

His fingers laced through mine as we rounded the final corner to the inn's main gathering area. Jair stood against the bar with a large bag strapped tightly across his back. I frowned; it was a new one I hadn't seen before.

"Picked up a second tent," his deep voice confirmed. He did well to try to not meet my eye as my cheeks heated. "Traded the mare for it. I prefer to run, anyway."

I opened my mouth to say that was not necessary, but before I could, Kade said, "Good idea."

"Besides, the locals threw in a lot of extra supplies. Seems that was not the Ostara Festival that they were accustomed to."

"Poison has its hold on Spring, and I'm not talking about whatever has Lord Brexton down and out," Kade said.

Not long after, I found myself atop Malvasia as Jair and Kade walked alongside as we left the edges of Arnprior. Teal, in her new full-body coat, sat atop my shoulder, still tucked inside my wide hood. She was listing off the ingredients in Nightale Tea when the loud caw of a bird pierced the air, causing Malvasia to startle. It threw my attention upwards as Kaderyn calmed the mare.

"Easy, easy." He coaxed Malvasia as well as my racing heart.

I blocked the sun with a curved hand. A massive tawny hawk with beautiful blue eyes landed a few meters in front of us, blowing out loose snow with the gust of its great wings. I clutched Malvasia's mane, trying to stay upright. Before I had time to process what I was seeing, it shifted into a blond, spiky-haired male who looked more pissed off than a nuckelavee with a dagger in its back.

"I've been searching the northern lands for you," he said, cocking his head to the side in a purely avian fashion like the canaries I coaxed over Spring Court lines back in Summer.

But far more hostile.

"We had a couple of detours. How are the courts faring?" Kaderyn asked.

This new male's sharp eyes met mine. How was I supposed to greet a Shifterfae? Jair greeted me by snapping the neck of an Autumn Court spy. I hoped this meeting went nothing like that.

"Rhett, you can trust Valentina," Jair said, now at his side, but it came out as more of a command.

I gave a little wave from atop Malvasia. Because what else do you do when being stared at like that?

Rhett scrutinized my hand and promptly ignored me altogether. "The Court of Shadows is fine. Trading is slow. Summer has retreated the caravans—"

"We heard about the Summerfae going missing—does Lord Grigory think it's us again?" Kade asked.

"Don't ask me to guess what that budgie is thinking," Rhett snapped, seemingly as an insult.

"And the Courtless?" Jair asked, moving his arms to cross over his chest.

Rhett's eyes moved to Jair and submitted, or at least softened. "Courtless is holding the mountains. Skulhad is demanding more food in compensation for keeping the mountain passage clear. Says he doesn't much care for the taste of Autumnfae anymore." Rhett clicked his tongue. "Say's he's had rather far too much."

"So, they've escalated their attacks?" Jair asked.

"Well, they seem pissed off about something," Rhett said,

his eyes shooting to me, but shadows curled up from Kaderyn in a warning. "And Deryn says the . . . plan should work, but for my sake, you two, no more detours." But he looked away from us all like he didn't have the authority to make these demands. "Running one court in your stead is enough responsibility, let alone two."

"I owe you more than you know, and I'll repay you when this is all over," Kaderyn said.

"You know what I want, Kaderyn."

Jair gave a large laugh as Rhett moved back a few steps. "I don't know, Rhett, you'd make a fine lord."

"Rather be a general," he said.

"How's Deryn doing?" Kade asked.

"I've got her," Rhett said as his blue eyes challenged him before looking up into the skies he'd descended from. "Keep your eyes up. Something big lives in the Northern clouds."

And with that, he shifted back into a hawk and took off. Within seconds, he was lost to the rays of the sun with an ear-piercing caw.

Kade clicked Malvasia on as I watched where Rhett disappeared over the tree line.

"He doesn't know what to make of me," I said softly.

"He's Jairek's second-in-command, and he's running both Shadow Court and the Courtless right now," Kade answered, eyes full of sympathy.

"Don't take it to heart
Rhett's been cross from the start.
Can't say he gets better with age.
Avoid if you can
Ignore if you can't.
There's only one who quells his rage," Teal said from my shoulder.

"Is it because of Autumn?" I asked.

"They've done a fine job trying to slaughter the Courtless," Kade said as Jair tossed his boots back to him. Kaderyn tied the laces together and slung them over Malvasia's neck.

"Why won't Autumn leave them alone?" I asked, watching Jair shift into a golden lion in the span of one breath.

"It's steeped in traditions they're reluctant to change," Kade said, thinking for a moment. "A new lord is needed, maybe."

I thought back to Terna in Autumn's Fortress. "Or lady."

Kade's dark eyes looked up at me, a smile on his lips. "Or lady," he agreed.

HOURS LATER, WE FOLLOWED JAIR—IN LION FORM— up the northern path to the bridge that led into Winter Court. Across the island, I'd found nothing hollower than the Winter sun above us. There was no heat in its rays, and its brightness seemed to mock me. Kade had kicked a grumbling Teal off his shoulder ages ago, so she had perched on mine, where we cursed the snow together until she fell asleep. I could feel the tight braids she'd weaved near my scalp.

Jair bound on ahead, unbothered by the slush-covered ground. But I felt ice on my fingers, and it wasn't from Winter's south-blowing wind.

Up ahead, a wooden bridge appeared with snowfall piled on the far side. A pair of Winterfae soldiers—with white eyebrows and eyelashes though their skin was the color of raw yew wood —stood at attention.

They watched us carefully as we walked Malvasia up to

them, their eyes flicking from Jair to us. I didn't think they'd ever seen lions in these parts of Eadha.

But Kade's patience had been far too tested already, and he cut right to the chase. "How many dimas will it take to get you two to ignore our passing?"

The mouth of the smaller one twitched. "We've been ordered not to impede your travels."

We both looked at Jair, who kept his broad face away from us.

Kade turned back to the soldiers. "And how much to light a warning torch if the general of Autumn decides to go stargazing in Winter's tundra?"

They glanced at each other.

"Five thousand dimas," the larger one said.

Kade tossed him the coins that threatened to blow away on winter's winds, and we were off.

Not long after crossing into Winter, did the snow squalls really pick up. Jair lumbered up ahead. White flecks of snow got caught in his golden mane, but he still pointed his nose into the wind and led us on. On particularly icy spots, Kade would hop down and lead Malvasia across.

We reached a covering of pine trees and holly bushes, marked by their bright red berries that even I knew better than to touch. Jair shifted into fae form as Kade tossed him his boots and coat.

"Storm is coming. Can smell it on the air," Jair said, leaving his coat open to the elements.

He moved off to feed Malvasia while Kaderyn set up the tents, and I was tasked with finding firewood.

Teal felt she was of better use inside Kade's hood. 'Too cold even to braid his hair,' she'd said. But the minute the tents were up, he sent her in on tea duty.

The very thought of warm liquids sent a jolt through me.

We were only halfway across the tundra, and I didn't want to tell Kaderyn I was far more frozen than I ever wished to be again.

He glanced at me as he tugged on the last tie to the very large tent Jair had bought in Arnprior. "You can go inside," he said as he nodded to the kindling in my arms. "I'll finish this up."

I shook my head and continued to gather pine boughs. "I can do this, Kade," I said through chattering teeth.

I made a fire, a billowing one, that crackled with the sap of the pine. It was nothing close to a clean fire until the fallen holly branches lit. Then it burned well and created a steady fire. We were able to heat a pot of oats for Malvasia and a thick meat stew for us.

Teal shivered from where she sat back, closer to the tents.

I looked on, puzzled. "Teal, come closer to the fire. There's no need to sit so far away."

"Memories are stirring
Of ashes we searched in
When that city was burned to a hull.
I'll be fine by the next roast
Just need time to dissolve ghosts
Running rampant inside my dear skull," Teal said, and I froze.

"W-what city?" I turned to Kaderyn and Jair. A city that burned? *No.*

Kade looked down at his hands. "We went to find you. To convince you to come with us."

I stood up. "You went to Elaria?"

He nodded, and his stare flicked to me, tracking my movement.

But my brain was broken because they would have seen its ruin. The city I was trying so hard to get back to, the city I was trying to save, the city I damned to the wrath of the firefae for a stupid secret.

Oh gods, ashes.

"Is that what you were covered in, in Scarlotta? When you came to get me out of the cell."

Kade rubbed his neck, and I looked at Jair quickly, whose face told me he wasn't going to join this conversation.

"We sifted through the ashes until Jair caught the scent of Virtusa. It was a pretty good indication Mohr had been there and gave us an idea of where he was going."

"Was anyone alive?" I choked as tears rolled down my face.

His black eyes stayed steady with mine, and I respected him for it. I didn't need pity. I hated what I had caused already. He shook his head. "But there were track marks of a carriage making their way west that smelled nothing of Mohr."

I nodded. They might have gotten away; they might have left the city as it was burning. And I couldn't ask if they found bones or jewels that would mark life left in the ashes. I couldn't possibly come back from knowing that.

I sat back down, closer to Kade, and wrapped my fingers in his. We were getting his shadows. Then I was going to Hawrenthia to *make* Lord Grigory use Summer Court's army to defend its fae. I shouldn't have to give myself to Mohr for Summer Court to be safe.

Kade offered Solanci, his orange-scented alcohol, and I welcomed the burn. My self-pity turned to an anger I didn't want to quench, but Jair picked up the flute and went into a lovely melody that threatened to soothe my fury.

Easy, little lion, Kaderyn said via mindspeak. *Save your anger for when our enemies are near. I don't imagine we are in the clear yet.*

You went searching through the ashes for me? I asked again, incredulous.

He looked down at me from where I rested my head on his shoulder, around a billowing fire in a frozen court.

I prayed to every god I've ever cursed that you weren't in that town when it burned. I would search the ends of the world for you. In this life and the next. He kissed my head.

I closed my eyes to Kade's affection, but when I opened them again, something caught my attention. "Hey, Jair. That's a different flute."

He brought the reed down from his lips and flicked his hair out of his eyes. "Had to trade mine in Scarlotta, unfortunately."

"For what?"

"Information on where I could find a small blue-skinned pixie with a love for ships. And who was probably nursing a raging hangover."

We looked at Teal, who gave us a sheepish smile.

But before long, the winds had picked up, and the storm became a giant stomping over us with thick, calloused feet trying to squash us whole. Kade and I walked to the stark black tent that marked it as ours, and I stilled inside its opening. It was like the one we had when we were first traveling together, but bigger and with far more blankets lining the floors in shades of black and amethyst-hued pillows.

Kade sat down at the table and chairs that lined one end of the tent and went about lighting candles for warmth and light. But I wasn't tired, and the Solanci warmed my blood in a way fire magic never could. When Kade sauntered back to me, I welcomed his arms around me and his lips on mine. How utterly lucky I was to have found him.

His nostrils flared, and he stilled. I didn't know if he could sense how much I needed him, so I opened our mindspeak and flooded him with how I felt, how much I cared for him, and how desperate I was to love him completely. I pulled his curved mouth to mine with a passion I'd never felt before. Because it wasn't just knowing I'd found my family in the shadows, but knowing that he'd seen all my mistakes and still came for me. Still fought for me.

His hands rose to take off my undershirt of woven linen, but I stilled them, splaying them wide across my belly.

His brows met in confusion.

I pushed him back to the chair, and the candlelight threw his shadows to stir around him wildly. I swayed from one end of the tent to the other and back again, tapping my lips.

"I was wondering—" I said, pacing back again, but his brows smoothed out, and his stare grew intense.

His shadows flicked eerily still. "I'm a Hunter, Valentina. Stop pacing," he said, his voice full of restraint.

Which was exactly my problem. I thought back to the kiss in Spring Court's festival when we were in the illusion. The passion I held for him was Otherworldly, but I didn't want a stupid Citrine Tonic for him to be able to let go for me.

"But what if I didn't?"

His dark eyes flicked to mine, recognizing what I was asking. I was asking for him, all of him. To be with me—unrestrained. We stared at each other, bodies tense and all of a sudden way too hot.

The shadows froze in midair. "I might not be gentle."

Excitement flashed in my eyes, and a smile tugged at my lips before I turned and took another step just—

One.

More.

Step.

Shadows exploded, cascading darkness around us, and strong hands were there at once and had me pressed against his hard body. He tugged my head to the side, exposing my neck to his will as his fingers laced through my hair.

I pressed harder into him; the sound of his pleasureful growl edged me on.

"What could you possibly want with a darkness like mine?" His voice was hoarse, but it coaxed out a yearning inside me I didn't think was possible.

"You're a light, Kaderyn, and you're leading me home," I whispered into the dark.

He pressed his mouth to mine, full of desire I was never going to forget. My heart hurt with how badly I wanted him to know how much I loved him. And that leashing him to me that night in the Fortress was the best decision I'd ever made.

I brushed my thumbs against his cheeks, but they were met with dampness. I tried to pull back and see why, but he held tight and tugged at my clothes before hoisting me up in his arms. My back met something hard, and I realized it was the upright pole at the tent's center, strengthened by Kade's shadows. I traced my hands down his body, eager to undo his pants. One of his arms held me to him, but his other batted mine away, undoing buckles for me. His warm solid body met mine, and he pressed into me, hard, at my center.

He was full of an intoxicating drive I couldn't get enough of as I looped my arms around his neck, a little curious and a little victorious.

I was going to need to hold on.

"Show me your darkness, Kaderyn," I breathed, tossing my head back.

Shadows snaked up the sturdy pole, pulling my hands with them and restraining them as Kade moved inside me. Friction was building, and I was panting into his mouth.

Because here I was, giving all of myself to him, trusting him. And trusting myself that in any shape or form, I was never going to be alone again. I was going to love the ones that loved me and follow my heart to where I belonged.

"Kaderyn," I said in desperation as my toes curled and my nails etched into the pole at my back.

His thrusts were rhythmic, but his teeth and hands were—as promised—not gentle.

And I came, shrouded in shadows with loving hands and a beautiful body against me and inside me.

The shadows released their grip on my wrists, and I dropped my arms to his hard shoulders.

I leaned my head on his chest as he walked us over to the bed, and I sunk comfortably into its soft sheets in sated bliss.

Kaderyn kissed his way up my chest. "I am *just* not through with you, Valentina."

He lined himself up between my legs, and I pulled him in tighter to me. "You mean tonight?"

"I mean forever," he whispered, and thrust back into me in a beautiful embrace.

22

KADERYN

I WOKE TO THE SOUND of snapping pine boughs with Valentina tucked in tight beside me. The smell of a campfire filtered in through the flaps of the tent. I crawled out of her embrace as softly as I could; regret paining me to leave her warmth.

I'd let her sleep just a bit longer. I opened the flap of the tent and recoiled when a foot of powdery snow fell onto my feet. *Fuck Winter,* I grumbled, dropping the flap down behind me.

It was a gamble, wasting time like this with Mohr hunting her down and my shadows so close, but I hadn't let her sleep much last night. Because *fuck*, I loved everything about her; her sweetness, her ability to see the world through the cobwebs, and I was going to destroy anyone who would try to take that from her. But something was bothering me, something that lay at the end of my journey, and as such, I was only half listening to Teal and Jair as they talked around the morning campfire.

"My toes were embossed
In ever-hating hoarfrost
I might as well have been sleeping in a horse trough,"
Teal growled, her words barely audible over the thick
scarf around her tiny neck.

Malvasia snorted. I knew they'd kept her inside with them
during the storm. The smell couldn't have been pleasant.

Jairek stirred the fire, sending sparks shooting like fireflies
into the chilly morning air. Their embers died out before they
had a chance to reach the ground. I leaned over the fire, grabbed
the snow-covered ladle, and scooped more of last night's stew
out of the pot before finding a spot to sit next to Jair.

My throat felt thick, and it had nothing to do with the stew.
"Jair, there's something I need to ask of you, and I wouldn't
hold it against you if you're inclined to say no," I said.

Jair met my eyes before pushing the embers again, sending
sparks to fizzle. He pursed his lips. "Go on."

"There's a chance the Hunt will be triggered when I regain
the last of my shadows. If my brothers join me and the power of
the Hunt pulls me under . . . I don't know if I will be able to
hold off enough to get you all—"

I cleared my throat because fuck, this was it, wasn't it? If it
did, I was leaving her in the very court that fractured her world
as a faeling. I looked to the tent where my love and my heart lay
asleep.

"—to get Valentina, home."

"I will keep Valentina safe until you return," he said, sniffing
once. His breath came out in a fog in the cool morning air, and
some part of Teal knew enough to keep quiet for once. "I have
enough to show her, anyway. We'll go visit Port Tayou in the
Courtless if she enjoys warm water springs. Get a break from
this chill."

"There are springs in the Courtless?" came Valentina's voice from near the tent.

I looked over at her, and swallowing became impossible. *Could I come back?* I wondered. *Would I still be fae?*

Jair sat with his shirt unbuttoned, and I could tell by the lines on his face that he, too, was worried. Valentina came and sat near me, huddling close as I wrapped an arm around her and passed her the stew. Teal passed around mugs of Nightale, shivering in her little cream snowsuit Valentina made. *I was going to come back,* I thought with resolve. *I had to come back.*

"Listen, this is a part of the journey I haven't mapped out yet. I don't know what lies ahead but a bay to cross and a cave to enter." My eyes shot to Teal, who, for a very good reason, had an aversion to caves. "I couldn't ask for a better family." And when I heard Valentina's breath hitch and her heartbeat skip, I couldn't rightly look at her. Any strength of heart I had melted around her. "This all being said, Arnprior can give you safety. There's enough food to make the trek back until—"

"Aren't you on dishes, Teal? I'm sure I did it last," Jair said, tossing down the poking stick.

Teal scoffed.

"Washing one pan
That held a hind lamb
Does not equal the mess of a stew.
Once Kaderyn's done spewing this gods-awful spam
I'll have a map to turn to," she seethed, pulling a rag—
oh, *nope*, it was the map—from deep within the coat
Valentina made. Her small foot jutted out and kicked
the bronze pan.
"And you'd BEST get to unsticking this glue!"

But Jair's eyes were taunting, and a smile graced his face. "I suppose you'll be feeding Malvasia, then."

And off they went, into an argument that included Teal thrusting her wrinkled, stained map into Jair's face squealing something only he could decipher.

"How much farther?" Valentina asked beside me.

I tucked her in closer. "We're chasing shadows at this point, little lion. This is what I feel." I opened our mindspeak to show her the gut-wrenching pull of my shadows that were split so grossly before. It guided me on like a compass.

She gasped beside me as I let her feel what I felt; how much it hurt to be split from them.

I was trusting her with this. "A day or two, depending if the bay is frozen."

I followed my shadows to where the northern bay was and could tell that solid land gave out, but I couldn't tell if it was frozen or not. I had much the same problem in the Narrows. Ice was fickle and tricky, and it wasn't the same as seeing Jair down a hallway in Scarlotta's castle.

With renewed purpose, I let go of her and dusted the fallen snow off my hands. We were just going to have to see for ourselves. Valentina grabbed the warmed feed for Malvasia while the other two kept up their bickering. Jair laughed into the cold morning air, swatting a flying Teal off from around his head. I sent my shadows to dismantle the tents and watched Valentina pat the mare that had taken me so far across the island. Steady and loyal, Malvasia was good company, and I hoped to get her back to Auris safely when the time came.

23

VALENTINA

WE WERE PACKED UP before the sun had risen much higher in the sky. Not that it did much to heat the chill. A few hours in and the crashing waves told us all we needed to know about the bay.

"For the love of the gods, Kade, they didn't make this easy for you," Jair shouted from in front of us as he found his footing on the ice-covered ground.

I huddled into Malvasia's neck, bracing from the winds, and Teal squatted in my hood as Kade led us on.

"How's your boat-making skills?" Kade shouted back to him as we carried on closer to the angry coast.

Beyond the water, I could make out snow-covered land, trees, and a small mountain. We were almost there.

"Only big enough for Teal, unfortunately."

But before we could grumble some more, Teal let out a deafening squeal into my ear that had me grimacing. She began speaking in broken rhymes and darted from my hood as cold air rushed in to fill her spot.

Kade picked up Malvasia's pace, following her as we rounded a small bunch of pines to see a . . . boat?

It was a massive wooden ship as big as the ones I'd seen docked in Autumn for what felt like so long ago. A thick layer of translucent ice covered it in a sheen as it sat immobile in five feet of frozen shoreline. Waves broke over the edge and onto the hull as we stared, dumbfounded.

Teal was off, zipping up to the steering wheel, dipping below deck, and was back up circling a pole in the center that I didn't know its name. Her clear wings flapped with vigor, and in the white puffy coat, she looked like a flying marshmallow.

"It's called a mast," Kaderyn said as he passed me Malvasia's reins. "Jair, unstick the rudders. Teal, see to the condition of the sails. I'll clear the way." Kade trudged on, full of purpose and determination, like a black mark against the screaming white North.

Jair managed to move to the back of the ship and smashed his boot over and over again into what I had to assume were the rudders.

"The pass couldn't have been frozen," he shouted to no one in particular over the crashing waves and the sound of his boot hitting the wooden planks. "It *had* to be a damn boat."

Teal zipped up the mast again and blasted blue sparks from her hand. Ice chunks rained down onto the deck as pale azure sails fluttered open in the wind. But the rumbling came from Kaderyn as shadows danced up in front of the ship's pointed nose and crashed down in jagged spikes piercing the frozen coastline.

There was nothing quiet about it. And when it didn't give him the result he wanted, he turned his shadows to form blunt hammers and smashed them down again.

Malvasia stirred under my hands, and I calmed her with

gentle words I'd learned over our travels together. We'd be out of here soon.

Shadows slithered through small crevices between the ship and the ice, finding grooves the ice hadn't filled and with a squeeze of Kaderyn's hands, they expanded, blasting the ice off into flying shards. The boat rocked from side to side as it became unstuck in the waters.

Jair came back around and jacked up a ramp of icy wood that led from the shoreline to the railing of the ship. Malvasia and I stared at it as Teal shouted for us to get on the gangplank.

"After you," Jair said, grimacing.

It took courage to hop down off Malvasia, but if I wasn't calm, she wouldn't be either. "Come on," I said, patting her side, and led the large horse uneasily up the bridge.

Kaderyn turned his shadows into an opaque mass and attempted to push through crevices in the shoreline out to sea. By the second run, he broke through the ice with a cracking fury. He looked at me, determination and sweat ran across his face, but his eyes stayed concerned.

This was going to be a tricky way back.

"Kaderyn! The sail is whole.
The path is set.
Everything is in good accord.
Jairek!
Stop being a coward
And climb aboard!" Teal shrieked.

And the look Jair shot her from the gangplank had me nervous for Teal's welfare.

I tied Malvasia to a railing near the middle of the ship, hoping the rocking would die down once we had begun moving forward.

Kade leapt up past the walkway entirely and danced along the railing. He brushed by me, giving me a quick, breathless kiss. "Jair prefers four paws on solid land," he explained as the chill of frozen wood seeped up into my boots. "Did you pull the anchor?" Kade asked Jair.

Jair pulled the gangplank up after him. "Couldn't find one."

"Let's hope we only need this one way," Kade answered, unfazed. "Just a little push . . ."

Shadows swirled into the sails, pushing them out as though they were filling with wind. I grabbed the railing, steadying my footing as the ship lurched forward. Jair used some colorful words I'd only heard leave Kade's mouth.

But once we cleared the shore, it became smooth and glorious sailing across the passage. And even so, once we reached deeper, rougher waters, the ice floes that bumped against the hull stopped sounding like they were going to break through below. It wasn't far to travel, but there were things in the sea I did not wish to meet. Like more nuckelavees.

We spent half an hour watching the shoreline come closer and closer before Kade moved to my side and said, "Teal, you best fly out of the way entirely. Jair, hold on to something."

"You're going to crash the ship?" I puffed as his arms encircled me and latched onto the railing on either side, enclosing me in his powerful embrace.

His breath was hot in my ear. "The raft seems to be missing, and we aren't stepping foot in these waters. We're running her aground."

"No!" shrieked Teal.

"To the air, Teal." Kade's grip tightened around me as shadows circled Malvasia, holding her firm. "Jair. Here we go."

I sucked in a breath as we crashed into the shore with a deafening thud. Wood splintered around us, and the force threatened to tip the back up over the front. I didn't think Kaderyn knew how to do anything subtly. Once the dust, wood, and ice settled back down into disarray, an eerie quiet came over us. Kade released me from his arms, and I went to untie Malvasia, stepping over broken boards.

"That wasn't so bad," he said as an enormous chunk of wood fell into the churning, frothy waters below.

"The stern is in shards
The mast is in half.
You crashed it with ill regards
For passage on our way back."

"Hush, Teal. I'll get you your own ship when we've returned home. Let's get moving before we meet the sea floor and the creatures that would call us dinner. The sun visits the sky for such a short period of time here," Jair said as he launched—in one massive leap—to the land beyond.

Sleet started falling like it was welcoming us to the northern isles; a terrible, wet, cold greeting.

Kade used his shadows and a broken plank to lead Malvasia off. I climbed down a chunk of wood that looked like it had been used as shelving below deck. My mittens snagged on the splintered edges and pulled loose threads apart. The ground was icy and broken, but a new fortitude hit us all. Even Teal stopped going on about the ship.

Eventually.

We could see a bulbous lump in the landscape beyond a pine and holly forest. I was in awe.

We stopped to camp near the closest edge of the forest where the spray of the bay couldn't reach us. We were running low on stored food at this point and tried to stretch the last of the jerky.

"We'll have to hunt by this time tomorrow," Jair said as the fire rose high in the sky. "I hope this icy terrain has something meaty living on it."

I curled in close to the fire on a pile of linen blankets I pulled from the satchels on Malvasia's back. I watched Jair, coat undone, hair covered in freshly fallen snow, cheeks rosy, and *still* relaxed in Eadha's north. "You're warm enough?"

"The cold never much bothered me."

I contemplated this. "What season rules you, Jair?"

His head shot up with an aloofness I treasured. "I'll show you. One day, when we are back across our court lines."

"It's jungles and deserts
And marshlands and mountains.
They have all the seasons
Wrapped up in one like the Mainland," Teal added as
she sat on Kade's shoulder, curling her fingers in his
hair; not in a move of affection but gripping it tightly—
like trying to pull it out.

"The Mainland? You mean south of The Court of Shadows. Who lives there?" I asked.

"Only two," Kade answered, prying Teal's fingers out of his hair. "One is Deryn Ironside. The one who gave me the Faebric. She's faeless and lives in a home of her own creation near the shores of the Galeairy Strait."

"Deryn lives in an iron tower
Away from other fae.
To others, she's bound to cower
Hiding away in the Mainland's bay.
But she's chock-full of her own power
Just not the kind we'd normally say."

"She's smart," clarified Kaderyn.

"She lives in iron?" I asked. I couldn't even imagine it. The first bit of iron I ever saw was Kade's key, where I learned iron wouldn't harm me like other fae. Then there was the chest that held his shadows in the nuckelavee cave. I didn't think it couldn't be mined in Autumn's northern mountains as they couldn't touch iron either. I didn't know enough about this. "Is there iron in the Anduat Mountains?"

"Shifters from the Courtless do not mine, and we stay as far away from the Anduats as we can," Jair answered with a chuff of his shoulders. "We defend our territory, but we do not attack the court to our north."

Autumn Court.

I knew I should have kept my mouth shut, but I asked anyway. "Why?"

"Because we are not Autumn." Jair's voice, though not harsh, had turned solemn.

I was going to have to ask him another time.

"So, who's the other?" I asked, trying to lighten the conversation. "Who is the other one that lives on the Mainland?"

Teal opened her mouth to answer, but before she could get out a rhyme through the eternal haze of Winter's storms, a spark shot across the sky like a falling star. A flame of blue and white soared to our right, far off in the distance, back over the bay— back the way we came. A flame that Kaderyn had paid Winter's soldiers to signal.

My heart stopped entirely as we watched the blue embers disappear against Winter's chill.

"Time to go," Kade said, dusting off his hands and reaching for me.

Jair kicked—with untied boots—heaps of snow on the fire, smothering it entirely. It hissed an awful sound, like fire scorching raw skin. Mohr was coming.

We had to move.

24

KADERYN

ONCE MORE, THE STORM was howling, and I wished it had something more to say than such utter disdain for me. Mohr was coming, hunting down the light that carved through my darkness. I knew, this close to my shadows with Valentina on Malvasia before me, that I would risk a war with Winter to end Mohr's chase once and for all.

My shadows snaked out and curled around my love, encasing her in all that I was. All they wanted to do was soak into Valentina's skin, her hair, her very soul. Because without her, there wasn't much point. I thought I'd feel whole getting my shadows back, but the truth was, was that something happened when I found her in that tavern in Autumn Court. A release of a burden I'd been carrying. A recognition of an otherness I could stare at forever.

She was here, and I was never going to let her go.

I might not have been meant for this island.

But maybe I was meant for her.

25

VALENTINA

THERE WAS SOMETHING ominous in the way the air smelled up here that had us moving faster across the open plain, especially as the sun set low, pulling the light out with it. Something unafraid of the icy rain that pelted us sideways; something the storm fled from as well. We moved as one across the land—pensive. There was a silence here I didn't much like.

"What are you thinking, Jair?" Kade asked from where he walked alongside Malvasia, upon whom I sat. His voice had lowered, and I had a feeling he didn't like the quiet either.

"Tree line for cover from the wind and whatever that smell is," Jair answered, all aloofness gone.

Kade pulled the wide onyx hood over his head. "Teal, to my hood."

I brought breath in through my nose and smelled a sourness in the air. "What is it?"

"I don't want to find out," Kade answered, but he jerked to a dead stop before the words left his mouth. And before I could look back and see why, he slapped Malvasia's rear so hard she bucked. "Get to the trees!"

I scrambled to grip the reins as she bolted.

Kade! I screamed via mindspeak.

She's faster with one. Hide in the tree cover, he answered, rushed. Worry pierced his words as Jair and he ran alongside Malvasia almost as fast.

A deafening roar sent my heart skittering. I looked back to see a beast twice the size of Jair in his lion form. Our broken ship was a brown spot on the horizon now, sinking into the bay behind the beast as it charged across the snowy plain with its gaze locked on us.

The creature was covered in thick, iridescent scales, shining different shades of black in the trailing sunlight, like glass. Its jowls—though snub-nosed—looked wide enough for Teal to climb in and dance a jig without reaching top or bottom.

In one smooth motion, Jair shifted; his arms became fur clad and clawed, and his golden hair became a flopping mane. He shifted so close to Malvasia that she jolted sideways hard, and I flexed my thighs to stay on.

To the tree line, little lion, Kade said again when I scrambled to find a clear head. This wasn't a firefae or a Winter lord. This was a monster. Beyond talk and reason.

I focused ahead on the snow-covered boughs of silver pines and the ruby-red berries of thick holly bushes. It looked dense enough that I could hide Malvasia in there.

Something glimmered against the brown trunk of a thick, high-boughed pine near the edge of the forest. I squinted through fear and snow as the beast growled again, closer than before. A curved, white-wooded bow lay against it, not yet covered by snowfall. Arrowheads poked out of a pale blue sheath beside it.

I looked back at the ones I loved, the leader of the Wild

Hunt, a lionshifter, and a feisty pixie as they raced behind me from a beast of the North. Something heart-wrenching showed in Kaderyn's eyes right before he pivoted, then halted entirely.

Adrenaline surged through me as Malvasia carried me farther from him. "Kaderyn!" I screamed.

Jair followed Kaderyn's lead. His tail flicked through thick snow as he turned and sunk his head low toward the oncoming beast.

They were going to face off against it.

I had my daggers strapped to my back, but using them would require me to get far too close to it. But an arrow? I looked to the slender, intricately carved bow sitting like a gift under the tree. Nausea rolled in my gut. I'd never trained with a bow.

I spurred Malvasia on as the beast growled again. This time it was so loud that it shook the snow from the pines in front of me before all that filled the air was battle sound. I gripped the saddle and turned to see Kaderyn slash at its hindquarters as it lunged for Jair. His sword pierced its skin, but it didn't seem to slow it.

We were close enough now. I whipped forward and jumped from Malvasia, stumbling into the dense snow, her reins in my hand. I pulled her into a thicket of holly brambles big enough to cover her. The beautiful brown mare didn't belong out here, and I didn't want her lost or hurt. I tried not to meet her panicked stare and found a sturdy branch to tie her to before I dove for the bow.

A grunt and a whine snapped my attention to the battle. Kaderyn grimaced against the ground before he shot to his feet, cutting off the beast from bowling into a limping Jair. Kade crashed his sword down again at its back, and sparkling scales flew off its armored skin as blue pixie magic blasted it square in the face. The beast shook itself out of Kade's reach and launched at Teal, whose magic seemed to annoy it the most. I froze because little Teal was far too close.

Teal took off toward the tree line as fast as her wings would carry her against the slush and hail. She aimed her thin arm backward, firing blue magic when she could as I notched the first white arrow, tightened my hand on the bronze grip, and sent a prayer to Angus that this would work. Jair was up and running now behind the beast with Kaderyn hot on his heels. Oh gods, my hands were shaking. Teal wasn't fast enough.

I pulled the string back, my fingers slick with sweat, and aimed.

Best case, I shot it between the eyes. Worst case—I swallowed thickly—I shot Teal.

Fuck! Why couldn't Petri have needed a bow partner?

I sucked in a breath and let the arrow loose, and watched as it skittered to the ground between my target and me.

A flush ran through my body, and I tossed off my mitts. I had to hit it. I grabbed another arrow from where they lay scattered on the pine-covered ground.

The monster was seconds from biting down on Teal. I pulled back, my throat dry and—

I shot it too far.

It soared over them all and almost clipped Jair as he stumbled behind.

Enough of this, I thought as I dropped everything and ran, pulling my daggers out of the holster on my back.

"Faster, Teal!" I screamed; my voice was pitchy from panic.

Its black snout puffed out air close enough to Teal that her hood blew off. It was following her blue sparks through the fading light, and I was going for it. She shot her arm out one last time as I pushed with all my strength and leapt over Teal, readying to land on the beast's back. I looked down as if in slow motion, as the beast's jowls clamped down on Teal's extended arm with a sickening crunch.

An awful scream left Teal's lips as I landed on its back half a second later, sinking Angus's daggers into its shoulder blades.

The beast threw its head back in pain, howling, though I could hardly hear it over the pounding of my blood through my veins. I sank to my knees, digging the daggers in as the beast dropped onto its belly.

Its large feet with thick black claws were well adapted for its environment, no doubt allowing it to stay on top of the snow. But it didn't matter now as its legs were now splayed out on both sides.

Nothing survived Angus's daggers.

I whipped my head around, searching through twilight for Teal to see a small outline of a homemade off-white snowsuit laying in the snow. Surrounded by blue-splattered slush.

Pixie blood.

I was too late.

The creature's tongue flopped out as I jumped off its back. The scales had lost their shine and faded to a matte black. I'd seen these scales before, but couldn't think straight as I scrambled to Teal.

Jair—now in fae form—Kade and I all met at Teal's crumpled body. Her poor arm was completely missing. The guilt pulled at me, knocking my feet out from under me. Snot bubbled in my throat, and my heart left my chest entirely. If only I knew how to work an arrow.

"Teal! Teal! Can you hear me? Wake up!" Jair shouted as he ripped off fabric from his beige and white shirt.

Kaderyn scooped her into his arms as Jair tied off the stump of her arm near her shoulder.

I brushed fallen snow off her little forehead, but she stayed quiet, and it was the most peaceful I'd ever seen her. She wasn't spewing gossip about the islands, carrying on about her map, or seething at anyone. Even sleeping, she used to snore to wake the dead.

But now, nothing.

And it was awful.

"Teal!" Kade growled.

"Come on, Teal. Who's going to play the flutes with me? Don't make me get that damn cousin of yours," Jair sniffled as her eyes fluttered open. "There you are, sweetheart. Stay with us."

"Kaderyn?
I should have known
I'd be destined for the Hunter's home.
When I go
Please don't leave me there alone." Her small voice
broke.

Kade let out a strangled laugh. "You're not dead just yet. I'm taking you back to Auris. Don't cry, Teal. It's going to be all right."

"Kaderyn, your shadows," Jair warned once and loud, pulling Teal from Kade's arms and bringing her tighter to his chest.

"It doesn't matter." Kade ran his hands through his hair.

And I looked into his face as I realized his fears—the ones he tried to block out of our mindspeak—had come true. Someone got hurt. I moved closer, my frozen fingers inches from her little head, because this was what I was for; this was what I was good at. I was going to take her pain away.

But her bloodshot eyes turned to me.

"Restrain from siphoning my pain.

I'll carry this burden
Because one thing's for certain
You're not leaving my map-making days in vain."

Jair must have thought the same because he said, "I'm going to shift. Tie Teal to my back when I'm ready, and I'll get her to Arnprior."

I pulled back my hand and choked down the lump in my throat. "The ship, Jair. It's in shambles."

"Fuck's sake!" he yelled. He looked around once, searching for a way out of this before locking his eyes on Kade's in the promise of a threat. "I'll never forgive you if you give up now."

Kade shot to his feet in one frustrated motion. He dropped his head back and sucked in a deep breath before righting himself to focus on me. "Valentina, get closer to Jair and Teal."

Shadows grew thick, coating Jair, Teal, and me in layer upon layer. Until they were all I could see and breathe. *What was he doing?* I looked at him as he stood outside the thick shadows. Instinct had me scrambling to my feet and out of the magic he was pulling.

If he wasn't in shadows, then neither was I.

"Take Teal to the castle. Send for Deryn. She'll know how to help," Kade said, his voice strained.

"I can't protect her if I'm an island away," Jair warned, nodding to me as the shadows picked up their pace, circling around them.

I furrowed my brows before righting my posture. "I'll be fine."

"What about the cloud cover?" Jair asked. Shadows were stirring now as one solid moving force, billowing faster than I'd ever seen them.

"I can't let Teal—I won't let her die. Get her to safety. We'll meet you in Auris when it's over," Kade choked out.

Shadows thickened again, swirling like a vortex, with Jair and Teal at the epicenter until the darkness blocked them out entirely and closed in on itself. I blinked at the vast tundra before us, now gray with shining moonlight. Jair and Teal were gone, and only blue-stained snow remained.

Kaderyn dropped to his knees, breathing heavily. Black-stricken veins traced up his face.

I dragged him close to me, holding him steady. "Kaderyn? Talk to me. What's happened?"

He pulled his face into my stomach, nuzzling there until he caught his breath. "Valentina, if you get hurt . . ."

His grip tightened around my waist, and that's when I knew Teal and Jair were very far away.

"I won't. Come on."

26

VALENTINA

W E COULDN'T STAY in the open like that, unprotected on all sides. No matter how much my heart broke for Teal or how badly I wished I'd killed it sooner. I had to get Kade to the last chest. But first, to safety.

We leaned on each other; our feet heavy with snow as we reached Malvasia in the tree cover. Her eyes were wide, and her reins were a tangled mess. She didn't enjoy being here anymore than we did. I leaned Kaderyn against a pine and got to work setting up the tent—wooden poles with canvas and ties. I was glad I'd watched his shadows do it all those times before.

Kaderyn slumped against the tree and looked at the bow. But at one point, I couldn't reach the top of the peak in the center. So, I focused on his shadows, pulling them to me like living things. They grew, wound up my legs, and danced on my fingertips before I sent them out like I'd seen him do countless times before, and tied the top peak of the tent.

Once the tent was sturdy, I led Malvasia in from the cold, patting her nose before I went back for Kaderyn. He met me at the entrance, hands shaking, and I stared up into his weary eyes. "Go lie down. I'll get us food."

I had the packs off and the saddle on its rack before I heard shuffling behind the cloth divider where Kade was. I searched through the food bag, but my heart sank. It must have opened in our frantic gallop away from the creature. It was empty, save a few apples in the bottom.

I looked at the shiny, red, dappled surface of my *favorite* food. And sure, I could have eaten them, but Kaderyn needed more sustenance; he needed to regain his strength. I sucked in a breath, steeled my courage, and turned around the soft cloth divider between Malvasia and our area. Kaderyn had used shadow magic to create the bed which sat in its usual position, though it was nothing fancy this time. He laid facedown, asleep, and the deep groves of his back rose and fell with each passing breath.

We were in the most northern point of fae lands, alone in the dark and fearing for little Teal's life. And now, no food. I leaned down and kissed Kade's sweaty forehead before leaving, returning to where I had set Malvasia up for the night. Her eyes were still wide with fear.

"Shh, Malvasia. It's going to be okay," I said as I held one apple out for her. The other I'd tucked under the crook of my arm.

She sniffed loudly, then opened her mouth and took it whole.

I brushed my fingers along her neck, trying to ease her anxiety. But one apple would not feed Kade and me both, so I tucked the juicy apple in my pocket and left the safety of the tent.

I was going to have to hunt.

Not half an hour later, I sat cold and anxious under the canopy of a sprawling silver pine. My back rested against its sturdy trunk. I wasn't good with a bow like Kade. I couldn't run them down like Jair. But I had built that picture frame in Otti Theater—the one that allowed me to take the audience's pain all at once, I had gotten Sloane out of her ice tomb, and I could do this, too.

I slunk shadows out like Kaderyn had taught me, slow and steady, and sat in Winter's dark night. Still as a rock, as Kaderyn had done. My fingers froze, no matter the cream-colored layers I now wore, and it took every fiber of my being not to run into the safety and warmth of the tent on the other side of the clearing. The one I had shadows monitoring.

But I had to do this for Kaderyn.

Using the light of the moon, I slunk them out to blend in with the natural shadows of the surrounding trees. Eventually, when I hadn't scared off everything with my chattering teeth, I felt a heaviness press upon the shadows.

Something was there.

For a brief second, I panicked and thought of the black-scaled beast that took Teal's arm. Or at the very least, it might even have been a moose, the giant hulking creature that Kade took down in Autumn's Forest, which felt so very long ago.

Could I do that? I slowly and silently pulled my red and yellow daggers out. What were my options? Kaderyn needed me now, and Jair and Teal were counting on me. I tightened my grip, bracing for whatever came out from behind the trees—

—and let out a breath when I saw the pointed, flicking ear of a white-furred hare. I watched it hop pensively once more. Though I was relieved it wasn't a monster, my heart fell because it *wasn't* a monster. It would have been much easier to kill if it were.

My nostrils flared as I tried to swallow my conscience. Being helpful was hard, dirty, and often (did I *ever* know) thankless. The hare nibbled the broken apple I had placed for bait. I'd put it in the shadow of a tree trunk, then layered my own—or Kaderyn's—shadows out under it.

I curled the shadows up quickly, trapping the hare as if in a net. It snapped to attention just as fast, and its powerful paws tried to kick free. But the shadows held, much to my relief and dismay; it hurt my heart so very much to see the hare struggle.

I sulked as I walked up to it. The stars shone brightly through the pointed needles overhead, guiding me to its body, now writhing under the inky opaque shadows I clung to. What was I to do now? Petting it didn't seem right, nor consoling it; I couldn't lull it into a false sense of safety.

The only monster here was me.

I leaned down and buried my face in its fur—my soul felt dirtier than anything this creature could have on it. I drew my dagger and thanked the hare, sent a prayer up to Angus for it, and with my face still pressed against my prey, nicked its paw with the red dagger.

It might have squirmed, it might have noticed, but I had magic of my own and I took its pain before it settled in. I was the help, after all.

It stilled in my arms within seconds.

Teal said that death was a circle, and as a fae, I knew this deep down in my core, but I'd been sheltered for too long and this hurt so much.

I sobbed as I built the necessary fire to cook it. I heaved into the snow before I prepared the hare, like I had seen Jairek and Kaderyn do so many times before. Wishing things were easier did not make it so, and dwelling on all we'd been through was causing a fire to brew in my belly that I didn't want. So, I thought of how thankful I was to catch the hare at all. I focused on how lucky I was to have found Kaderyn in Iradown Tavern in Autumn Court, right when I thought my days were over.

I sucked in a deep breath as I rotated the rabbit, thinking about how strong I felt around Jairek and how much I loved that little seething pixie—who I hoped to see alive again. How much I loved Kaderyn, the very darkness embodied, who was my lifeline and held my heart in his. I was here because I *wanted* to be. Not because I was forced to or felt indebted to be. And I would do this for him.

When I thought it was cooked enough, I took it off the spit to cool and threw our last oats in a pot for Malvasia with some snow that would melt to soften them.

I didn't get that sinking feeling that would always crop up when I couldn't use water magic. I was a Siphon, of pain and magic, and I'd been hidden in a dusty theater in Summer Court for far too long.

I fed Malvasia her oats, which she thanked me for with a snort, before bringing the cooked meat in for Kade. I rubbed a hand across his dewy back and brushed the onyx hair off his face.

He sucked in a deep breath through his nose at my touch and leaned up to his elbows. His head hung heavy as he looked at me through sweaty strands of hair. "What did you cook?" he asked.

I cradled a little bowl of meat in my hands, feeling like a bird providing food for its mate. "It's rabbit," I said, helping him up to a sitting position.

He stretched his neck before leaning his forearms on his knees and looking at me clearly. "You hunted?"

I nodded, swallowing thickly, not trusting myself to talk about it.

Understanding dawned on his face. "By my hounds, Valentina. I do not deserve you."

"Eat. Please." I ignored his nonsense and passed him the bowl.

I refilled it three times for him until there was nothing left and deflected his question when he asked if I'd had some.

Once he was done, he wrapped his arms around me and pulled me closer to his bare chest, where I nuzzled in. The shadows swirled up around us in comfort and familiarity, but I couldn't wait any longer.

"Kaderyn, are you all right? Is Teal . . ." I asked, pulling back to look into his face.

And I knew he wasn't. Teal was a part of us. I didn't know if she was going to make it or if he could tell if she was alive.

"I shadowfaded them to Auris," he said. "It took shadows and energy to do it, and I had to pull from shadows I was holding elsewhere."

I thought back to what Jair said before Kade sent them away. "The cloud cover above Shadow Court?"

He nodded. "I hold it in place to keep prying eyes off our court. I had to pull part of them back to get Teal and Jair out." A bit softer, he added, "Oir's going to be pissed."

"Your adviser?"

He nodded again.

"Can Deryn really help Teal?"

"We have the best medicines across the island for creatures that can't heal as well as fae. Oir will do what she can with them, and Deryn will do what she can about the arm. As long as Teal did her part and survived the shadowfade home. It can be a bit . . . bumpy."

Did her part, he'd said. Nausea rolled in my gut at the thought of Teal dying. "I'm sorry, Kade. I'm sorry I never learned to work a bow."

His lips met mine in a kiss to silence the doubt. "Don't blame yourself. I was the one who dragged them up here. I should have known baliroqs would have found a way to cross the bay."

Baliroq must be what the scaled black beasts were called.

"Jair and Teal would follow you anywhere." I looked up into his black eyes, now ringed with tired shadows underneath, as I helped him lie back down. "And so would I."

But he stilled against the soft linen fabric of the bed. "Valentina, I don't know that I can get you home when—*if*—we reach my shadows. There's a chance—and I should have told you sooner—but there's a chance the Hunt will sound, and I'll be gone, scavenging the lands for souls meant for the Underworld. It's been two hundred years, and I don't know if I can hold it off long enough to get you home."

I swallowed stiffly and tried to hold in my worry from even our mindspeak. "Malvasia and I will get to Auris. We've come this far. We're not giving up on your shadows."

I had far too much on my mind to worry about keeling over in the isles of northern Eadha. And I would not be a victim anymore. I'd find a way back to them all.

But right now, my place was here, where I was helpful, beside Kaderyn. Helping him become whole again on the quest for his shadows. Compliancy was no longer an option. There was no going back to life on the sidelines, so I rubbed his arm and pulled his head into the softness of my chest. Right now, this was where I needed to be. Where I wanted to be.

Once he was asleep again, I slunk out of bed. I still had work to do. I had to figure out how to set up the shadows as lookouts. Not long after, I stood just outside the tent's entrance, and darkness greeted me with a stillness I'd grown accustomed to. No bugs chirped in the night; no leaves rustled in the wind, so I focused on shadows and sent them out along the white-powdered ground in a wide circle around the tent.

Holding them there took concentration. If any thought wandered to Teal, they dissipated, toddled away, undisciplined, like unruly faelings. So, I sent them again and again and again until I felt confident that they'd hold. A Winter's arrow lay close from where we inspected it earlier and once I felt like I had the shadows controlled, I tossed it out into the night and felt it pang against my mind.

Good.

I would know if anyone, or anything, was coming.

When everything was set and both Malvasia and Kaderyn were calm and asleep, I lay down next to him, sinking into the comfort his closeness provided. I clenched a bowl in my hand and drooped it over the bedside. If I dropped it, it'd wake me enough to check if I'd lost the shadows surrounding our camp. I prayed to Angus I could hold the lines while I slept.

I was going to get Kade to his shadows. Even if it left me stuck in the North.

Alone.

27

VALENTINA

I DREAMT OF BLOOMS ON TREES and buds breaking from the soft earth, but I opened the tent flap the next morning to see nothing but desolate white. The sun sat high and clear in the sky, and it seemed almost cruel to see it so clearly and not feel its rays. Why was it shining at all? What was its point?

I had us packed up within the early hours and forced Kade to ride Malvasia for the first half of the trek as I trudged beside them through the heavy snow. We trailed along the tree line, keeping to the outer reaches of the dense forest, and pushed in when the branches allowed us passage and cover.

After an hour or so of clomping through the thick snow, I climbed onto Malvasia in front of him to rest my legs before we braved the cave.

The steep side of the mountain was peeking through the tree cover above us. Occasionally, I caught glimpses of the black recesses of a cave mouth through the heavy pines. And here it looked back at us now, seeming to stare us down. The cave's large mouth was wide enough to fit three horses side by side.

I felt Kaderyn lean over Malvasia's side and looked down to the scuffed snow below.

This was it.

This was where Kaderyn's shadows were stuck. Though his black eyes now held anticipation and worry as they sparkled like onyx gems off the sun-soaked snow.

"Once upon a time there was a lover on a cliffside." I softly sang the song I made up during Spring's festival.

Kade's battle-worn arms tightened across my torso, telling me more than his words could.

"Who searched the night stars for her Hunter on the high tide," I continued, quieter now, as the hair on my neck rose.

We didn't know what was going to happen when we opened that chest. And I double-checked the iron key in my pocket. We'd kept it from the cave in Spring Court because this part of the journey held secrets even to Kaderyn.

Trepidation followed Malvasia's steps as we closed in on the cave mouth. There was no color of life on this mountainside but frigid, desolate snow and a slate-gray rock face.

I watched as the soft snow fell and my fingers froze. *"She waited by the shores for the sea to bring him back."* I'd never get used to Winter Court. I'd never like the cold. *"Searching through the darkness for those eyes of shadows, black . . ."*

I leaned forward, peering into the cave mouth—a giant echoing thing—as Malvasia carried us closer. When suddenly, Kaderyn's strong hands went from holding me on to tossing me off.

A yelp escaped my mouth before I landed in a heap beside jagged rocks that hid under a thick layer of snow. I looked up in time to see a massive three-headed, flying creature carry off Malvasia and Kaderyn in its razor-sharp claws. I stared in horror as Malvasia tried in vain to kick her hooves, whinnying and braying, to free herself as it lifted her upwards still.

The sounds of Malvasia panicking were going to be permanently etched into my mind. I screamed into the open air as the creature's three heads swiveled in different directions.

It was a brown-feathered creature, like a bird but with necks as long as trees, and a body the size of three horses. Its necks held round heads with orange beaks.

It swooped once, and I saw Kaderyn had moved and was now clinging atop its matted, feathered back, holding onto the center neck and dodging the pecking of the two other beaks.

He looked down at me and growled, "Get to the chest!"

I forced myself to move. I scrambled down the covered rock face, sifting through snow to find solid ground. My battered knees ached as I ran as fast as I could through the whistling air. I had the key, and I could touch iron. My purpose was becoming clear. I wiped the tears away I shed for Malvasia and wished Kaderyn would save her.

But the cave tunnel was dark and isolated, and my steps faltered as fear licked down my spine. A thick layer of ice coated the floors and walls, and every third step I spent trying not to fall on my butt.

Kaderyn! I sobbed once in mindspeak desperate to hear his voice, but all stayed quiet. And I'd never cursed him more.

About twenty feet in, every step became warmer in a weird change that battered my senses. Slowly, small buds of leaves appeared on long-growing vines reaching out along the cave walls as they searched for sunlight. I followed them as they trailed deeper until the ice-covered walls gave way to a thick padding of rich green vines, and the ground turned spongy under my feet.

I focused on any shadows I could still feel, like gentle fingers down my spine, and pulled them to me, trailing them out in front, searching. But if a chest of Kade's shadows was close, it wasn't for me to feel it.

It became an oasis of sorts as the tunnel opened into a large, lush green cavern. I'd expected to see plants like these in Summer Court only, back by the Robinswallow River's edge in Elaria. Large flowers, ones unfamiliar to me, bloomed on their stalks, and tiny insects flew through the humid air to their center. Horror struck me quick and swift when I noticed that a boulder lay in the center of the oasis. Because I knew enough about birds to guess it wasn't a boulder at all. It was an egg.

A large opening above me told me how the three-headed bird came and went. By all the gods, this was a nest.

And I was standing in the middle of it.

If there was a chest here, it had to be buried under dense foliage. I dropped to my knees and wasted no time searching, pulling up vines, sifting through small bushes for what we needed to find. I heard the shriek of the creature and crawled quicker, digging through the plant matter faster. On my second trip around, I'd gotten too close to the egg and scrambled to back up when my palm felt the coolness of something hard and rough.

I pulled the green vines away to see the black rusted lid of Kaderyn's chest. I flipped over to my knees and dug around it, scraping off moss, when another caw of the bird stole my attention. The feathered beast, with long necks thrusting forward—but one head missing entirely—came through the opening.

I leaned over the chest and searched for the keyhole. We were running out of time. I glanced up once more in relief to see Kaderyn holding on with one of his boot daggers lodged in its back for leverage. We were here; we were so close. Where was the stupid hole?!

One of its heads must have seen me next to the egg, and it soared down, chomping out, searching to take a bite. I dove to the side, falling into lush, tangling vines as I raced through all my winter layers to find the key.

Kade, in a show of inky shadows, tumbled off to land on his feet beside me. His thick hands pulled my tangled hair off my face. "Are you all right?" he frantically asked, panting heavily as it circled above us.

It cawed an ear-splitting sound full of pain and anger as one of its heads tried to reach its back for the dagger lodged there. The remaining head stayed locked on us.

"What is that thing?" I shouted, looking up at the bird where it landed on a rock ledge. Its bloody claws were as long as my torso where they dug into the rock face. Its dark-brown feathered body confused me. I'd expected the beasts of the North to be white-furred like the hare I'd killed. But I supposed that was the difference between predator and prey.

Predators didn't need to hide.

"That bastard is called an Aileen. And it looks like she's having young—"

But whatever Kade was going to say got cut off when his eyes fell to the chest, and he sucked in a deep breath. His arms stilled on mine, but I didn't waste another second and pulled away, crawling over mossy plants to set free his shadows.

The bond between us opened up unexpectedly in his distraction, flooding me with his thoughts of relief, with love for me, and with unease at the creature above us.

You can focus on all that later, I mindspoke as I grabbed onto the chest. This was it. What he needed.

I went to thrust the key into its home, but his large hand landed atop mine, holding me still. "Wait. If I go, if I turn to shadows..." He looked up sharply to the Aileen that began circling again as it tried to remove his dagger. "You'd be stuck here. With that beast. I won't leave you like this."

He stood, materialized his shadowsword and stepped defiantly between me and the monster.

If the Wild Hunt forced him to ride, I would be left here in the nest of a three—now two-headed—beast in the most northern point of Eadha Island.

No horse and no magic.

But this was what we came for, and I'd known the rules coming in. Adrenaline surged as I ignored his wishes and thrust the key into its cold iron home. I had the ability to take away pain to help others. And better now, I could do it on my terms. I wasn't leaving Kaderyn when he needed my help.

But the stupid lid was just as stuck as the first one in the nuckelavee cave, and I jabbed one of Angus's daggers into the crack between the chest and its lid.

"Stupid iron. Stupid monsters. Stupid cold Winter!" I grumbled as I heard Kade block the shrieking claws at my back with a clang of his sword.

The Aileen flapped its wings above us, sending humid air against my face as it lifted itself off the ground, dodged Kade's sword, and snapped its claws toward us again.

"Valentina! *No!*" he yelled.

But I'd made my decision. Kade turned and dove for me, but I slammed my fist into the hilt of the dagger, forcing the lid open. All at once, my dagger pushed through entirely, and the lid jolted open in a rush. Instantly smothering Kaderyn in inky darkness, like a faeling jumping into a parent's arms, swallowing him whole, just like it did with the first chest.

I covered my head out of instinct as the last thing I saw were the razor-sharp claws of the creature coming toward me. But when nothing pierced my skin, I looked up into the eyes of my love, standing above me. His eyes were completely black from iris to ends now, and his face was stony, void of any emotion. A wall of black shadows behind him blocked the flapping wings of the shrieking bird and its tan, sharp, blood-covered claws.

Screeching voices surrounded us, moans of the dead, and I covered my ears. I couldn't think straight through the wicked noise, with awful thoughts not my own.

The force and strength of his shadows whipped around us in a flurry as the Aileen continued to hack at the wall of shadows between us.

Kaderyn? I yelled mind to mind, though pensively because his mind was not like before. There felt a single goal now, and it had nothing to do with me. Tears welled in my eyes and swept down my face as his pure black eyes locked on mine. And from somewhere, I saw recognition click in the smallest of movements as he lowered his brows.

Kade? I asked again, desperate, as the bird cawed behind us and pecked at the wall of shadows with a new fury. If he left me here, fine. But if he didn't remember me . . . or what we'd been through—

I heaved out a sob.

His eyes moved to the passage I'd come in through and he blinked once. I instinctively knew he was telling me to leave, but I scrambled to my feet and risked a step toward him instead. Toward this *other* creature that I wished was still my Kaderyn. I leaned up and kissed his hard lips, wet from my tears. But he stood motionless before me, even when I pulled back.

My stomach gutted as he stretched out an arm and pointed toward the tunnel.

Please come, I mindspoke, not trusting my voice. I pulled on his hands, linking his fingers in mine, but he was an immovable stone, no different from the jagged rocks that surrounded us.

The bird pecked furiously as shadows swirled into a nightmare of a storm. A flurry of horses galloping echoed all around us, drowning out the wailing of the dead.

Oh gods, his Hunters were coming.

The tears poured down my face harder because, though I wished to stay with him, I couldn't fight this Aileen alone, and I had to make it back to Auris. I had to check on Teal.

I had to make my way back home and even more—I had to hope he'd remember me and the love we shared.

I stumbled backward, away, through the thick vines.

Don't run, came a deep, powerful husky voice I barely recognized as Kaderyn's.

And the tears overflowed again as I tripped my heavy legs through winding vines and vegetation, too scared to turn away from him entirely. Too scared that this was the last time I'd ever see him.

Will you come back? I asked, feet moving out of instinct as I hesitated on the edge of the tunnel.

In this life and the next, came his voice as I ducked around the corner of the icy cave and ran until the vines trailed away.

My tears became frozen beads on my cheeks as I burst out of the cave opening, and the cold air threatened to freeze my lungs.

No amount of exhaustion or distress meant my trials were over. I still had Winter Court to get across. I squinted out across the white tundra, and my eyes caught on a brown lump sticking out of the snow. And if my heart wasn't ripped out of its home before, it was now.

I stumbled to Malvasia's side where she lay covered in snow, unmoving. Her saddle and gear were stuck, half attached under her, as long claw marks scarred her side. She deserved a proper burial, not this icy tomb. But it was not within my abilities to get her out, and I was going to have to be strong enough to carry this hurt I felt at leaving her. Because that was what my role was: to carry the pain.

I sucked in a breath, unlatched the sacks, and kissed her stained nose. I brushed blasphemous snow from her muzzle.

She was such a noble mare.

My fingers froze in their mittens as I looked back in time to see a tornado of shadows swirl out from the top of the cave.

There was no other option; I had to start my trek home or be a victim as well. But we'd crashed the ship, broken it to pieces on the shore, or at the bottom of the bay by now.

I started to jog. I was going to have to trail the shoreline and brave the northern beasts until I found a way across. The bow and arrows we'd found had been laid there recently, which told me someone else was out here. And that *someone* must have known a way back. My thoughts were so far from my current predicament as I wallowed in sadness for Malvasia and Teal and the gut-wrenching misery I felt at leaving Kade's side, that I hadn't realized I'd made it through the pine forest where we'd set up camp. Pure sadness and anger had carried me far across the small island. But *something* was strong enough to pull me out of it all.

I started sweating.

I pulled at the collar of the warm fleece coats, and by the second time of undoing a button, I'd realized this heat wasn't from exertion. No, I was tinder, dry leaves near a lit match. I looked around wildly because this was magic. Fire magic. My eyes settled on the deep brown furs of an Autumnfae standing in a blizzard of Winter's frigid snow.

Hope sparks the fire
Fury fans the flames
And courage carried Mohr through the frozen court to stand before me now.

A bobbing raft lay beyond him beside the broken ship, covered now in a layer of frothy ice.

He stared at me against a white-blue sea, and I could feel the jagged pain of the god's sword throbbing in his back like it was in my own. Of all the places I thought this would happen—from my first days with him in a desert to a desert of a different kind now—I didn't imagine we'd meet again here.

And I'd always thought when this moment—this reconciling—happened, fear would consume me. But it didn't. Instead, annoyance bubbled up like trapped bubbles in a hot spring. After all, we'd been through to get Kade to his shadows, I still had this fucking firefae trailing me like I was his property.

Then Mohr, from across the white tundra, did something even worse. He gave me that look; that ugly, greedy, demanding grimace like I was disappointing him, and it lit me up from the inside out like a flowing river of flaming torch oil.

I had a pissed-off momma Aileen behind me and no idea of the state of the one I loved, and Mohr now stood between me and my way to Teal and Jairek.

I dropped the sacks I took from Malvasia—who I just left dead in a frozen foreign court—and tossed them to the ground. Fury inside me roared into a moving force as my feet carried me forward. Our family was split again, and this Autumnfae tracked me down across an island. All because he felt I was owed to him.

He lumbered closer with that damn clip in his step, and I shook my head. "You chased me across an island," I said, matching his pace as I pulled my daggers out of their holsters. "You drugged me."

"I warned you, Valentina. I will not let you go," he said.

The very sound of his voice had me gripping the hilts of my daggers tighter. "You burned my home down. You killed everyone I know," I screamed, as the fire brewed inside me like a storm I refused to hide from. I pulled at any shadows I could still feel, and they fanned off me in anxious snaps, like waves off a black sand beach.

His eyes narrowed at them as he lumbered forward. "I did. And now, thanks to you, we have negotiated a ceasefire with Lady Fede. Who knew? Decades of fighting to be ended with a brothel female from Summer Court."

I shook my head. He would not unnerve me with insults. I'd been through too much. "Only one of us is leaving this court, Mohr."

His hand twitched, and I felt the fire magic try to course through me. I felt its seductive power try to control me, but I had it brewing inside me from the first moment I saw him, and we both looked down at my hands, which were now consumed by fire magic.

"The Siphon never worried me, Valentina. Not when it showed up in the form of a scared Summer female," he said, full of confidence, but I could feel him trying to pull back his fire magic, nonetheless.

I reveled in it and kept it siphoned to me, fueling the fire with my own anger. What did Gael in the Fortress say? Anger breeds action, and action brings change. And I was learning the usefulness of fire magic.

He muttered something else, but I walked forward faster as he pulled his massive sword from the sheath on his back.

"Think about what will happen if I hurt you, Valentina. Nothing here will ease *your* pain. And I won't stop to give you rest as you take mine until we're back in my court."

I let out a guttural scream from my chest. I would not be going nicely.

We were so close now I could see the snowflakes as they landed on Mohr's blade. He looked me over in a fashion that made my skin crawl and my hands shake. No, only one of us was making it out of here alive.

I slashed my daggers at his face, wanting to carve his smug mouth off entirely. The anger built into a palpable thing, forcing me onwards. I just had to nick his skin once and Angus's daggers would take care of the rest. If only I could find a way past his reaching sword. I dropped down looking for the injured leg; it would do as a good target. I sliced my daggers forward, but he pulled back in time. I tried a second and a third time, getting closer to his body each time.

"The blonde wasn't there," he said between thrusts, dancing back.

I froze, but couldn't speak.

"She wasn't there when the theater burned."

Sisaria? Was he saying she was still alive? Had Roshan got there in time? But his eyes went wide at the sight of my daggers, and it dawned on me that he was just trying to buy time.

I crouched, slashing at his ankles before ducking the blow of his sword, thankful for those lessons with Kade. I reached up quickly and brought both daggers down to smash the large bronze sword out of his grip. I froze one dagger inches from the skin of his neck and the other near his bulbous belly as his sword skittered to the snow, too far from his reach.

"Taking a life marks you for the Underworld. That Spring Court guard may have been in self-defense, but I'm not aiming to kill you now. Don't do anything you're going to regret, Valentina," he panted before leaning in. His breath was disgustingly hot on my face. "But I guess taking the leader of the Wild Hunt himself as a lover would have done that, anyway."

I met his golden eyes with courage and a promise. "Then I guess I will meet you there."

And I could have nicked his skin; I could have dug through the furs into his lower belly slowly and just brushed the surface of his skin. But I didn't. I thrust forward straight to the hilt, squelching the dagger in and dug up, through muscle, through tissue, and into the softness beyond that. His eyes went wide and his mouth fell open.

Mohr did not deserve kindness, and if I was destined for the Underworld for his death, then so be it. He flopped backward to the snow, stumbling, trying to stay on his feet, holding a hand to his bleeding stomach.

The thundering of horse hooves thumping and hounds barking sounded behind me. I pulled the swirling shadows to me in comfort before I gained the courage to look back. Kaderyn was almost translucent, like a ghost of black smoke and shadows as he charged onwards, mounted on the largest midnight-black horse I'd ever seen. Deathmarch, he had said her name was. Three white-haired hounds with red-tipped ears had their lips curled back in a snarl near the horse's feet and kept up with the charging company. Behind him, in an organized group, were five other Hunters covered in shadows, mounted on their own horses. Shadows in mixed shades of black and purple swirled around them as they ran straight for me and a dying Mohr faster than any creature I'd seen move before. Pure panic set me on my feet, begging me to run, but I knew—*I knew*—you never run from the Wild Hunt.

One day, I'd have to answer for the lives I'd taken and for the harm I'd caused this island. But I planted my feet and refused to die the same day as the fucking firefae on his knees beside me.

Kaderyn's black eyes locked on mine with a vacancy that might as well have smashed my heart to pieces. Did he recognize me? An unknown frenzy stirred across his beautiful face, and I desperately searched our bond for any hope he remembered who I was.

He was there. But quiet—so painfully quiet. I watched him charge at me as a peaceful fog rolled over our bond that smelled purely of him and briefly closed my eyes to it. Letting it calm my racing heart. They were yards away now as I came to terms with whatever would happen, but I braced myself and held my breath all the same.

The hounds flanked Kaderyn as he sat atop Deathmarch and charged the Wild Hunt straight through me, sifting like ghosts through castle walls; like running my hands through patchouli incense in Otti Theater's back rooms.

Only one Hunter looked down at me, the one with gold buckles on his boots, but I watched as they all had eyes as black as Kaderyn's. The shadows hit me in a peaceful embrace no different than they had any other time we'd traveled the court, tied together by the Caterina del Aamod ties. The wind swirled, and the ground rumbled, but still—I felt no ill will.

I threw my head back to watch as Kaderyn's hounds circled Mohr, barking and snarling, with spit dripping from their jowls. Kaderyn reached a shadowy hand down—impossibly down the side of the black horse—and reached deep inside Mohr's body; a ghost hand searching for purchase on a corrupt soul only meant for one place. And without slowing, Kaderyn pulled Mohr's essence—his soul—straight out from the body I'd gutted only moments before.

Without faltering, the company charged on across the tundra like a lunar eclipse overtakes the sun. A band led by the Hunter I loved galloped out and over the ground in a parade of black smoke and shadows. They were so incredibly fast that they were halfway to the ship when I watched as Kade slowed and pulled Deathmarch around to face me. His expression drew down into a sadness I wanted to kiss away. I left the bond open, desperate for him to know I loved him, and that I would wait for him in Auris. My breath caught in my throat as shadows caressed down the bond and into my very soul.

Tears rolled down my face faster than the snowy air could freeze them, and I wiped them with the back of my hand. I'd find a way across this island and meet him in Auris when he was done. I ignored the doubt in my mind that reminded me just how far away Auris, The Court of Shadows city, was from us.

Deathmarch snorted once and tossed her head. She stomped her massive front hoof hard against the powdery snow, sending it billowing out in a wave around her. Kaderyn, without a word, leaned forward and ushered her on, charging her straight toward me again.

Panic sent a warm flush through my body as the rest of the band of Hunters turned as one and followed behind like a pack of wolves. I locked my eyes with Kades.

I planted my feet hard and deep, and furiously brushed tears away as shadows grew thicker and thicker around me, growing into a chaotic frenzy that whipped my hair around my face. Kaderyn leaned down and reached out a hand, just like he did with Mohr, but instead of it moving through me, it circled around my waist and lifted in one go. I was being pushed and pulled every which way like bread dough being kneaded as Kade sat me before him on the impossibly tall horse. His arm stayed locked around me, holding me as I joined the Wild Hunt. We rode across Eadha Island like falling black stars.

In all the lands I've seen destroyed, in all the worlds I've seen reborn, you are the greatest wonder I've ever known. In this life or the next, I will always come back to you, Kaderyn said through our bond.

I reached a hand back and caressed Kaderyn's face, *my* Kaderyn, and he tightened his grip. I was where I belonged.

Kaderyn's shadows morphed and flowed, spreading their way as the six Hunters and I charged through cities, through the countryside, across lands I'd never seen. There was a peace to it I'd never expected, so I closed my eyes and trusted him. Trusted them.

Even when everything went black.

28

VALENTINA

I WOKE TO THE sound of an owl calling from somewhere high in the misty trees above me. It let out a long, screeching cry, and I blinked up into the thick green trees and beyond to the sparkling, swirling deep-purple and black cloud cover. I wasn't hurt per se, but a dull ache was settling into my head. My body still felt like it was moving, even though my hands sank into the squishy green moss below me.

I leaned up to look around. The trees were ominous and called seductively to me, but I wasn't naive enough anymore to believe they meant me no harm.

This must be Gillies Forest.

I brushed the moss off my hands against the cream-white pants I'd gotten to keep me warm in winter, but now, in the humidity of The Court of Shadows, they were sweltering. Suffocating even.

I pulled a blade of grass from beside me. It was deep green, the color of life and vitality. And a laugh bubbled in my throat at all the false rumors that spread about Shadow Court and its desolate fae. No doubt spread by Kaderyn himself.

A small stone-walled shack sat to my right, and the smell of herbs wafted out from the cracks in its foundation. I looked down across the hillside to a sprawling black wall, and I could see a castle beyond and rooftops surrounding it. My heart snagged in my chest.

Auris.

I tried to stand, but my shaky legs felt not of my own, so I plopped back down and shucked off my coat; it was neither needed nor appropriate in Kaderyn's Court. I threw it across the mushroom-strewn ground; Gillies Forest could keep it. I would not need it ever again.

And as if by thought alone, I watched as a golden-maned lion bounded up and over the hillside from the black-walled city below. His piercing brown eyes stayed locked on me as a boldness warmed my heart, and a smile spread across my face in relief.

Jairek was coming.

Jair shifted mid-stride; his bare feet landed softly on the moss, and I looked up at my friend.

"You could never shift in your shoes," I said as I blinked up at him. Exhausted and worn, but happy.

He reached down a hand and pulled me to my feet. "And the clothes are for your benefit," he said with a wide smile.

"How's Teal?" I brought him into an embrace, content to have one member of our family back.

We started walking down the hill toward Auris, and the globular city lights surrounding it. "Come see her for yourself. But don't ask her about the map. It seemed to have been tossed aside when Kaderyn shadowfaded us here." He winked, and I knew exactly who it was who did the tossing.

But at the mention of Kaderyn, my throat closed. I wanted

him here. Jair seemed to know as much and squeezed my shoulder tighter. Kaderyn promised he would come back.

The city walls groaned as swirling black and gray marble doors swung open, and I was thrust into the daily life of a Shadowfae.

Dozens of fae, recognizable by the twirling shadows that spiraled around them, hustled about their business down Auris's main street. Jair held my shoulders as we passed a storefront to the right called The Malt Seas. An overflowing pile of purple, sparkling salt was on display in the front window with smaller mounds of spices beside it in varying shades of neon. A fluffy, cranky-looking owl sat perched on a narrow rod above it. I caught the end of a conversation happening out front.

"Edlyn, once more, The Malt Seas thanks you for your patronage, but I am out of casha salt until this time next month," the female—in loose black linen pants with thick straps holding them up—said to the male harassing her.

"And what am I to use for my curing salts until then? Don't you dare say use that ochinack you have in the back there. The flavor comes out all wrong."

"Then, I encourage *you* to travel to the tide pools in Port Tayou. After, of course, you negotiate a bargain with the court to even *be* there in the first place. Then, you must skim it off the shallow waters, avoiding the beetles that live in it, lug it back, and dry it properly." Little hairs wisped out of her low ponytail as her eyes flicked up once to Jair and me.

"Oh, Juniper Hatch," the male grumbled with a shake of his head. His shadows snapped the air like he was going to convulse in on himself. "I do hate your sense of humor!"

She blinked at him as we walked by, and I had a very good idea that she didn't think she was being funny at all.

"Why do they have to cure meat at all here, Jairek?"

"Auris is a sprawling city and many live far from the castle and the magic Kaderyn holds. These Shadowfae, while powerful in their own right, were once faeless. And with it, comes some limits on their magic."

"Oh," I said, dismayed.

"Don't feel bad for them, Valentina. They lived full lives having no magic at all. Sometimes traditions and habits are hard to change."

I looked up at my friend and wished Autumn Court would consider changing theirs.

To our left was a shop called The Lucky Owl Tearoom. Its name glinted in big, swirling, gold letters. The scent of fresh tea leaves wafted out as a group of young Shadowfae piled out, laughing.

Passersby glanced up at Jair, who walked through a crowd of Shadowfae like sunshine in a thunderstorm. They smiled and waved, and he nodded cordially back. I balked at how normal everything was. Their lord had been gone, out searching for his shadows, and his court stayed functioning, thriving even. I was going to have to give Rhett, the hawkshifter, more credit.

"Come on," Jair said, leading me down a path to the left, toward the colossal black and gray castle that looked like it was carved out of one enormous block of marble.

I looked under Jair's shoulder, down the opposite road, desperate to see as much as I could, and noted a large group of faelings being corralled by three Shadowfae. They must have a school, even. I was going to have to give Rhett *a lot* more credit.

The walkway toward the castle grounds was carved of polished marble, and I looked up at the sheer mass of strength it would have taken to build such a home. My heart ached for Kaderyn.

Jair pushed open the main double doors, and I gasped at the beauty that greeted me. Everything was the color of Kaderyn's shadows or his clouds. From onyx black to bright violet.

Everything was *him*.

"I'll show you where he'd want you to stay. You can get changed, then I'll bring you to Teal," Jair said, moving through the large foyer, past flickering candles in sconces on the walls.

The staircase posts were the snarling heads of teeth-bared hounds carved out of black wood. We wound our way up the stairs. Candles flickered on either side as we climbed until we were met with a large hallway with doors on both sides. Jair stopped at the very end of the hallway and pushed open the heavy black walnut door.

"You'll find clothes in the dresser and a warm bath through the door to the right. I'll meet you in the foyer when you're ready."

"I'll be quick. I want to see Teal," I said, moving inside the room.

A fireplace flickered to life, illuminating a tray full of summer fruits and honeyed pastries I'd smell a mile away. I gasped and looked back at Jair, who gave me that silent smirk.

But he sobered to say, "Teal's alive and as feisty as ever, but she might look a little . . . different from when you last saw her." His eyes flicked away, then back again. "Please, Valentina, take your time. The journey is over, and the dead can rest easy. Kaderyn will find a way back to you."

Jair closed the door shortly after, and I started for the baths. And he was right, it was over. Kaderyn was going to meet us back here when he was done riding in the Wild Hunt, and we would all be together again.

A soft noise akin to a sigh spread down my bond with Kaderyn. I closed my eyes, focusing on the all-consuming love we shared that was proving to withstand distance and time itself. A heaviness sat on my heart; one of safety, love, and companionship because I never needed to be alone again.

But as much as Jair wanted me to linger, it was going to be a quick bath. I still had to see to an absent lord about attacks in Summer Court; I had to see what I could do to help the faeless; and, if Mohr was telling the truth, Sisaria, and Petri might still be alive.

But first, there was a frantic, squealing pixie somewhere here I had to hug.

READ ON FOR CHAPTER ONE OF RISE OF A HUNTRESS, THE WILD HUNT BOOK 3

CHAPTER ONE: RISE OF A HUNTRESS

VALENTINA

"**S**HE CALLED YOU A MANGY CAT?"

"Among other colorful names," Jair answered with a deep laugh as we strolled side by side through Auris's bustling main street. He nodded to the Shadowfae guard to close and lock the large marble doors behind us on our way out of the Shadow Court's capital.

We were heading towards the old medicine hut, which was now used to store and dry herbs harvested from Gillies Forest.

"Teal wasn't nearly as unhappy with me when I visited. Even though I deserved her wrath most of all," I said, glancing up towards the black and violet sky. Kaderyn was out there. Somewhere.

Jair rested his heavy arm around my shoulders. "You took down a Baliroq, Valentina. Don't discount yourself."

I thought back to the white-wooded bow and arrow leaning against the tree the day Teal got her arm bit off by a Baliroq, a massive four-legged, scaled, snub-nosed beast of the northern plains in Winter Court. If I was a better shot, if I had *any* shot at all, she'd still have an arm. Instead of that . . . *thing*. "Jair, where can I learn to shoot a bow and arrow?"

"Ah," he scoffed. "We were all there. We were all too slow."

"Yeah," I answered, but I'd live with that guilt for the rest of my life. The beast only dropped to the ground when my gods' daggers sunk into its back.

It died in the same tundra I killed General Mohr in. Both their bodies were now locked in Winter's clutches. And Kaderyn—*my* Kaderyn—dragged Mohr's soul out of his body before shadowfading me to Auris.

Home.

Was Autumn Court going to retaliate against me for killing its general? I was definitely going to need to learn to shoot a bow.

It had been a week since we got Kaderyn's shadows back, and the Wild Hunt was still out riding across the lands. Occasionally I could hear them, the baying of the hounds and the braying of the horses as the six Hunters scoured the lands for souls destined for the Underworld, the darkness in the next life. Jairek didn't know how long it would take for them to finish. The Hunt had been split for so long. So instead, he had been giving me a tour of The Court of Shadows with quick visits every day to a healing Teal.

Jair and I were on our way to collect more herbs for Oir, Kaderyn's advisor, to make more Virtusa, a pain-relieving tonic for Teal. I struggled to keep down the nausea every time I smelled it. But we were moving on past our plights, and I'd already talked Jair into heading to Hawrenthia in Summer Court to make Lord Grigory protect his fae better. Especially since Mohr burned Elaria and my old theater to the ground in an attempt to give me nowhere to go back to, except back to him.

We stopped just outside the doorway of the old hut.

"Mind if I wait out here?" I clamped my mouth shut as the bile rose.

Jair turned to me quickly. "It's the smell again, isn't it?"

And my face must have been green because he gave me a brief nod and went in. I watched from the doorway as Jair gathered the herbs needed for Oir from baskets and drying racks on makeshift tables. The hut was full of hung roots and drying stalks. Their faded purple petals swayed in the breeze of the open door, sending out floral and bitter smells; their stalks looked crunchy to the touch. I didn't know what they were all for, but I had an idea some would kill quite quickly.

And not nicely.

I turned to the sprawling midnight black forest where all these were harvested. Small lights, maybe fireflies, floated throughout the dewy air. I wandered closer, but it wasn't any place I was going without Kaderyn by my side. A slow mist crawled along the edge, and though I knew Summer lay on the other side, I knew all who went in never came back out.

A tingling started in my toes, and I wiggled them in my black calf-high laced linen boots. Shadow boots repelled the rain nicely. But the tingling continued until my body was humming, buzzing with an energy I only associated back to my time at the theater. My heart started racing as my vision faded. I whipped around best I could for the medicine hut door. For Jairek.

"Jair!" I shouted and watched as he turned to me just as quick.

His face blanched, and his normal calm brown eyes shot wide. The Virtusa herbs dropped to the floor and crunched under his boots as the lionshifter dove for my outstretched hand.

I willed myself forward, I reached for him, but my body

wouldn't respond. I tried again, clawing, crawling at the air, but fell.

And fell and fell and fell.

WHEN THE SPINNING, THE ENDLESS CHURNING, stopped, cold marble—not unlike cold cobblestone when I was six—pressed against my cheek. I curled in on myself with the memories it brought with it. I couldn't stand the cold. Not then —not now.

I opened my eyes, groggy and dizzy, and peeked through my forearms to see white.

So much white.

"What—" I shielded my eyes as best I could with a hand that felt not my own.

"Welcome, Valentina."

I flipped over, pressing my entire body against the floor, bowing away from that voice. Lord Aborys, in his pristine white and pale blue regalia, stood over top of me with his hands clasped together.

His tongue flicked over his teeth. "Welcome to Winter Court," he said, leaning down as the power of ice, steady and quick, ran through my body. "Siphon."

ALSO BY H J REESE

Dancing With Darkness

Shadows of Solace

Rise of a Huntress

Coming 2024

King of the Courtless

Coming 2024

<u>Short Stories on Eadha Island</u>

(Available for free if you're on my newsletter or in paperback at your favorite retailer) Sign up for my newsletter at www.hjreese.com/newsletter/

Haven of Feathers and Ore

Skies of Onyx

Origins of Shadowfae

ABOUT THE AUTHOR

H J Reese is a left-handed, second-born, Sagittarius, who often falls into all the stereotypes these represent. She lives in a small town in Ontario, Canada but her dreams take her around the world. She is the author of the Wild Hunt books. Visit her website at www.hjreese.com for more information.